MARY ROSIE'S WAR

Catherine M Byrne

Email Catherinbyrne@aol.com

Published by
Overtheord Publishing

ISBN 978-1-9995830-0-2

Artwork by

https://www.selfpubbookcovers.com/Acapellabookcoverdesign

Acknowledgements

I wish to thank the following people for their help and advice in getting this book ready for publication.

As always, friends willing to pre-read, comment and give editorial advice when needed.

Margaret Mackay, Margaret Wood, Sheona Campbell.

Chapter One

Mary

'There they are now,' said an excited Mary to her mother, but before she reached the door, it flew open and Great Aunt Agatha, a tall, elegant woman, burst in with the wind at her back. Her fur-collared coat, open at the front, almost reached the floor. In one hand she carried a cane with a brass horse's head and in the other, an oversized handbag made of leather with a tapestry inlay. A flowery scent mixed with that of cigarette smoke wafted around her.

'I'll put yer luggage in the ben end, Auntie.' Mary's brother Peter, who had met the aunt at the railway station in Wick, came in behind her carrying her suitcase.

'You do that, my boy. Chrissie, you haven't changed much.' Agatha, speaking in a voice that rasped like a saw on wood, grasped her niece's hand and kissed her on the cheek. 'Now, where's that girl of yours?' Her eyes fell on Mary who, self-conscious of her aunt's scrutiny, tucked an unruly curl behind her ear and gave a shy smile.

'What a pretty girl you've turned out to be. Rather reminds me of myself all those years ago. All that hair and what lovely blue eyes.' Agatha rested her cane against the table, put a hand on Mary's shoulder and pressed dry, papery lips to her cheek.

'Good to see ye,' said Mary, suppressing an embarrassed giggle. She was pleased to be compared to Aunt Agatha in looks. Remnants of the old woman's youthful beauty still lurked in the planes of her face.

Agatha took a bout of coughing and patted her mouth with a lace handkerchief she'd pulled from her sleeve.

'Are you alright, Auntie?' asked Chrissie, concern in her eyes.

'Fine, fine, dear.' She flapped her hand. 'And now, Christina, a cup of your good highland tea and a flour scone, if I'm not mistaken.' She nodded at the plate of bannocks fresh from the oven, looked round the room and gave a sigh. 'You really should get something better than this. Have you tried for a place in town?' She pulled a packet of cigarettes from her pocket and lit one.

Very few local women smoked and Chrissie disapproved of those who did. Mary was surprised at her great aunt, but maybe things were different in London where Agatha had made her home.

'A better place costs money and with no man at my back we have little enough of that,' Chrissie said. 'And in any case I like my wee house.'

The cottage in John O' Groats was much like many others, a typical Scottish croft house, a but and ben. The design was simple, an oblong brick building with three downstairs rooms and an attic space in the loft. The 'but', an all-purpose room, a place to eat, sleep and sit of an evening, was spotless and welcoming. Great Aunt Agatha would no find fault with that, thought Mary, but knew her mother worried about the lavatory, a shed with a tin bucket beneath a wooden bench with a hole in it. Toilet paper comprised of newspaper cut into squares, laced with string and hung within easy reach. A bottle of green sanitiser with the cork raised to show some sort of material that absorbed the disinfectant and dispensed a strong odour, often marginally better than the contents of the bucket, sat on the

2

floor. Great Aunt Agatha owned a proper bathroom in her home in London, with a toilet that flushed.

At least the bucket was clean, Mary thought. Chrissie made sure of that before the aunt's arrival. Not only had she scrubbed it, but polished it to a shine. Then she warned her daughter and son that if they used it, they would have to clean it right away.

'Well, I'm not going to use the byre,' declared Mary, although she shared her mother's concerns about the aunt's scorn. Luckily she had not felt the need. In any case, this was not the aunt's first visit. She should know what to expect.

Aunt Agatha removed her hat and took a seat by the table. Her hair, once as red as flame, lay short and silver and waved, pink scalp showing through. 'How have you been, Christina?'

'We're well, Aunt. It's grand you could manage home after all these years.' She took the aunt's hat and coat and hung them in the passageway, then returned to pour the tea.

'Home? Oh, yes. Though, of course I no longer think of Scotland as home.'

Pusskins, an ancient ginger tom, jumped on her lap. Chrissie reached out to remove him, but Agatha waved her away. 'Leave the poor dear,' she said. 'You know I'm fond of cats. I've got three myself.' She stroked Pusskin's head and he closed his eyes, a deep rumble beginning in his throat. 'Poor old fellow,' said Agatha. 'You just stay right there.'

As Peter re-entered, she held out her hand. 'You will sit beside me, dear boy, and tell your old aunt all about your life.'

Peter, looking mildly embarrassed, allowed her to draw him down on the chair beside her.

'Christina, dear, some tea for your lad.' Aunt Agatha gave a single nod in Chrissie's direction and turned her eyes back to Peter. 'Such a handsome boy, so like his grandfather, my dear brother. I must say, Christina, you have done well in your children.'

'I'm proud of them.' Chrissie smiled as she pulled the kettle over the hottest part of the range.

3

Aunt Agatha sighed. 'I wanted to see you one more time, Christina, that's true, but I have another reason for coming north.' She sipped her tea, her hand shaking. 'You mustn't mind me, my dear. The journey has been arduous, all the way from one end of the country to the other and I am very old.' This time she lifted her cup with both hands and took a long swallow before setting it down.

'As you know, apart from Katrine, my cook, I live alone in a large house in Belgrave Square. My health is not good and I fear for the future.' She looked at Mary. 'Would you consider coming back with me? I need a companion. I need someone to be there for me since I've no family of my own. A young presence in the house will bring it back to life. We've grown old, Katrine and I, old and dry and dusty, like cobwebs.' She continued to stroke the cat, who now purred loudly.

Mary didn't think she could live with her aunt, but it would be a chance to see more of the world. However, her mother's next words dashed any hope of that.

'It's awful kind of ye, Auntie, but Mary's just got a job at the mill and she's settled in fine. Furthermore, ye've that many nieces and nephews, we don't want to cause any ill-feeling by ye favouring her.'

'Don't concern yourself about the others. How often do you see them? I'm offering your daughter a good opportunity. Who in their right mind would stay in this God-forsaken backwater when they could be comfortable for life?'

'It's just... so sudden and Mary is very young,' said Chrissie.

'But Mam, we could go for a visit. I would like to see London,' said Mary.

Peter winked at her. 'With things the way they are in Europe, *I* wouldn't be going to London.'

'Britain's not at war. Even if it happens, it'll be fought in Europe and it's not as if Mary'll be alone,' continued Aunt

Agatha. 'She'll still be with family. I think she'll manage very well.'

Getting out of Caithness, seeing more of the world appealed to Mary. It was something she'd often hankered after, but given the state of the family's finances her only escape lay in the many books she read.

'Can I give it a wee bit thought?' Mary knew she'd no hope of being able to accept, but didn't want to appear ungrateful.

'By all means, child. And if not,' Agatha turned her eyes to Chrissie, 'I'm a lonely old woman. You could all come and live with me, God knows, my house is big enough. There's work in London, too, for all of you.'

'Thanks for the offer, Auntie. Ye've aye been kind to us. But I can't see myself living in a city,' said Chrissie.

'I could give you all a much better life. Mary might even snare a rich husband. I'm sure she could be quite sophisticated with a little coaching. Of course, she would have to lose some of that puppy fat.'

Mary glanced at her mother, rounded her eyes and made a moue of horror. She saw herself as reasonably slim, carrying no 'puppy-fat' at all. Her breasts were perhaps on the large side for her age, but she did her best to conceal them by rounding her shoulders and often folding her arms across her chest.

'That's kind of you to say so, Auntie.' Chrissie spoke solemnly enough, but her eyes and lips showed suppressed amusement.

Agatha stood up and lowered the cat to the floor. 'It's the best option. Since your husband died, I've been worried about you. Now show me where the toilet is then bring me a basin of warm water. I need to wash. Those trains get worse the further north you come. I suppose the facilities have not been upgraded since I was last here?'

'I'm afraid not, Auntie,' said Chrissie.

Once Aunt Agatha was outside, Mary burst out laughing. 'Yer face is a picture, Mam. *The facilities!* Much as I would love to see London, I can't imagine *living* with Great Aunt Agatha for long. I mean I do love her and all, but...'

'Now hush, Mary. Ye know she means well. Show some respect.' At the same time Chrissie's eyes twinkled.

'But can't we go for a wee holiday if she pays? We've never had one.'

'No, we'll no ask for charity or take it either. Anyway, these big cities are dangerous places for young lassies. And see how she smokes? It's clear she's no got the same principles as I do. Furthermore, Katrine is getting on a bit, probably no so fit any more and Agatha needs someone to run after her. Always did. I hope our *'facilities'* don't offend her too much. She aye forgets where she came from.'

'I don't want to smoke,' said Mary, but there was no use arguing with her mother. She *would* go one day, just to visit, when she was older.

Later, as the family took their places at the table, Aunt Agatha stubbed out her latest cigarette. 'As the guest, I shall say grace.' She waited until Chrissie sat down before lowering her head and clasping bony fingers.

Peter leaned back rolling his eyes. Mary fought down the urge to giggle. Aunt Agatha's grace was usually extensive and Peter's face plainly showed his dread of the ordeal to come. She nudged him with her knee and he pulled a face at her. Chrissie shot a warning glance in their direction.

Mary *was* fond of Aunt Agatha in her way, but had always been glad to see her leave after her few visits north. Nothing seemed good enough for her, yet she was kind, too. They all looked forward to the box of goodies that arrived every Christmas: chocolates, second-hand clothes that smelt of moth-balls, a toy for each of the bairns when they were younger and a small gift now that they were older. Once she sent a fur stole which looked like an elongated fox complete with head and tail, and Chrissie gave it to Peter and Mary to play with. They tied a string around its neck and dragged it about the floor.

6

'Amen,' the old lady said at last.

A communal intake of relieved breath passed round the table.

'This soup smells quite delicious,' Agatha said as if surprised, picked up her spoon and stirred the broth. 'Maybe a bit too much barley, Christina.'

Mary avoided her brother's eyes. To take a fit of giggles now would be rude. Agatha finished, cleaned her plate and picked up one of the ham sandwiches Chrissie prepared earlier. They were triangular shaped with the crusts trimmed. Despite Chrissie's best efforts, Agatha wrinkled her nose. 'I'm sure these taste very nice, but if you don't mind, that soup was quite enough for my delicate digestion.' She slipped a piece of ham from between the slices and fed it to the cats who sat by her side, watching her hopefully.

'Well, there's nothing wrong with my digestion.' Peter, ignoring his mother's glower, grabbed a sandwich and began stuffing it into his mouth.

'Delicate digestion indeed,' muttered Chrissie as she helped Mary clear away the plates. 'Ye wait and see, despite her uppity ways, she'll eat like a horse in foal.'

Mary sniggered, putting her hand over her mouth as another fit of giggles fought to be free.

Chapter Two

Mary

After the dishes had been put away and Chrissie had read a passage from the bible, the family sat around the peat fire in the ben end, toasting bread on long forks and listening to Peter's stories about the coopering, the lads he worked with and the mischief they got up to. Yet no matter how hard he tried to keep Agatha's interest elsewhere, the talk eventually turned to her favourite subject, an account of how much better life was in London.

'Europe's in turmoil. Hitler will be looking at Britain next, as sure as eggs is eggs,' Chrissie said. 'I think we'll be safer here.'

'With Scapa Flow just across the water?' asked Agatha. 'If we do get embroiled in this war, they'll be dropping bombs on you long before they touch us. Anyway, Belgrave Square will be safe enough. We're nowhere near the docks. If there is any danger, we can move to my bungalow in Wales.'

'Ach, Scapa Flow's far enough away. Thanks for the offer, Auntie, but we're just fine here for the minute,' said Chrissie.

Agatha took a deep breath, disappointment visible on her wrinkled face.

Mary cleared her throat. 'We *will* come for a visit someday. But I don't want a rich husband. I already have a sweetheart.'

Mary smiled as she knew she was meant to do. Both her family and that of Johnny Allan seemed to be under the assumption that the childhood friends would marry one day. Their future, it appeared, was already sealed without permission from either of the two people involved. She *was* very fond of Johnny and she had yet to meet a lad she liked better, but she wasn't sure if she wanted to spend her life with him.

'Really? Just what prospects has this *sweetheart* got?'

Johnny was a good catch, steady as a rock. A bonny lad, too, with his black curls, soft grey eyes and wide lips. The freckles that once covered his face were hardly in evidence now and a dark shadow ghosted on his upper lip and chin where he'd begun to shave. This last year he'd grown taller than her and he'd filled out, his gangling boyish body a thing of the past. Many of the young lassies giggled and preened when he was around. Mary was glad he didn't flirt back. Although unsure of her feelings, she still didn't want him to fall for someone else. If only he wasn't so cautious. He saw the future laid out, his life no better and no worse than his parents before him.

'Johnny's a fine chiel,' said Chrissie. 'He'll be good to our Mary and he's a hard worker and all. He has an apprenticeship as a miller.'

Agatha gave a snort. 'Miller's apprentice! You could do so much better, my dear.' She put a hand over Mary's.

Mary stood up. 'More tea, anyone?' she asked, keen to change the subject. Agatha wasn't all that bad really. Sometimes she could be good company, talking of long ago and her time in university, how strange it was after life on a croft, about the young men she could have married and about her late husband, a law student at the time. He moved on to become a very successful lawyer in the city, hence Agatha's wealth. Her only regret, she said, was that there had been no children. Some of her stories were funny and made them laugh. Yes, Mary thought, she could cope with a short visit, might enjoy it even.

As the week went on, the way Agatha belittled life in the Highlands, became wearying and they all sighed with relief when they saw her off at the station. Chrissie was a bit concerned about Agatha's health as she seemed to cough a lot, but Agatha assured her it was caused by the chill winds of the north.

'If you change your mind, dear girl, you will be welcome any time,' she said as she kissed Mary's cheek.

'Thank you,' Mary replied.

'Did ye not want to take her up on her offer?' asked Peter with a chuckle, as the train puffed out a cloud of steam. 'She could teach "our Mary" to be quite the lady, maybe snare a rich man.'

'Are ye wise?' replied Mary, and laughed.

'Ye never know, think of all that money. She must be ninety if she's a day and she doesn't look that well. It could be a step in the right direction.' His eyes twinkled with mischief.

'Will ye two stop it. She means well,' said Chrissie.

'If we went, we could say goodbye to poverty,' said Peter, still smiling.

Chrissie shook her head. 'If Agatha's that lonely, she should move north.'

'Why doesn't she pay for a companion?' asked Mary.

'She has done, many a time. None stayed very long.'

'She must be very lonely.' Mary suddenly felt a bit ashamed at having laughed earlier. 'I...I would like to go for a visit.'

'Maybe one day ... when you're a lot older,' said Chrissie. 'Anyway, she can't be that lonely. The cook, the one from Scotland, she's been there for nigh on twenty years, I believe. No, I was right. They're both getting on and she needs a slave.'

The train disappeared in a haze of smoke, steam, clacking wheels and warning whistle. Chrissie searched in the depths of her bag. 'I think there's enough money for a cup of tea in that new Italian café by the harbour.'

Mary slipped an arm through her mother's as they made their way to Bank Row and down to the sea. Most of the fishing boats were out at this time of day, but the area was still busy. The herring gutters worked at their barrels, row upon row of them, their voices rising in tune as they sang cheerful songs to the ring of the coopers' hammers. A few hands rose to give Peter a swift wave, their nimble fingers pausing for less than a second, and one girl called his name, her smile wide, her eyes bright.

'Bonny lassie,' said Mary.

'Jess Duncan,' said Peter. 'She's fine and all.'

'Is there something we should know about?' asked Mary.

'Maybe. Ye'll get to meet her soon enough.'

'I hope so,' said Chrissie. 'I would love to see ye married and settled.'

'I just said she was fine. Don't go hearing wedding bells, Mam.' As they passed, Peter greeted his workmates at the coopering.

'A day off in the middle of the week, aye, favouritism that is,' called one of the lads in a good-natured tone.

Peter laughed. 'I'd rather work than take care of my Great Aunt Agatha, I'd tell ye that. I'll be back on the hammer as soon as I've seen these two ladies to the café yonder.'

He said goodbye to his sister and mother at the café door. 'See you on Sunday.' He lodged in town during the week. For a long time after Chrissie had been widowed nine years ago, the three of them had clung together, an inseparable unit. But now the gaps between Peter's visits home were becoming longer and Mary could sense him breaking away, leaving her to be the focus of her mother's world.

'Did you mean what you said, about wanting to see him settled and wed?' Mary asked as they sipped their tea.

'It's got to happen one day,' said Chrissie. 'Thank goodness I still have you for a few years yet. I'll be able to help with the bairns too, once ye marry Johnny and get a house nearby.'

11

'But what if we don't get married?' said Mary.

'Don't be daft. Ye'll no get a better chiel than Johnny and that's a fact. And ye get on so well. It's important, ye know, to get on like friends. Me and yer dad were like that.' Her eyes grew wistful. 'It's what I want for ye too.'

'I suppose so,' said Mary, feeling more trapped than ever.

Chapter Three

Johnny

'So ye got rid of the old aunt, then,' said Johnny next day, after running to catch up with Mary.

She turned and greeted him with a smile, making his heart flip over. 'Aye, we did.'

They walked in silence for a while through the blustery morning as Johnny searched his mind for something clever to say. Mary was so smart and bonny and he wanted to impress her.

As children they'd been inseparable, but then, about a year ago he detected a subtle shift in the relationship, something that made him tongue-tied in her presence, made them less easy together. Johnny's mother died when he was a baby and he had been brought up with his father and two older brothers, which he believed contributed to his awkwardness around girls, especially since hitting his teens. Everyone expected that he and Mary would get married one day and it was what he wanted too, but he'd never broached the subject with her. He had another year to go as a miller's apprentice and with Benjie soon to retire and having lost both his sons to the Great War, Johnny would be his successor.

With his job and his boat and Mary working in the bakery which was run as a side-line to the mill, they would soon save up for a croft of their own. Of course she would have to give up her job once they were wed.

Mary gave a little cough, jolting him from his daydream. 'Aunt Agatha wants me to live with her in London.'

'Ye're no leaving are ye?' Shocked, he stopped and stared at her.

'Maybe I should, ye know. It's a chance to get away from here, see another place.'

His blood ran cold. 'I always thought ye were happy enough.'

'I am, but Agatha's stories make me realise there's a big world out there.'

'Surely ye're no thinking on it?'

'It's just that, well, maybe I shouldn't settle for living here all my life. I mean, we don't have to do what our parents want, do we?'

'Well, they are sensible and...and they know what's best,' Johnny said miserably. She couldn't leave, she just couldn't.

'Ye're so serious!' Mary laughed and shook her head. 'I could never live with Agatha for long. She'd dress me up and parade me in front of,' here she placed one hand on her hip, cocked her head and changed her voice to mimic her aunt, "several suitable young men." Apparently I could be "quite sophisticated" if I got the chance.' She laughed some more. 'Can ye imagine?'

What Johnny couldn't imagine was life without Mary. She had turned Agatha's suggestion into a joke, but there had been a certain wistfulness in her voice. Maybe he'd assumed too much. Maybe he should make his feelings clear, but there were things he found impossible to say. *Mary, I want to marry ye, I thought ye wanted that too.* The words raced round in his head but he was unable to form them in his mouth. What if he blurted them out and she laughed? Told him she had no such intentions after all? He would never be able to stand the hurt and humiliation.

14

'Ye'll no go, then?' Hardly daring to breathe, he waited for her answer.

She pulled a face and shrugged her shoulders. 'I've no really got a choice right now, but maybe someday I'll go for a wee holiday.'

'I...I would miss ye.' His fists clenched, blood rose up into his face.

When his eyes trapped hers, Mary saw love in them. It was obvious he assumed the same as his family and hers, and that gave her a strong sense of unease. 'I would miss ye too. Ye're my best friend,' she said.

'But we're more than friends, aren't we?'

'I... yes we are,' said Mary. 'But I'm thinking about the future.' As a young girl, she had often seen herself and Johnny in a fine wee house with bairns at her knee. She'd even chosen the name for her first-born son, Charlie, after her dad. But back then, she didn't see many choices for a girl in her position. Plenty lads would have her, she knew that, but none were as steady as Johnny. However, Agatha's offer had fed a growing restlessness in her soul and she no longer wanted to think about marriage or settling down, at least not for a while yet.

She and Johnny spent a lot of time together and everyone saw them as a couple and she did love him in her way, but he didn't stir her blood like the heroes and heroines in the books she read.

Johnny looked crestfallen, making her feel a bit guilty. He had always been there for her and, deep down, she couldn't imagine life without him. But was that enough?

'Look, why don't we go out on Saturday night? We could go to Wick. There's a good film on in the Pavilion,' she said.

'Yes, yes, if you like.' He cleared his throat and his face brightened slightly.

She was glad she had appeased him and she was keen to go to the Pavilion. It wasn't the film that she wanted to see

15

particularly, but the town buzzed with preparations for an invasion that might never happen. By now they had reached the mill door.

'I need to get on before Benjie comes or I'll be for it. Ye'd best be off and all, Mary.' Johnny scratched his neck.

'Aye, see ye Saturday.' She wished there was someone she could confide in, someone whose advice she could ask. Her mother was no use. She thought the sun rose and set on Johnny Allan.

'He's a steady, sensible lad,' Chrissie said whenever Mary tried to voice her doubts. 'Ye hang in there, our Mary. Ye'll never do better.'

Her friends weren't much help either. She could imagine Rita saying, '*I'll have him. Pass him over to me.*' In spite of her misgivings, she wouldn't want to see him with someone else. Then there was Peter. They'd been close as children, but now she could hardly get him on his own. When he came home at weekends, her mother seldom left his side.

She'd heard the other girls talk. Seemed the lads were always after them for a bit of fumbling in the long grass or anywhere come to think of it. Johnny wasn't like that. They had kissed once, a brief brushing of lips, innocent and awkward. She wondered whether, if he kissed her, really kissed her, she would hear those violins. Then she would know for sure. She had to be the only girl her age who had not yet experienced the so-called passionate embrace.

On Saturday night Johnny and Mary sat in the back row in the cinema. He put an arm along the back of her chair and she waited, hoping he would kiss her, that's what boys did, wasn't it? But he was more intent on watching the film and eating popcorn. Now and then she sneaked a glance his way.

'Are ye all right?' he asked, turning to look at her before slipping another bit of popcorn into his mouth. He held the bag towards her. 'Want some?'

16

'No thanks. I'm fine,' she replied, and turned her head away.

Perhaps he was like her, she thought; going along with what had been planned for them, with no strong feelings in either direction.

'I enjoyed that,' he said, as they walked out into the night air.

'I couldn't hear the film for people fumbling around us.' That wasn't exactly true. Longing to be held and kissed too, she had listened and felt envious.

'They shouldn't go to the pictures if they didn't want to see the film,' said Johnny, startling her with his disapproval.

'Could we go to the coffee shop and get a later bus?' she asked. The street was alive with young people, laughing and larking about. Music spilled from bar-room doors.

'I only have enough for our fare,' he mumbled.

Disappointment brought her mood further down. She had her fare and enough for one glass of lemonade.

'Can't we stay for a wee bit longer anyway?' If nothing more, it would be nice to just walk about and soak up the atmosphere.

'I've got to get up early tomorrow. I'm working on my boat,' he said.

As they passed the café windows, Mary gazed longingly at the people inside and thought it would be good to live in the town.

'Well, if you really want to,' he said at last.

'Doesn't matter,' she replied, huffily.

They didn't say much to each other on the way home and when he walked her to her door, she didn't invite him in, but stood against the wall, waiting for *the* kiss.

He pulled her against him for a brief awkward moment and let her go just as quickly. 'A year's no that long,' he murmured.

'For what?' she asked.

'Till I finish my apprenticeship.'

Without speaking, Mary gave a snort of derision, spun on her heel and shut the door with some force behind her, leaving Johnny standing there looking perplexed.

Chapter Four

Chrissie

'Hello, Mam,' Peter shouted as he came in the door that Sunday, the wee herring gutter who had waved at him at the harbour clinging to his arm. 'Hope ye've got enough meat for an extra one. I've brought someone with me.'

'Aye, ye know I'll always make do for one of yer friends.' Chrissie grinned, both pleased and surprised. This was the first time Peter had brought a lassie home. It had to be a good sign.

'This is Jess,' he said, his face slightly flushed.

'I'm glad to meet ye.' Chrissie clasped the girl's hand. 'Come away in. It's lentil soup and smoked ham. I've just put it on to warm up.'

Small and slim with bobbed dark hair and enormous eyes, Jess smiled shyly. 'Sounds good.' She glanced up at Peter, and Chrissie saw adoration in her eyes and hoped Peter wouldn't let her down.

'Where's Mary?' Peter looked around the room.

'She's up the stairs, changing out of her best clothes.' Chrissie gave a laugh. 'Ye should have known she wouldn't be far away, no when the meat's almost ready.' She began to set an extra place at the table.

Mary burst in through the door. 'I thought I heard my name mentioned.' Her eyes flew from Peter to Jess and a smile spread across her face. 'Hello, I'm Mary,' she said with enthusiasm.

'Aye, the bane of my life.' Peter tousled her hair and she batted him off.

'Come on now, the soup's warm,' said Chrissie.

'We'd better do as she says.' Mary winked at Jess. 'My Mam's good at wielding a dishcloth when we don't answer.'

As they ate, they chatted. Jess, an only child, lived on a croft with her parents. She was quiet, but pleasant and blushed easily. From the looks she and Peter exchanged, it was plain that they cared deeply for each other.

Chrissie warmed to her immediately. She didn't want to appear too nosey, but longed to get Peter on his own so that she could find out how serious this was.

After the food had been eaten and the dishes cleared away, she got that chance.

'One of our ewes birthed three lambs last night. One of them's awful wee. Would ye like to come and see him?' Mary said to Jess.

'Aye, I would.' Jess removed the apron she'd borrowed from Chrissie so she could help with the dishes. 'Will ye be making a pet of him?'

'We'll likely have to,' said Mary as they walked through the doorway.

'Fine lassie,' said Chrissie when they were out of earshot. 'Are ye serious about this one?'

'I think I am, Mam. But don't go getting ideas. It'll be a while before I'm ready to settle, and Jess, she loves going off to Yarmouth and up to Shetland with the other gutters. So she'll no be around all the time.'

They spent a pleasant Sunday afternoon together. All too soon the time came for the young couple to catch their bus to Wick.

'Ye'll come back and see us again,' called Chrissie as they parted.

'Aye, I will and all,' answered Jess.

As the bus pulled away, Chrissie turned to Mary. 'What do ye think of that?'

'Oh, I hope they get married. I really like her.'

'Me and all.' Chrissie linked arms with her daughter and they walked back to the house.

She was happy about Peter, and Jess seemed just right for him. The afternoon had gone a little way to taking her uneasy mind off the unrest in Europe for a while.

Early Monday evening a sharp knock came to the door. Mary grabbed Sandy's collar and pulled the collie backwards. 'Be quiet yapping pup.' She raised her eyes and looked at the man whose frame filled the doorway. 'Sinclair, come away in. Mam's just making tea.'

'How are ye, bonny lassie?' He grinned and threw her a wink. Sinclair Mackay was a big man with kind brown eyes and a square chin, his hair thin on top and white where it once was black.

His face softened as he greeted Chrissie who was pouring water into the teapot. He took a seat at the whitewood table, removed a folded newspaper from below his arm and set it down. 'Got a letter from Billy Inkster yesterday. He's enjoying the navy, but there's lots of talk.'

'What kind of talk?' Chrissie's green eyes narrowed as she set a steaming mug before him. 'Ye'll have a bere bannock with that?'

'Thanks, Chrissie, there's no one makes a bannock like ye. Well, Billy says they're getting all the ships ready and commissioning more. They don't tell the men much, but there's lot of new recruits. To be honest, I don't give much for Chamberlain's claim that there'll be peace in our time.'

'Ach, ye're always full of doom and gloom. It'll maybe be something and nothing. It's good that they're prepared though.' Nevertheless, a shadow crossed Chrissie's normally cheery face.

Mary set out a plate of bannocks cut into quarters and slathered with home churned butter and rhubarb jam. She took a seat at the table beside Chrissie and Sinclair, eager to hear the latest news.

In spite of her apparent optimism, Chrissie wasn't herself these days. But then everyone was living on edge, hoping for the best, fearing the worst. Like many others, Chrissie Rosie had lived through a war before.

'What else was he saying?' asked Chrissie.

'Not much, pet, but reading between the lines, it looks bad. I mean can you see a man like Hitler stopping at Austria and Czechoslovakia?'

'Surely the rest of Europe won't let him off with it.' Chrissie poured the tea into mugs. The china tea set used for Aunt Agatha had been put away for another time.

Sinclair ran his hand over a stubbled chin making a rasping sound. 'It's no just him. There's Franco in Spain and Mussolini in Italy and then you've got Stalin. They're all evil men. I tell ye, the world is going to pot and it's a pot that's about to boil over.'

'Surely no sane person wants war, no after the last time,' said Chrissie.

'Aye, but I'd hardly call Hitler sane. Look what he's doing to the Jews. A madman that's what he is,' Sinclair said.

'What has he got against Jews?' Mary had been listening. She was born after the Great War and her mother spoke little of it, but she knew her dad suffered ill health and disfiguration because of his experiences there and that ill-health finally took him from her when she was just eight years old.

'Some people are just plain evil,' said Chrissie. 'I never understood why Jews were persecuted in the first place. Now can't we talk about something else? I can't stand the thought of Peter and all those young lads being called up, especially after what happened to Charlie. Have ye had many lambs this year?'

Sinclair wasn't to be swayed. 'What he's doing to the Jews is beyond belief. Turning people out of their homes and setting fire to synagogues just because they're of a different faith. Makes me ashamed to be called a Christian. And they're no more welcome here. I was just reading the other day how any caught coming into the country illegally are deported and anyone harbouring them, well, they're imprisoned!'

'I don't know if that's the whole story, but in any case he's no Christian,' declared Chrissie, her voice rising. 'The de'il himself, that's who he is.' She slapped her cup on the table so that some of the contents spilled out. 'Damn it! God forgive me that I should say such words indeed.' She rose, grabbed a tea towel from the brass rod above the mantle and dabbed at the spill.

Mary took a fit of giggles and immediately covered her mouth with her hands.

'Ye'll be laughing on the other side o' yer face, my lassie, if we go to war,' Chrissie said.

'Sorry, Mam, but ye always ask God to forgive ye after ye swear.'

'Ye make it sound as if I'm aye swearing. But seriously, this is no laughing matter.'

'No, it's a swearing matter.' Mary fought down another burst of laughter. She looked at Sinclair. His eyes never left Chrissie and, Mary realised with a start, there was more than amusement there. It was the way Johnny Allan looked at her. Mary felt a frisson of surprise. Her mam was just that, her mam. It was the first time she saw her as a woman and the realisation that she could still be attractive to man was a new concept. But why not? Although a bit on the plump side, her mam was still a good-looking woman with her normally cheery face and reddish brown hair now flecked with grey.

Mary realised something else too, that she didn't mind her mother being over friendly with Sinclair Mackay. She liked him and a man around the place would help a lot. In his fifties, amazingly still single given his eligibility, he earned a wage on the ferry and ran a croft as well. He was not bad looking either, for a man of his age. Now that she thought about it, Sinclair was a regular visitor these days and Chrissie did seem in better spirits after he left.

Furthermore, if her mam was with a man, Mary wouldn't have to worry so much about seizing her independence. Feeling a bit more optimistic, she asked, 'Do you think Hitler and his forces'll come to Britain, Sinclair?' Knowing how worried Chrissie had become these last few months, Mary willed him to give the right answer, to put her mother's fears to rest.

'I'm afraid they will, bonny lassie,' said Sinclair.

'Go collect the eggs, Mary, will ye?' Sharpness sprung into Chrissie's voice. All this talk of war obviously annoyed her. Either that, or she wanted her daughter out of the way for some reason.

Mary stood up and glanced at Sinclair who was studying the remains of his tea, both hands around the mug.

'I'll get the basket, then.' She went through to the back porch.

From there she could overhear the conversation in the other room. 'The young don't realise the seriousness of the situation. I'm not sleeping with the worry of it,' Chrissie said.

'Maybe I shouldn't talk about it so much, but it's on my mind too,' said Sinclair. Silence reigned for a beat. 'Have ye thought of what we spoke about the other night? I'm having a proper toilet that flushes built on. If the lamb prices are good next year, I might even stretch to a bath and all.'

Chrissie replied, 'Ye've a grand house, no doubt about it, but this wee cottage is fine for me and the bairns. It's the kind of thing I've been used to all my life. But with what's going on in

Europe and all…. Ach, Sinclair, ye know the situation I'm in and my feelings on the matter.'

'Just think about it, that's all I'm saying.'

It was a strange conversation, Mary thought. Could there already be more going on here than her mam let on?

Chapter Five

Chrissie

Once Mary left the house, Chrissie sat down and rubbed her hands on her knees. Then leaning towards Sinclair, she said, 'I am flattered, really I am, but why would a fine upstanding man such as yourself want the likes of me?' She laughed as if she'd said something funny. The more time she spent with Sinclair, the harder it was to deny that her feelings for him were growing stronger, but giving him any encouragement was a bad idea. As long as her bairns were in the house she'd sworn to never get involved with another man. Furthermore, although he hadn't asked it of her, she'd promised Charlie on his deathbed that there'd never be anyone else.

'Ye're still a good looking woman and ye've got a lot to give.' Then, as if he'd read her mind, he said, 'Would Charlie really want you to be on your own?'

She had no answer to that. Knowing Charlie as well as she did, she knew he would want what was best for her.

'It's too soon. I've still got the bairns...'

'They're hardly bairns,' said Sinclair. 'Peter's practically left home and it won't be long until Mary has a ring on her finger if that young Johnny's got any say in it. What'll be yer excuse then?'

'It's just the way things are. With all this war business, I can't turn my mind to anything else.' She studied his face, willing him to understand.

The way his eyes drank her in stirred something deep within her, something both pleasing, yet scary. When he spoke his voice was low and soft. 'I really like ye and it's time I found myself a wife, but I'll no wait forever.'

'Time to find a wife?' she said, and stood up, her heart sinking. In spite of her words, she had hoped that she was special, that what was between them was more than just "because he needed a wife". 'If that's all ye want I'm sure there's plenty more willing than me,' she snapped.

'I'm sorry, that came out wrong. I didn't mean it like that and you know I didn't.' He stood up and turned to go. 'It's ye I want, but I'll no keep going where I'm no welcome. Think on it.' Then he was gone, the door shut behind him.

Chrissie rubbed her forehead. She hadn't meant to be so sharp. Sinclair had been a good friend to her over the years — in the beginning, to both her and Charlie and afterwards, when she found herself alone, it was Sinclair who helped her pick up the pieces. He was still ready to help with any repairs that needed doing round the house: the thatch beginning to leak, the chimney sooted up, the window rattling in its frame. Sinclair would have it mended without her having to ask. He wanted nothing in return, but she was always ready with a cup of tea and a bannock, or a plate of her delicious soup. She was only too happy to do mending for him and they enjoyed each other's company. Why couldn't he just leave it at that? Why did he have to declare himself forcing her to make a choice?

There had been three men in her life and they had all hurt her in different ways. Davie had left her for another, Jack had hurt her physically, Charlie had been her soul mate but he had died, causing the greatest heartbreak of all. Britain faced another war and Sinclair could very well be called on to serve for a second time. She swore she would never again open herself up to that

27

degree of hurt. But, she asked herself, was she just looking for excuses?

Her thoughts turned to her children. She'd have Mary for a few years yet, but her lovely son was of an age to fight for his country. She would have to speak to Peter, try to persuade him to get a restricted position somewhere, the fire or ambulance service for example. If only she owned a proper farm, not just one cow and a puckle of sheep, he could have claimed to be needed on the land.

What was the matter with her? She wasn't the only woman facing the same threat, but knowing that didn't make it any easier.

She thought again of the way Sinclair had come into her house less than a week ago. 'Chrissie,' he'd started, and a tingle ran down her spine at the way he'd said it. Then he'd licked his lips and lowered his eyes. 'Ye must know how I feel about ye.'

Shaking her head, she'd willed him not to say more. She didn't know what she would do without Sinclair, but she didn't want to be faced with a decision she was unable to make. It was totally the wrong time.

Chapter Six

Mary

Meanwhile, instead of going towards the henhouse, Mary headed to the beach only yards away. A soft wind stirred the air and a few clouds moved lazily across a mother-of-pearl sky as the dying sun bleached away the day. Johnny Allan was where she thought he would be this time in the evening, on the beach tarring the bottom of his upturned boat. He looked up as she approached and a wide grin split his face. Before rising to his full height, he set down the tar pot and brush and wiped his fingers on the legs of his dungarees.

'Mary, good to see ye.' A faint flush spread up his cheeks.

Mary gave a little laugh. 'Were ye hard worked at the mill the day? I didn't see much of ye.'

'Aye, I was.' He stopped and scratched his head. 'I...I thought ye were a bit annoyed with me on Saturday night. Did ye no enjoy the picture?'

'The picture was fine. I was tired, that's all.' She couldn't say what was really on her mind, that she was beginning to find Johnny boring and too staid for his age. She moved on to a safer subject. 'He can be a bit of a slave driver, that Benjie.'

'Aye. Ye know, the mill's a decent enough job, but I'd rather go to sea full time.'

'There's no the same money in it now.'

'I know. I'll no give up my boat though. I'm doing well at the lobsters and I'm saving every penny.' His eyes caught hers for longer than they normally would and there was a wealth of meaning there. Ignoring the look, she said, 'Sinclair was in. He says there's going to be war.'

'Like as not.' Johnny dropped his eyes to his tar-stained fingers.

Mary pushed a strand of hair away from her face and gazed across the crumpled blue of the Pentland Firth towards the islands. 'We'll be safe enough up here though, won't we? We're at the other end of the country, pretty far from Europe. Sinclair's always full of doom and gloom.'

Johnny shook his head. 'Don't be so quick to think that. They'll hide the fleet just across the water in Scapa Flow, like they did last time.' He took a step towards her so that they stood together and their arms touched. 'But don't look like that. It might never happen. Are we going to the next dance? Folks are saying there's going to be a real band.'

Mary enjoyed the dances. Last week she danced with nearly every lad in the hall, but turned down any offer to walk her home. Johnny was not one for the dancing, preferring to stand and watch from the sidelines, but he always waited for her at the end of the night.

'Of course,' she said.

'Hi, ye two,' came a call from the ridge above.

Rita and Ellie were picking their way down the narrow path towards her.

'Day off?' asked Mary.

'Aye,' answered Rita. 'His lordship and lady Muck are visiting relations in Sutherland this week. All the staff aren't needed.'

Rita was a kitchen maid in the Provost's house in Wick.

'This is my night off anyway,' said Ellie. 'I'm glad. I hate that laundry. I can't wait to find somewhere else.'

30

'It's no often we all manage to be free at the same time. We're going for a walk along the sea front,' said Ellie, tossing her head. 'Up by the hotel. Come on.' She linked her arm through Mary's, but her eyes were on Johnny. 'Ye coming? I'm sure some of the lads'll be there.'

'I've got to finish this.' Johnny picked up his brush.

Mary held up her basket. 'I came out for eggs.'

'We'll get them on the way back. Come away.' Ellie pulled on her arm.

'Ye're going with them?' said Johnny, looking sullen. 'I thought we could talk.'

'I wouldn't want to keep ye back from yer *work*,' she replied.

'I'll see ye later, then,' Johnny snapped, and turned back to his boat.

'Johnny's so good-looking,' said Rita, 'but he's no much fun, is he?'

'Ach, he's just a wee bit shy.' Although Mary defended him, she was also exasperated by his careful nature.

The three girls skipped along the shore road to the harbour where, legs dangling, they sat on the sea wall. The soft wind protected them from the biting midges, the sun sat on the horizon, and the hotel cast a long shadow. Mary loved that building. When Peter was taken on at the coopering, her mam and da treated them to tea as a special treat. She'd been overwhelmed by what she saw as the poshness of the place with its octagonal front, high corniced ceilings, and massive fireplaces. Along with tea served in little china cups, there was white bread cut into thin slices spread with shop-bought butter and small cakes. Mary thought it tasted very good indeed. It was not a treat that was ever repeated because, shortly after, her da became too ill to work.

'How did the night at the pictures go?' asked Rita.

'It went fine. The picture was good.'

'Are ye being careful?' asked Ellie, with a sly look.

'Careful about what?'

'Ach, Mary, ye're no that innocent that ye don't know what I mean.'

Mary felt her face flood with heat as Rita's meaning sank in. 'I'm not like that,' she said. 'I'll wait till I'm married.'

'Do you really love Johnny?' Rita asked.

Mary thought for a minute. 'I think so, but I honestly don't know.' She wanted to confess her true feelings to her friends and Rita had given her the opportunity, but before she could say another word, Rita elbowed her in the ribs, set her other hand against her own heart and feigned a swoon.

'Oh my goodness, see what's over there!'

'Ouch.' Mary pushed her friend's shoulder. 'Is that why ye brought us here? Who are they anyway?'

A couple of men in air force uniforms strode down to the pier and stood looking over the water towards Orkney.

'I don't know, but I think there's something important going on. My dad says when the Germans come they'll take the easiest way in, invade from the north. I reckon there's going to be a lot more servicemen coming up to protect us.' Rita pushed her hair back from her face. 'It'll be good, eh? There's no enough lads to go round, less if the call-up starts. I wonder if these men'll be at the dance? I think I'll ask them. Ye coming?'

Mary giggled and shook her head. 'Don't be so forward.'

'Aye, ye go. Let us know what they say,' said Ellie.

'Ye two are so dull.' Rita slipped off the wall and sashayed along the pier. She stopped when she drew level with the pilots and tilted her head to one side, her glossy auburn hair falling over her shoulder.

Mary and Ellie looked at each other and sniggered. Rita was attractive with her curly red hair, turned-up nose and large green eyes. If anyone could get information out of a man she could.

Within minutes, she returned with the young men in tow. 'This is Greg and Robert, and they're pilots in the RAF.' She indicated her friends. 'This is Ellie and Mary.'

The pilots shook the girls' hands in turn. 'I believe we'll be meeting up at the dance,' said the one called Robert.

Greg held Mary's hand a little too long, his eyes looking straight into hers, ensnaring her in his gaze. It was as if a jolt of lightning shot through her. Before her stood the most beautiful man she'd ever seen and he was a man, not a boy. His jaw was square, his mouth generous, his nose slightly bent and a mite too long for perfection, but his eyes...losing the power to speak, she turned her head away. What was the matter with her? She'd no right to feel like this. At least not with someone she'd just met.

'Are there more of ye?' asked Ellie, her voice a pitch higher than before.

'Eventually I'm sure there will be.'

'Nice to meet you, girls,' said Robert. 'We'll see you around.' They nodded and strolled towards the hotel. Greg walked slightly bent forward, his hands clutched behind his back. The two men seemed to be in deep conversation.

'Wow,' said Rita, releasing the word on a rush of air.

The girls put their hands over their mouths and shook with silent glee. 'Well, what did ye find out?' Ellie turned to Rita once the pilots were out of earshot.

'Ach, they're tight-lipped. But, hey, did ye see the way Greg looked at ye, Mary? I'm here swinging my legs and giving him my best smile and he hardly glanced my way.' Rita pulled up her dress to reveal a smooth knee above a shapely calf. 'Maybe I should have done this sooner.' She batted her eyelids.

'Oh, Rita. Ye're that daft!' Mary pushed her friend playfully and laughed out loud.

'Is it the dance, then?' asked Ellie.

'I'll have to ask my ma,' said Mary, knowing Chrissie would be willing enough if she went with Johnny. She liked him and

Mary did love to dance. Her dad taught her the steps on the kitchen floor when she was wee, before his collapsing lungs forced him to stop. Her parents had often danced together, holding each other close. 'It won't be a good thing, war,' she said, thinking about her father's injuries.

Rita rubbed her friend's shoulder. 'I'm sorry, I forgot. I know how yer dad got hurt bad the last time.'

'It's fine.' Mary grew up with her father's scars. She hadn't even noticed them until she took her first friend home. Jessica had taken one look at Charlie's face and screamed, ran outside and cried for her mam. Next day it was all round the school that a monster lived in Mary's house.

Afterwards, Chrissie took her sobbing daughter in her arms, explained about the brave, handsome man her father had been and about the war and the fire that ruined his looks.

Once more the pain of his loss cast a shadow over her mood. 'War's a terrible thing,' she said. 'I can see why my mam's so worried.'

Rita, not one to be down for long, shrugged. 'My folks are worried too, but there's nothing we can do to stop it, so we might as well enjoy the benefits.' Her eyes were still on the pilots who had stopped by the hotel door. Rita lifted one hand in a wave and they waved back before going inside.

It was alright for her, Mary thought. Her dad was too old to be called up and she'd no brothers nor a steady sweetheart.

'I don't know why yer mam's so protective over ye anyway,' said Rita. 'It's no as if ye're a bairn. Ye're the same age as me, and mine can't wait till I'm married off.'

'Mam brought me and Peter up on her own after my da died.' Mary felt the need to explain why things were different for her. She plucked at the material of her skirt. 'I know she feels responsible for me, but since Peter's all but moved out, I feel sort of responsible for her.'

'Ye can't live with her all yer life,' said Ellie.

'I think I'll always be nearby,' Mary replied.

Chapter Seven

Mary

Chrissie was a bit reticent about Mary to going to the dance, especially since she'd asked if Chrissie knew anything about the airmen.

'I know nothing about them,' Chrissie answered. 'But there's a couple of soldiers in the county too. It'll be something to do with the threat of war. Someone said they were going to start issuing gas masks and all.' She stopped and looked steadily at her daughter. 'Those men'll be after the good-time girls. Just ye see ye've nothing to do with them.'

'Oh, Mam, ye're no wise! Why should I be anywhere near them? Anyway, they must be quite old.'

'Ye're only seventeen, lassie, but ye do look older and bonny with it. I'd come to the dance myself if I wasn't so busy.'

'Aye, ye are a bonny lassie,' said Chrissie's neighbour, Dolly, from her seat next to the fire. 'Ye just be careful with those airmen. Dinna ye end up with a fatherless bairn.'

'I'm only going to the dance. I don't think there'll be any fatherless bairns there. They'll no be allowed in,' said Mary with a chuckle.

'Ye may well laugh.' Dolly, spare as a rod, with short, wispy hair as yellow at the front as her nicotine-stained fingers, rose to go, 'but ye wouldn't be the first nor the last.' She nodded wisely. 'Keep yer hand on yer ha'penny, that's my advice.'

'But I'll have to pay my ha'penny to get in,' said Mary.

'Mary, ye're being a wee bit cheeky now,' said Chrissie.

'Sorry, Dolly, I know what ye mean,' said Mary, still smiling.

'The young think they know it all,' muttered Dolly as she opened the door. 'I'd better get the tea on. Jock'll be in soon. I'll see ye later, Chrissie. And ye, young lady,' She waggled a finger at Mary, 'mind my words.'

'Aye, I will and all.'

The door closed behind Dolly. Mary turned to her mother. 'Please, Ma. There's a real band. Johnny's coming. He'll keep an eye on me. No that I need it, mind. All the other lassies are going. Rita and Ellie got time off specially. I promise if I find any fatherless bairns, I'll no take them home, or,' she gave her mother a sly glance, 'Let go of my ha'penny.'

Chrissie grinned then sighed. 'I suppose it'll be alright. But ye're to come straight back.'

Mary clapped her hands and, grabbing her mother's arms, whirled her round the kitchen.

'Och, my,' said Chrissie, when Mary released her. 'Ye're fair knocking the wind from me.'

'If ye're lonely, ye can always ask Sinclair in, for a bit of company, like.' Mary burst out laughing at the sudden shock on her mother's face.

'Sinclair and I are no more than friends.'

'*I know* that.' Mary giggled as she spoke. There were times when she had no control over the giggles that sprung from nowhere and often at inopportune moments. 'But,' she continued, 'he's soon to have a bonny new bathroom.'

'What? Ye've been listening at the door, ye wee limmer!' Chrissie pulled a dishcloth from the brass rod and cracked it at her daughter. Mary yelped when it caught her hand and jumped away, still laughing. No one could turn a dishcloth into a whip the way Chrissie Rosie could.

'Seriously, Mam, I don't mind if ye and Sinclair get together.' She rubbed her hand where the dishcloth had stung. 'Ye're too young to be on yer own.'

Chrissie's face turned pink. 'I'll no be looking at another man and that's that.'

Mary shrugged. 'I'm just saying I don't mind. Don't stay single because of me or our Peter. We want ye to be happy and Peter'll be gone soon enough judging by the looks he gave that wee herring gutter. I'd better get to bed before ye come at me with the dish-cloth again. I'm starting at six tomorrow. It's a good job the mill's within cycling distance.' Still grinning, she climbed the steep wooden staircase to the room beneath the rafters where she slept on a mattress stuffed with chaff.

With Johnny's help, Benjie Mowat the miller, a bent old man with sinewy arms and a constant cough, carried all the grain sacks up two flights of stairs. Once all the grain was gathered, Benjie opened the first sack and brought up a double handful. 'This is a goukinful,' he said, 'Ye've got to recognise the finest grain.'

'Aye,' said Johnny with a wink at Mary who had taken a break to follow them up, 'Ye tell me that every day.'

Benjie dropped the grain back in the sack and tapped his forehead with a yellowed finger. 'It's to get it in here, laddie, get it in here.'

'I've got it.' Johnny picked up a handful and let it run through his fingers. 'I know the difference between the good stuff and the grist.'

'They say there's going to be a war,' said Mary.

'They'd better no take the lads from the land,' said Benjie. 'Else all we'll be getting is grist. Now get yerself down to the kitchen, Mary, enough o' keeping my apprentice from his work. My good wife needs a hand with the bread.'

'Yes, sir,' said Mary with a laugh. 'I'll see ye at half-yoking time, Johnny.'

'Well, if ye don't get a move on, there'll be no half-yoking.' Benjie took a fit of coughing, turning his head away from the grain as his face reddened and beads of sweat trickled along his cheeks.

He wasn't a bad sort, Mary thought as she climbed down to the kitchen. He and his wife Daisy were salt of the earth. She was lucky to get a job with them.

'Will ye be going to the dance, Daisy?' Mary opened the kitchen door.

Daisy heaved her massive body round so that she could push a tray of loaves into the oven, her face red and damp, her breath laboured. 'I'm too glad to get my feet up of a night, I'll no be wearing them out on a dance floor. Mind ye, I was aye nimble on my feet when I was a lassie.'

Benjie's hacking cough reached their ears.

'He sounds bad the day,' said Mary.

'It's the dust from the grain. He's no fit to be carrying all these sacks either.' Daisy shook her head. 'But there's nothing else for it, lassie, nothing else for it. Now get these loaves bagged up and delivered to the shops. There's a dozen for Groats and a dozen for Canisbay. Then come back for the eggs. Don't try to take everything at once like ye did last time. Customers don't want their goods all over the road.'

'I'll no try that again,' said Mary. 'I was only trying to save time.'

'Well-meaning or no, ye'd best not, else it'll be coming off yer wages. But I will say, ye've been working like a wee slave ever since to make up for it.'

A week ago she'd run over a stone and the bicycle careered into the ditch spilling the contents of the basket and breaking all the eggs. It might not have been so bad if they had not been balanced on top of the loaves causing them all to fall out.

Mary sang as she cycled along the road, enjoying the wind in her hair and the sun on her skin. Somewhere in the distance she heard the drone of aeroplanes. As they drew nearer, she realised there were three. She stopped and watched them as they flew over Orkney, circled and came back, swooping low over the land then disappearing into the distance. *If I was a boy, I'd join the air force. It must be wonderful to soar through the sky*, she thought as she resumed her pedalling.

Chapter Eight

Mary

Saturday night came round at last and Mary took extra care with her looks. She dressed in her best frock and curled her hair, taking care not to overheat the tongs. She even borrowed a bit of make up from Rita. Deep down she wondered who she was really doing this for. Johnny wouldn't care if she came in a sack. She thought about the airman's striking eyes and laughed at herself. He must be somewhere in his twenties and he'd sounded posh, not someone who would ever be interested in her with her broad, flat accent and country ways. Anyway, if she did marry Johnny, years down the line when they were old and settled with several bairns, it might be good to sometimes remember a handsome pilot who had once held her hand too long. That's *if* she married Johnny.

Mary was disappointed that the promised band failed to turn up. Instead, the music was provided by a gramophone, but she was in such high spirits just to be there, that the scratchy records could not dampen her mood. She turned to Rita to say just that, then stopped, the words instantly frozen inside her.

The two young pilots, looking smart and polished in their uniforms, walked through the door. Mary was surprised at her own reaction. There was something about this man that gave her a squeamish sensation in her belly, made her heart beat high in her chest and dried her mouth, all of which were new, embarrassing, but exciting sensations, sensations that Johnny never raised in her. Aware that she was staring, she snatched her gaze away, then sneaked a sideways glance at Greg. He was watching her, a slightly amused look on his face.

Was he laughing at her — pleased that yet another silly young lassie had fallen for his smooth good looks and wonderful eyes? Well, she would show him how disinterested she was. Pulling her shoulders back and tilting her head, she looked around for Johnny who was in the far corner, seemingly not noticing her at all.

'Let's go get some lemonade,' she said to Rita, who stood next to her, swaying to the beat of Glenn Miller.

Rita shrugged. 'That's if Lily's made any.' Lily was the caretaker of the hall and usually laced beakers of water with whatever berries she could get her hands on, berries and her home-made wine. The word 'lemonade' covered a variety of flavours.

They were about to go when she heard the voice at her shoulder. 'May I have this dance?'

Even before she turned, she knew it was him. She tried, unsuccessfully, to look nonchalant when she nodded. He slipped an arm around her waist and clasped her hand in his. Greg was taller than she thought and he led her effortlessly onto the floor.

'Penny for them,' he said.

'I thought it was a band tonight. I'm a bit disappointed.' She spoke in a little rush through dry lips.

He smiled. 'Not too disappointed, I hope.'

Not now, she thought, aware of the pressure of his arm and the minty smell of his breath. She laughed, a silly giggly little sound.

'We'd best introduce ourselves properly if we're to dance all night. I'm Greg Cunningham.'

Dance all night? A pleasant shiver ran through her. 'Mary Rosie.' Should she tell him she was here with her boyfriend or

41

just enjoy the moment? She decided on the latter. Serve Johnny right for leaving her alone. He was supposed to care for her, but didn't actions speak louder than words? He did look at her the way Greg Cunningham was looking at her now – but Greg, he made her all tingly inside.

'Have you lived here all your life?'

'I was born on Raumsey, an island over there.' She nodded over her shoulder in a northern direction. 'We moved to the mainland when I was still small. My dad was injured in the last war and often needed a doctor and there was none on the island. My mother knows about herbs and things; she was the island howdie, but, well, there's new-fangled medicines that work better than hers. My cousins still live on Raumsey.' Realising she was babbling, she snapped her mouth shut.

'Your mother was a what?'

'A howdie. I suppose you'd call her a midwife.'

'Ah, I see. And you, do you like living here? I imagine it's very quiet.'

She loved his voice. It was soft and deep and proper, like they taught in school. 'We do have dances and sometimes go to town to the dances there or the pictures.' Her mouth dried again and she gave a little cough. 'What's it like to fly? I've always wondered. I envied the birds when I was small. I used to jump off walls and flap my arms and wonder how the birds could do it and I couldn't. Sometimes I used the tails of my coat to make wings. I bruised my knees and hurt my back. My mam shouted at me, "If God meant us to fly, he'd have given us wings."' She laughed as if she'd said something funny, then clamped her lips shut again. Why did her rebellious tongue always run away when she was nervous?

He chuckled. 'I think we've all done that. I certainly did. To answer your question, flying's amazing.'

'Do you think I could do it? Be a pilot, I mean?' Why did she say that?

'Unlikely, though I believe there were women flying planes in the last war and I foresee a time when we might need them again. But you'd have to be a trained as a pilot and that takes money. Maybe someday I'll take you up.'

'Really? Could you?'

'Right now I'd probably get into big trouble, but someday.'

Her heart thundered. He was talking as if they had a future together. That thought was ridiculous, of course, but it made her want to laugh out loud. She knew he was merely flirting, but she loved it.

The conversation went on. Mary forgot Johnny, forgot the other people in the hall, forgot her mother's warnings and was only aware of the strength of the arm around her, the way he made her laugh and the way they moved in perfect step together. Taught by her dad, she was an excellent dancer. Johnny on the other hand, suffered two left feet. When the dance ended, Greg continued to hold onto her.

'Stay with me,' he said.

Forever, she thought dreamily as they waited for the music to begin again. Mary watched the others gathered in the hall. Mostly people she knew, but a few other servicemen too.

'Why are you lot here?' she asked.

'There are things I can't tell you, little one.' The music started again. He tightened his arm so that she felt his heartbeat and he bent forward so he could talk right into her ear. 'I always wanted to fly. I'd have joined up even if there was no war.' He put his lips even closer and she felt the heat from his breath. 'But, you know, this is the first time I've flown without wings.'

She knew exactly what he meant, because she felt it too. And she longed to stay in his arms with his breath in her ear forever.

But this time, when the dance ended, he thanked her. 'I've got to go now, I just saw one of the lads signalling to me'. There was a twinkle in his eye. 'But I'll be back for *you* again.'

She walked, or rather floated towards Rita who raised her eyebrows. 'I could've drunk a gallon of Lily's potion and ye'd never have noticed. Have a sip, some of the lads have managed to get something a wee bit stronger to put in it and all.' She held out the tin mug.

'I don't need anything stronger, but…' Mary took the mug anyway and took a long drink. 'Eeh, that's pretty strong.' She coughed, wiped her mouth on the back of her hand and, aware that she still wore a silly grin, she giggled.

'Did ye get his full name?' whispered Ellie.

'Greg Cunningham.'

'Flight Lieutenant Greg Cunningham,' echoed Ellie.

'Flight Lieutenant?'

'Did ye no see the stripes on his arm? Oh come on, bet ye didn't see another thing but his eyes. I saw the way ye were gazing at each other, so did Johnny. If looks could kill, that poor man would be stone dead.' She gave her friend a little push.

Mary ignored the comment, not caring whether she made Johnny jealous or not. 'How do ye know about the stripes?'

Ellie gave a loud laugh. 'I've been dancing with Robert. He told me.' She handed her friend another cup. 'Want some more? I think I've had enough.'

Johnny marched across the floor, his face like thunder. 'What do you think you're doing?' He grabbed her arm and spun her round to face him.

'I was dancing. What do you mean? The drink?' Shocked by his reaction, Mary jerked away from him, took the cup from her friend and, although she'd not meant to drink any more, lifted it to her lips and emptied it before handing it back. The liquid slipped down her throat burning a little as it went.

'I promised yer ma I'd keep an eye on ye. That guy's pretty old.' Johnny's mouth pursed, his cheeks, red.

'Probably…in his twenties.' Her voice was already beginning to slur and she wished she hadn't been so hasty drinking the contents of Rita's mug as well as her own.

'Well, ye're not dancing with him again.'

44

'I danced with a man, took a drink, what's wrong with that? I didn't even think you'd notice.'

'Ye're supposed to be with me.'

'And where were ye? Away with the lads sampling some illegal brew no doubt. Stop being such a grump, Johnny. I'll dance with who I want.' The alcohol had gone to her head and she did a twirl, staggering against him as she stopped.

'For God's sake, Mary. You're drunk.'

'I think I am. But just a teenie weenie bit.' Suddenly the whole thing seemed hilarious and, throwing head back, she dissolved in a fit of giggles.

'Take your partners for a Gay Gordons,' said the compere. Johnny grabbed Mary's arm again. 'Come on, have this dance with me. With any luck it might sober ye up.'

She'd never seen him like this and she didn't like it. His face was scarlet, his eyes angry.

'Are ye jealous? 'Oh my goodness, ye are, aren't ye?' From the tail of her eye she saw Greg and the other men in uniform heading for the door and her high spirits plummeted. He could have at least said goodbye, or asked for her address, anything. Suddenly she didn't want to be near Johnny any more.

'Don't be ridiculous. This isn't like ye, Mary. Come on, we're going home.'

'What? Oh.' Her attention was drawn back to the boy everyone expected her to marry. 'I don't want to go home.' She looked at Johnny, staid, predictable, boring Johnny who never whispered in her ear, who held her like a brother when they stumbled round the dance floor. In the last few hours she experienced something exciting and in that short time, she knew she really didn't want to marry him. 'I'm not going home.'

'I don't know what's got into ye the night. We'll go for a walk in the fresh air, see if ye'll sober up. Carry on like this and ye'll be no better than Maudie Blackstockings.'

If he hadn't said that, she would have gone with him, they would have perhaps made up, remained friends and said no

45

more about it, but *Maudie Blackstockings*! She was a drunken old woman who seldom washed by the state of her clothes and had a reputation of having enjoyed several sexual partners. Being compared to her made Mary's temper boil. Johnny had never behaved like this before, but then, neither had she. He was right though. She should go home. Since Greg left, the night had been ruined for her.

Johnny followed her out and tried to put his arm around her as they walked along the road.

Still smarting at being compared to Maudie Blackstockings, she shook him off. 'I think I'd rather walk by myself,' she said.

'Don't be daft. You can't walk all that way on yer own. Anyway I promised yer mam and she wouldn't be happy that ye were cavorting with that airman.'

'I was only dancing for God's sake.'

'Ye're *not* walking home alone.'

'Why not? What do ye care?' She started marching along the road. *Maudie Blackstockings*. How could he?

Johnny quickened his step until his pace matched hers. 'Look, I'm sorry if I upset ye, but the way that guy was looking at ye, like ye'd no clothes on. I hate seeing ye disrespected like that.'

For a short time Mary had felt special, but the way Greg left without a backward glance was like a knife in her heart. She couldn't understand why she felt like this. Was this love? But no one fell in and out of love as quickly as that did they? With tears threatening, she kept walking. Her shoes pinched her feet and she was cold.

'I shouldn't have taken the drink,' she said. 'It's made me all weepy and no myself at all.'

'I was just looking out for ye, that's all. As long as ye've learnt yer lesson.' Johnny's eyes were riveted on the road ahead, his face set.

'Aye, I've learnt a lot,' she said.

When they stopped outside her cottage, he grasped her arm. 'I was going to speak to ye tonight. I want to ask ye ...'

Mary's stomach roiled. She didn't want him to ask her anything, was afraid of what the question might be. She stopped and looked at his concerned face in the moonlight. He pulled her against him and bent forward as if he were going to kiss her, but why now when she no longer wanted him to? It was too late, had been since she first set eyes on Greg Cunningham.

'I'm sorry. I don't know what got into me, but I can't talk now. I'll be back to normal tomorrow probably.' She put her hands on his chest, pushed him away and hurried off.

Chrissie looked up from where she was knitting by the fire. 'Ye're early, love. Good dance was it?'

'It wasn't that great.' Mary sat down, shook off her shoes and held her numb feet to the fire. 'There was no band and the records were scratchy.'

'Didn't ye ask Johnny in for a cup of tea?'

She shook her head. 'He upset me the night. Acted like he owned me.'

'And why wouldn't he? He's got a soft spot for ye, a glass eye would see it and I'm sure ye feel the same.'

'I thought I did, but I hated the way he acted.'

'Mary, can I smell whisky?'

'No, it's just Lily's brew.'

'I'll have to have words with Lily. Her elderberry wine is getting aye stronger.'

'Mam,' Mary changed the subject. 'When ye first met Dad, how did ye feel?'

Chrissie gave a gentle laugh and her eyes went soft as she took a trip down memory lane. 'He was younger than me. I just thought of him as a daft wee laddie with a crush on an older woman.' She looked past Mary with a smile that spoke of long ago.

'Ye weren't *that* much older than me,' Mary said. She really wanted to ask whether he'd made the blood rush in her veins and if not, when did she know she loved him, but that was not the kind of question she could ask her mother.

'Have ye and Johnny fallen out?' Chrissie was suddenly back from her musing.

'No, not really. But why does everyone think we're a couple? I...' She searched for a word that would explain her emotional state and then found it. 'I feel pressured.' Yes that was exactly what it was.

'Mary, what happened? I thought... I hoped ye two were set on getting wed.'

'That's what I mean. Everyone takes it for granted.' Even Johnny, she thought. She didn't want to talk about it anymore.

The long walk home had sobered her, but left her tired. Normally she would have swung into the house full of news of the night and she and her mother would have a last cup of cocoa before bed. She also knew if her mother found out the reason behind her mood and Johnny's tantrum, she would be on his side.

'Ach, I'm going to my bed,' said Mary, rising.

'There's water in the jug in your room for a wash. There's hot in the kettle.' Chrissie usually kept clean water, soap and a towel by the basins in the bedrooms, to wash off the grime of the day.

'Thanks, Mam, but I'm used to washing in cold. Goodnight. I'll probably go right to sleep.'

Once in bed, sleep would not claim her. She was thinking about the pilot and how he made her feel. That she cared for Johnny was not in doubt, but tonight she discovered feelings that she never knew existed. She had to see Greg again. Only then she would know if what she felt was real or was it just the magic of the night. Her great aunt's words came back at her. There *was* a big world out there and she had barely sampled any of it.

Chapter Nine

Mary

Johnny wasn't a regular kirk goer, but that Sunday he was there, sitting with his family a few rows in front of Mary and her mother. He turned around when she entered, his eyes sorrowful, reminding her of a chastised pup. She gave him a wan smile and a slight nod.

After the service he was waiting by the door.

'Of ye go with him,' whispered Chrissie. 'I've a few folk I want to talk to.'

They walked without speaking for a few minutes. When Johnny took her hand, she let her own lie lifelessly in his and allowed herself to be led towards the shore.

'Are ye still huffing about last night?' he asked after a while.

'I'm no huffing.' But she didn't look at him. Instead she allowed her eyes to wander across the firth to the islands. 'I think I'll go across to Raumsey the day. See my cousin Annie and her new baby.'

'I could go with ye. Take ye in my boat.'

'Na. Sinclair's going. He's got business there. Ye can just honour the Sabbath day and keep it holy, since ye've seen fit to go to the kirk.' She grinned when she said that. Johnny would happily find a hundred other things to do rather than spend the day in rest. With crofts to supplement their income, few locals had the luxury of choosing how to spend a Sunday. Even with dinner cooked the day before and eaten cold, the women couldn't rest either. There were hens to feed and cows to milk.

Mary had made no arrangements to go to the island, but she didn't want to spend the day with Johnny.

'See ye tomorrow then.' He looked crestfallen and let her hand slip from his.

The whole of the following week they walked together to work, as usual. Mary laughed and joked, but kept a distance. Her feelings had changed. What was the matter with her? It couldn't be the pilot. She knew he was only here for a short time and she might never see him again, whereas she had been friends with Johnny since they were bairns. But war was on the horizon and deep within her, Mary knew everything was going to change and, in one way, she would welcome that change.

The following Sunday, when Mary returned home, the kitchen was full of neighbours, which wasn't unusual. Betsy, with her bulging belly and full bosom, her bairn due any day, filled the armchair before the fire. Dolly sat in the other. Myrtle who ran the wee shop up the road, sat at the table smoking a cigarette. She was wearing a white kerchief with red spots and her peroxide blonde hair was tightly curled. Chrissie didn't approve of Myrtle's styles, but Mary secretly admired her, thinking her very pretty and a good laugh. Johnny's father Donal sat at the other side of the table, his pipe in one side of his mouth, his greying hair standing on end where he no doubt had run his fingers through it, a habit of his when he was worried. Johnny leaned against the wall, his arms folded. Peter, home for the weekend, had pulled his chair close to the wireless beside his mother and, of course, there was Sinclair, sitting on the box by the bed, his long legs crossed. The only sound in the room was Donal's asthmatic wheeze, the steady tick of the clock and the fizzing of the wireless as Peter fiddled with the knobs.

'What are ye all listening to?' Mary set her basket on the wooden table and tried to avoid Johnny's eyes.

Chrissie flapped her hand. 'Wheesht.' She leaned closer to the crackling wireless as Peter found the station he was looking for.

'That's it,' she said as a voice broke over the miles, clear enough to be understood.

'It's Chamberlain,' Peter mouthed to Mary. And she knew at once it wasn't good news.

"This morning the British Ambassador in Berlin handed the German Government a final note stating that, unless we heard from them by 11 o'clock that they were prepared at once to withdraw their troops from Poland, a state of war would exist between us.

I have to tell you now that no such undertaking has been received, and that consequently this country is at war with Germany."

In silence they listened to the rest of the announcement. When it finished, Chrissie turned the wireless off and rubbed her hands down the skirt of her apron. For a moment there was relative silence in the room.

Chrissie was the first to speak. 'I'd hoped never to see another war.'

'Aye, lassie, we all hoped that,' said Sinclair. 'But little good did hoping do. And we'll no be safe, far from it. The government'll hide the battleships just across the water in Scapa Flow and with the new airstrip in Wick no twenty miles away, we'll be in the thick of it, mark my words.'

Chrissie moved to the stove and pulled the kettle over the flames. 'What's afore us, will no go past us,' she said with a sigh. She picked up a wooden spoon from where it lay on the table and brandished it. 'But I'll tell you this, if any Germans come near my door, they'll no be leaving unscathed.'

'Aye,' said Donal, removing the pipe from his mouth, 'If you were in charge of the army, Chrissie, Hitler would be high-

51

tailing it back home this very night!' He chuckled and replaced the pipe.

Johnny was still watching Mary, making her feel uneasy. To get away from his accusing gaze, she left the house and breathed in the damp air. War. What did this mean for them all? She heard footsteps behind her.

'I wondered where ye'd gone.'

'Johnny,' she turned. 'What do ye want?'

'Don't ye think this has gone far enough? Ye're a right thrawn bitch when ye want to be.'

'What do ye mean?'

'Mary Mary quite contrary. Ye've changed. Have ye gone off me? I'm sorry about the other night. I was thinking o' yer welfare. But I shouldn't have been such an idiot. Can we no go back the way we were? I'll like as not be called up and I don't want to leave things like this between us. There's something I wanted to say before everything got bad.'

'Ye'll no have to go, not till ye're done yer apprenticeship anyway and by then it might all be over.'

Johnny drew in a deep, shaky breath and his face grew red. 'I wanted to propose, ask ye to marry me.' The words came out in a rush

Not now, please not now, she thought. She didn't want to hurt him, but she didn't want to be tied to him either. 'I didn't think... this is a bit sudden.' Her cheeks grew hot. It wasn't sudden at all, but she had not envisaged it happening like this.

'It's the war. It changes everything.' Now that he had said it, his voice grew more confident.

She held up her hand, stopping him. 'Ye're right. The war has changed everything.'

'Then...then we'll get wed?'

Mary shook her head. 'I don't think we should make a commitment until the war is over.'

He stared at her. 'Things are going to get hard. Shortages and all that. My way o' thinking is, if the worst happens and ye were a war widow, ye'd get a pension from the state.'

'Oh Johnny, how can ye even imagine that?' Dear Johnny. Facing an uncertain future, his first thought was to make sure she was alright. Filled with a sudden rush of affection for him, she leaned forward and kissed him on the cheek, then wished she hadn't.

He put his arms around her and held her so tightly she could hardly breathe. When he let her go she pushed him away and stepped back. He had completely misread her action. At that moment she saw him as a much-loved friend, nothing more.

'It's awful good of ye to think of me, but it's best to make no decisions till after it's all over,' she said.

'So ye don't want to?' Hurt filled his eyes.

'Everything's changing…ye must see that.'

'Even what ye feel for me?'

'I don't know what I feel for ye,' she answered honestly.

'That's it then. I needed to know before I decided.'

'Decided what?'

'To volunteer for the army.'

'But yer apprenticeship…'

'I'll finish it when I come back.' He stared at his hands in silence. 'I was waiting until I'd some money put by, something to offer ye. But…' He waited, his eyes hopeful.

'Oh Johnny. I care for ye deeply, but everything's so scary. I can't say yes right now.'

'So there's still hope?'

She searched her mind for the right words. How could she let him down gently? 'I know how my dad's injuries affected my mam, affected them as a couple, changed their whole lives.'

'Ye're maybe right. I hadn't thought. I could come back maimed for life and then ye'd be shackled to me. And ye wouldn't want that, would ye?' His voice held a hint of bitterness.

53

'That wasn't what I meant, ye might feel different, everything might be different.' She covered his hand with hers and felt him flinch. She turned away and swallowed the lump in her throat. 'My dad didn't speak much about the last war, but I know he lost his twin brother and was badly injured in the same battle.'

'Are ye scared?' he asked.

'About what might happen, aye.'

'Ye look cold.' He moved closer and put his arm around her. She allowed the embrace, but when he tried to kiss her, she pulled away. She no longer needed that kiss to know how she felt. 'We'd best go in. They'll be wondering what happened to us.'

He gave a deep sigh. 'No, ye'll stay till we've sorted this. I need to know for certain…if there's no hope…'

'I can't marry ye, Johnny.' She began to lose patience. He wasn't listening to her. 'Have I not made that clear?'

'Well then, if ye're sure. I haven't joined up yet. I'll go into town later the day since there's little left for me here.'

'Don't be like that. I'm truly sorry I can't be what ye want,' she said.

'I hoped so much…' He shook his head and stared at the ground.

When she turned to go, he grabbed her arm. 'Mary?'

'What is it?'

'I want to have ye to come back to. It'll keep me going until it's over. And I'll pray every night that ye'll wait for me. Give me hope at least.' His demeanour changed and once again he was the Johnny she'd known all her life.

'I'll pray for ye too. And of course there's hope. Who knows how we'll feel after the war.'

Chapter Ten

Chrissie

Chrissie looked up from where she was peeling potatoes. 'Peter,' she gasped, 'is anything wrong?' He normally only came home at a weekend. This was Wednesday.

'Not a thing, Ma.' He hesitated for a beat, then said, 'Me and the lads were talking. We're not waiting to be called up. There were some soldiers in town the day and we've signed for the Seaforth Highlanders.' He fell silent, his eyes concerned. He rubbed a thumb and forefinger together.

The strength drained from Chrissie's legs. Although she knew he would have to go sooner or later, she could see no sense in anyone putting themselves in danger until it was compulsory.

'Oh Peter, are ye sure?' she said. 'When?'

'As soon as we get the shout. I'll be at home for the next couple of weeks. The fishing's no what it was. These waters are going to get dangerous. Most of the lads are joining up.'

'Ye don't have to explain, laddie. Let's hope it's over soon, eh?' She turned away, her eyes dry, yet her voice broke and she could say no more. It was useless to argue with her son, always had been and at his age he would not thank her for telling him what to do. 'What about Jess?' she asked.

'Jess understands. She's no happy, mind, but...' HHe walked over and gave her a hug. 'I know how you feel, Ma. But I'd rather go with my pals now than later and me and Jess, we've talked about it. She's promised to wait for me. We're engaged.'

'Engaged? That's ... great.' She was pleased about that, but the thought of him leaving marred any joy at his news. How could she argue with her first-born at a time like this? Every mother and wife in the land would have to face the worry soon, why should she be any different? She silently thanked God that Mary was still too young to get the call and that she was a girl. There were lots of different things women could do to help the war effort without putting themselves in obvious danger. 'Congratulations. Jess is a fine lassie,' she said, solemnly.

The night before Peter left, he and some of his friends gathered in Chrissie's ben end. Sinclair, Johnny, Dolly, Betsy, Daisy and Benjie, Myrtle and her man Bill, were all there to congratulate Peter and Jess on their engagement and wish the boys safe journey and early return. They drank a toast of home-brewed beer' Chrissie had cooked stovies with more gravy and potato than meat and served it with thick baked oatcakes.

When the lads started singing, Chrissie slipped outside into the still night. It was just like last time, when Charlie left, promising to be home before Christmas. This time there would be no such promises. Keen to get away from the forced bonhomie, she sat on the wooden bench Charlie made when they'd first come over from Raumsey. From here she was afforded a view over the grey, lacy tops of the waves, to the dark humps of the islands adorned with pinpricks of light from windows.

The door opened and closed and the sound of voices flowed into the night, louder for a moment. Soft footsteps sounded on the flagstone path and the seat creaked as someone sat beside her. She could smell nicotine smoke on the clean air. He dropped his cigarette and ground it out with the sole of his shoe.

'He'll be alright,' said Sinclair.

Without speaking, or turning, she nodded.

An arm snaked around her shoulders and she leaned back against his chest. 'I can't stop remembering,' she said.

'They've got to go, ye know that.' Sinclair tightened his grip.

'What did Charlie give his health for? What did all the young men die for in the last war? The war to end all wars, that was a laugh.' She turned to look at him and found his lips inches from hers. Although there was something warm and comforting about his bodily contact it also gave rise to feelings she constantly fought to forget.

He laid his cheek against her forehead and rubbed her arm. 'I can't answer that, all I can say is, I'll always be here for ye.'

'Until ye get the call as well.'

'No. I'll be needed on the land though the ferry'll probably stop running. They'll be planting mines in those waters and sending U-boats. The need to grow our own food'll be greater than ever and at my age I may be considered too old anyway.' He bent forward and tried to kiss her.

For a moment she was tempted, then pulled away. She'd promised Charlie. He hadn't asked for that promise and she knew he wouldn't have held her to it, but sitting here with another man and welcoming his embrace made her feel disloyal. Furthermore, if she dropped her defences, let him in, then by the time this war was over, would she be suffering the loss of two loves instead of one? No, it would be better by far to remain friends. 'We'd best go back, they'll be wondering where we are.'

'Chrissie,' he said her name like a moan. 'I'm sorry, I shouldn't have done that. But I want to love ye. Do ye no know?'

She thought of Mary's words, *I don't mind if ye and Sinclair get together*. Now Peter was leaving and she needed all the comfort she could get. The arguments raced round in her head. Charlie had been her soul mate and when he died she felt as if half of her had been ripped away and that never again on this earth would she be whole. Anyway, her daughter was still in the house. Yet all her reasons seemed weak when Sinclair was this close.

'Ye know I would marry ye in a heartbeat, if it's marriage ye want,' he said.

'And ye won't go to war?'

'No. And if ye'll have me, I'll make doubly sure I never leave yer side.' He bent towards her again. She felt the strength of his arms, breathed in his strong male scent and something stirred deep within her, a pure physical desire she'd thought long dead.

'I'm sorry, Sinclair. I can't ever marry again.' Terrified of her own rising emotion, she rose and almost ran into the house, the memory of his essence going with her.

One of Peter's friends took her hand and twirled her round on a floor where Mary, Peter and a few others were already dancing.

'Come on,' he said. 'Peter'll be fine, we'll look after him.'

'I'm sure ye will and all.' She gave a forced laugh.

She danced and sang along to her one and only record playing on the gramophone and tried to ignore the nagging certainty that all of these lads would never again congregate in her ben end.

Chrissie didn't sleep much that night. Mixed in with the fear of losing her son, was the longing that Sinclair Mackay reawakened in her. She often asked herself whether she should just satisfy that longing, but knowing how Sinclair felt about her, it would be wrong to raise his hopes when she could never fully return his feelings. She cared and respected him too much for that.

With a low groan she turned over. Her daughter was in the next room, her bairn. Then there was Peter, leaving tomorrow for God knew where. Her brain felt as if it were on fire, thoughts crowding upon desire, desire crowding on worries.

The scarred face of Charlie when he first came home and the way his nightmares had plagued him rose anew. Now Peter was going to face that same foe.

If only she could have Charlie back, just for one night, enjoy his strength next to her, tell him her fears, have him tell her what to do, she would be able to cope with the rest. But now, alone with the silence, she found it impossible to ignore a sense of dread.

She rose, brewed herself a cup of tea and sat wrapped in her quilt, huddled before the dying fire. Yet she knew that the next day she would wash, go to the shop, crack jokes and laugh with the others and no one would know about the demons that plagued her nights.

Mary and Chrissie travelled with Peter into Wick and saw him off at the railway station. Chrissie had insisted that they dress up in their Sunday best. Jess was there too, constantly blotting her eyes with a lace handkerchief. She was supported by a little knot of her friends from the herring gutting, who knew Peter well.

The platform was crowded; so many young men, so many partings. When the train came it drowned out the sounds of the many goodbyes, the sounds of the seagulls and the crows, the sheep in nearby fields and the sounds of laughter; the young men were in high spirits.

Peter, her little boy all grown up now and taller than her, was good at writing letters, but he didn't have a clue where he would be sent after his training. Both he and his mother were only too aware of the reality of war.

Swinging rucksacks onto their backs, the lads went laughing and joking, as if it were a grand adventure. Those they left behind hid their tears behind brave smiles that disappeared the minute the train pulled out and they stood in the billows of steam and smoke. They watched that train as it grew smaller until at last it was lost in the distance. Flo, the wee dairy maid from the mains, appeared behind Mary and Chrissie, took Mary's arm and said, 'Let's get a glass of lemonade in the café.'

'Ye go with yer friend, lassie.' Chrissie longed to be alone, to hide her worry from her daughter. 'I'll… I'll just catch the next bus home.'

'Thanks, Mam,' said Mary, 'Are ye alright?'

Nodding, Chrissie turned away. 'I'll be fine. I will.' She wiped her cheek and took a deep breath. She was, she really was. She had to be.

'Are ye coming to the dance this weekend?' asked Flo.

'Mam doesn't like me going to dances, especially now with Johnny going away and all those servicemen filling the town. Warned me against them, says only loose women go out with them.'

'Oh, thank you.' Flo wrinkled her nose. She'd already had one boyfriend from the air force and was flirting with another.

'Is yer mam and da okay with ye going with servicemen?' asked Mary, still concerned about her mother.

Flo giggled. I'm nineteen. Anyway, what the eye doesn't see the heart doesn't grieve over.'

'Ye're awful, Flo.'

'Well, are ye coming or no?'

'I'd best not. Mam's worried with Peter going off. I don't want to upset her anymore. I'd best bide in for a few nights.'

Chapter Eleven

Mary

Peter had been gone for over a month and Mary Rosie sat with three of her friends in the café in High Street.

'Do ye want to read my tea-leaves?' She asked Sally as she studied the dregs in her cup. Today was a rare outing to Wick and Sally, Rita and Ellie were off next week to join the forces. The girls were excited, sipping their tea and giggling at very little.

'Give's it here then.' Sally reached for the cup and peered into it. 'I can see ye're going to miss us so much when we've gone, ye're going to regret no coming too.' She lifted her eyes and looked at her friend. 'I don't know why ye're waiting. Ye'll be called up soon in any case.'

Rita took a long draw at her cigarette and blew a plume of smoke into the air. 'Ye'll *have* to go where they send ye. At least if ye volunteer, ye'll have a choice.'

'I've told my mam that, but she always says the same thing.' Mary toyed with the end of her auburn pleat. 'I'm too young. She would have to sign the forms and she'll no do that. Says she'll apply for a dispensation when they do call me up. She needs me on the croft.' Mary didn't want to hurt her mam, but she longed to be on that train with her friends. 'It'll no be the same without ye all,' she said.

Sally shook her head and her blonde curls bounced. 'Don't worry, she'll no get a dispensation. She's a fit woman and she doesn't need ye for all the size of yer couple of fields.'

'But what if she does get it?' Mary stared at her tea, more despondent than ever. This was the second time she had a chance to see that big world out there and the second time her mam said no. 'Maybe the war won't last long, anyway.' Her heart gave a lurch. Her mam appeared strong and able and she laughed and cracked jokes with the best of them, but Mary often heard her sobbing in the night, saw the lines of weariness around her eyes, knew how worried she was about Peter, her first born, her perfect boy.

'Who's for the dance this weekend?' Rita's voice broke into Mary's thoughts. 'Ye'll have to come. It'll be the last one before we leave.' Her face fell slightly. 'I met this lovely air force guy last week. He asked to see me again. Almost made me change my mind about leaving.'

'There'll be plenty lads in uniform where you're going,' Mary said with a dry laugh, knowing that it was the influx of air personnel which influenced her friends' choice of forces.

Sally continued to study the leaves in Mary's cup, turning her head this way and that. 'Someone new is coming into yer life,' she said.

Mary giggled. 'A man no doubt. Handsome and charming.' No one really took Sally's predictions seriously. No one, that was, except Sally herself. She lifted her eyes and shot Mary a withering look.

From the distance came the deep drone of a solitary plane.

'Doesn't sound like one of ours,' said Ellie, pulling a moue of distaste. 'Could that be Jerries?'

The girls looked at each other, smiles slipping, their hands clutching their cups. At dusk on 16th March an attack had been made on Scapa in Orkney by fifteen enemy bombers. Four officers were killed and several officers and ratings wounded. That event, though many miles to the north, made the war real.

'I'm no sure...' Rita's voice was lost as the thunder of the plane became so loud it could have been right outside. The girls rose as one and crossed to the window. 'Bloody hell, that's close,' said Sally.

Suddenly the world around them seemed to erupt. Cups rattled in saucers, the building trembled.

Customers leapt to their feet and ran out of the door into High Street, desperately looking for a place of safety. A pall of smoke belched from the direction of the harbour as another explosion rent the air and flashes of fire and thick black clouds rose from down-river.

'Oh my God,' someone screamed. 'They're bombing the town.'

A woman dropped her shopping basket and ran past the girls. 'Ma bairns,' she screamed, 'I left them playing...'

Everything seemed to happen at once. The clanging of the fire engine's bell, children crying, people running around like confused ants as the managers of shops and banks herded them into the relative safety of their cellars.

'It's personal now,' screeched Sally. 'Why are they bombing us?'

An old man stood with one hand against the wall, the other clutching his walking stick. 'I knew it'd happen,' he said, as he struggled to catch his breath. 'I knew that airport would attract them. The devil's work if you ask me. And all these servicemen. What are they doing here? They should be away fighting, not billeted in good folk's houses...' He stopped and coughed, phlegm rattling in his throat.

Mary didn't pause to answer him, but made to go across the bridge towards River Street.

'Get inside, in the basement,' someone shouted, grabbing her arm as air raid sirens, woken from their reverie, shrieked too late. She shook the hand off. Many of the lads and lassies she knew worked at the harbour which was the obvious target. Her uncle Jimmy ran his own coopering business there.

Nevertheless, she followed her friends into the cellar of the Royal Bank which was by now crowded with shocked pedestrians.

The all-clear sounded as, having unleashed its deadly cargo, the plane turned up river, guns rat-a-tat-tatting until they faded into the distance. The shaken shoppers emerged into the acrid afternoon. Coughing, Mary inhaled air dense with smoke. The sea of bodies scattered erratically as two heavy horses thundered towards them, ears flat, eyes white and rolling in terror. Mary squashed herself against the wall as they passed.

Word bounced from person to person, desperate voices shouting the news, 'They've hit Bank Row. They've hit Bank Row.'

There had been no warning, no siren, no previous bombs dropped anywhere on mainland Britain, no reason for folk to suspect that death and devastation would rain down from a sunny blue sky on a residential area. Bank Row was a busy place with several shops, kilns and a pub. It had been a toss-up whether the girls went to the tea rooms there or the cafe in High Street.

The air seemed to have been sucked from the day. All around her people were crying or standing motionless. An ashen-faced policeman with shocked eyes stepped in front of her holding out both arms, barring the way. 'Sorry, girls, no one's allowed down there. It's dangerous.'

She stopped and took a backward step. 'The harbour...?' she asked, icy fingers clutching a heart that beat all the way up to her neck. Apart from Uncle Jimmy, many of her friends worked down there gutting the herring.

'I've no idea. Now keep back. Please...just...keep back.'

Numb with shock, the girls watched until the first of the stretchers was carried towards the waiting ambulance. A small mound completely covered by a blanket. A child.

From the centre of town the clock struck the hour. 'I...I have to get my bus.' She didn't want to leave, wanted to know the extent of the devastation, needed to know. She would have gladly stayed in town had there been any way of getting word to her mam, who would be worried sick and, also, there was no other means of transport home to John O'Groats that night. She grabbed Rita's arm. 'I've got to go. Will ye phone me later?'

Rita nodded. 'Nine o'clock?'

On occasion, Mary was allowed the use of the telephone in the John O'Groats post office where they had a radio link to the rest of the world and tonight no one would deny her access.

The few passengers on the bus that day were full of the news. 'Aye,' said an old woman shaking her head and dabbing her eyes. 'When the Germans occupied Norway, I knew it wouldn't be long before they came here. Didn't I say it, Cissy?'

'You did, Bella. But no sirens, no warning. Animals, that's what they are.'

'Anyone heard how many were hurt?'

'I canna believe it.'

'We never expected it here.'

'It's terrible, just terrible.'

Mary said nothing. She was still shaking.

The bus shuddered to a halt startling Mary from her shattered thoughts. Without replying to the driver's sombre farewell, she climbed out, her legs as unsteady as saplings in the wind. The quiet of the countryside was a balm after the madness in town and the high pitched voices on the bus. The cottage where she lived with her mother sat solid and welcoming, the smoke from the chimney reaching upwards in a thin line, the breeze for once, being non-existent.

The steady boom of the ocean pulsed like a heartbeat, her heartbeat. She thought of the people who would be homeless tonight, who might even now be searching the wreckage of Bank Row for their loved ones and she shuddered. This was it. This was really war.

The minute she saw her, Chrissie ran to her daughter and clasped her hands. 'Mary, thank God you're alright. We were that worried when we heard. I'll swear ye could see the smoke from here.'

'I'm fine, Mam.' Mary, marvelled at how she could act so normally when all she wanted to do was to sob and rail against the unjustness of what had just happened, but her mam had visitors as she so often did and behaving with decorum was important in this house, so she'd always been taught. Neighbours sat around the room: Betsy Oag and her son. Allan, Constance and Gussy McLean and Sinclair Mackay.

'Where did they hit? The aerodrome?' asked Chrissie.

'I think they were aiming for the harbour.' Mary's voice shook.

Chrissie stepped back, her hand over her mouth. 'Did you hear… how many were hurt?'

Knowing Chrissie's first thought would be for Uncle Jimmy, Mary shook her head. Tears welled up and stung and she fought them back. 'I felt so helpless, so useless,' she said through half sobs. 'I wish I was going with the others, I want to fight that bloody man!'

'Mary, mind your mouth,' Chrissie said.

'I'm sorry…I'm angry…'

'I know, love, I know.' Chrissie led her to the armchair by the stove and set her down. 'I've just filled the tea-pot. I'll get ye a cup and we'll have no more o' that joining up nonsense. Yer place is here.'

Mary accepted it; a cup of tea was the balm for all ills, so it seemed, but she shook her head at the offer of salmon-paste sandwiches.

Sinclair drew deeply on his cigarette. 'Aye, we'd no long left the pub or we would have been in the thick of it.' He toyed with the last of his sandwich, seemingly without appetite.

Betsy Oag, her laughing mouth still for once, leaned forward. Betsy, no more than five feet tall and as broad as she

66

was long, befriended the Rosie family the day they moved into the district and, along with her man and five bairns, had been a constant visitor ever since. Now she stared vacantly at the window.

Martin, her eldest, just past his teens, tore his eyes away from Mary for a moment and said, 'I've been speaking to a couple of the lads. We ... we think we should join up.'

'Ye can't,' gasped Betsy spinning round to face him. 'Ye're needed on the land.' Her full face grew red, her chins shivered.

'There's no enough farm work for me and Dad as it is,' he answered.

Sinclair extinguished what was left of the cigarette by stabbing it onto the ashtray. 'I was the same last time, couldn't wait to do my bit.' He raised his eyes to look at Martin. 'There's no glamour in it, son. Mind that.'

'I'm no stupid.' Martin reddened and bristled.

'Ye canna stop the laddie, Betsy,' said Sinclair.

Mary needed to keep active. She rose, walked to the stove and moved the heavy kettle over the flames. 'Another cup o' tea anyone?' she asked, forcing brightness into her voice.

'Aye, and the lads will be having a drop of this added and all.' Sinclair pulled a half bottle of Johnny Walker from the pocket of his dungarees and set it on the table.

Mary could have done with a drop herself. Since Wick was a dry town, devoid of public houses, the only alcohol was available from the seamen who used the port, or from a variety of illegal stills throughout the county. There was aye a bottle being passed along the back row in the picture house on a Saturday night. Mary was no stranger to a taste of the craitur. She cast a longing glance at the bottle, knowing a dram would go at least some of the way to help steady her shattered nerves.

'Want some, bonny lassie?' asked Sinclair as if reading her mind.

Mary glanced at Chrissie and shook her head. 'Never touch it,' she lied, and she couldn't hold back her emotions any longer. Her breath came in short, desperate gasps over which she had no control, as visions of the small body beneath blanket, terrified horses, screaming people and the stench of burning flesh, rose in her mind again.

'I can't...' She ran from the room to the end of the house where she lowered herself onto the seat and gave vent to the tears that had been frozen within her for so long.

'Aw, lassie, lassie,' came her mother's voice and a strong hand rubbed her back.

'I'm fine, I'm fine,' hiccupped Mary, 'it's just the shock. It was awful, Mam, just awful.' She pressed the palm of her hand to her mouth to try and force normality into her breath.

Chrissie hadn't hugged her daughter for a long time, it was not the highland way, but now her arms went round the shuddering body and she rocked her gently making shushing noises as if she held a little girl again.

Once the storm subsided, Mary pushed her mother away and gave a shaky laugh. 'I'm fine, honest. I'm no a bairn. There's going to be a lot more of this isn't there?'

'Aye, lassie, I can't deny it.'

'They'll need all the volunteers they can get, won't they?'

'Thankfully we can do our bit right here,' said Chrissie, her voice hardening. 'There's no need to go joining the forces.'

Mary said nothing, but silently she hoped the compulsory call-up would not be too far away. It wasn't just that she wanted to do war work, she wanted out of Caithness. It hadn't seemed too important before when there was little option, but now everything was different.

They sat like that listening to the rush of the sea, the cry of the seagulls, the bleat of a sheep, the sounds of peace, and they looked south towards the distant cloud hovering above the horizon. A cloud or smoke from twenty miles away, rising from the still burning buildings of the town, she couldn't be certain.

About two hours later, Mary made her way to the post office where she waited for Rita's call. By the time the phone rang, Ethel, the postmistress, had already filled her in with what little she knew.

'It's not good,' she said. 'Fifteen killed and eight of them bairns. The bombers missed the harbour, although we think that was the target.'

At nine thirty exactly, Rita's call came through.

Mary listened to the list of names, a few of them known to the girls and she marvelled at how calm her friend sounded.

'We're going to have to get used to this. There'll be a lot more of it.' Rita's voice remained flat.

Mary trailed home, her heart heavy. The war had seemed a distant thing, now she had to face the reality of it.

In the gloaming, she took the path along the shore. Sheep bleated for their young, a seagull yelped in protest, black-eyed seals gazed at her from the water as if reading her secrets. She wondered about the pilot who dropped the bomb. Was he old or young? Did he have a wife and children of his own? She wondered whether he'd looked out of his window, down on the sleepy little town below. Had he seen the children in the streets, running with their hoops or kicking cans, the women with their shopping bags, babies in prams? The plane had been so low, he must have seen them. Even if the harbour was his target, what threat were a few fishing boats to the grand German army? Would the boys she knew who went to join the air force, rain that same terror on a small German town? The thought was unimaginable.

That night sleep evaded her. Each time she closed her eyes she heard the droning again, saw the smoke rise in a great cloud, saw terrified horses heading for her and she struggled to run, but her feet were slow and sluggish as if stuck in mud. The second before the hooves crushed her, she woke sweating and shaking.

At last she rose, pulled her jacket over her nightdress and went downstairs where she lit the tilly lamp, stirred the dying embers in the stove and added some drift wood. Maybe her mam was right. If one bomb affected her like this, how would she cope with being in the forces? She didn't know what a WAAF's role was, but she was pretty sure they never went into combat. Nevertheless, she needed to toughen up.

While she waited for the kettle to boil, her thoughts took her back to the previous year, when war had been no more than a niggling concern. She thought about Great Aunt Agatha. Much as she hated to admit it, the old woman's predictions had been right, the Germans did attack the north first. She wondered how the old lady was faring now.

Chapter Twelve

Mary

'Mary, Mary, have ye been here all night?' She woke up to the sound of her mother's voice. Early sunlight streamed through the window and when she tried to move she found herself stiff and cramped in the rigid chair.

'I couldn't stop thinking,' she said. 'What time is it?'

'Just gone six. Go back to bed, have another hour. Ye've a day off haven't ye?'

'Aye, but I'm awake now. Might as well do some work round the croft. Ye have a rest, Mam. Ye look done in these days.'

The cow was already bellowing and a hen was perched on the window ledge, her head moving from side to side. As well as tending to the animals, peats had to be brought in and potatoes peeled. Demanding attention, the cat meowed from her bed in a cardboard box.

'Oh, Tibby.' Mary bent down and looked into the box. Tibby had given birth to six kittens somewhere in the hours before the sun rose and now, as her mistress admired her brood, she purred in contentment, her eyes half shut, reminding Mary that life went on. The whole of Caithness and possibly beyond would be in mourning today, but the world didn't stop turning.

Later Mary sat in her favourite place by the shore staring over the firth. The skies were clear and blue and free of death-bringing bombers, the firth was unusually empty of sea-going traffic. The seals had begun their dirge and sandpipers waded along the place where the surf lapped over the sand. They didn't know there was a war on. She turned at the sound of someone sliding down the slope towards her.

'Are ye alright, Mary?' said Johnny.

She shook her head. 'It's so sad. All of it. Why can't people just get on with each other?'

'I ask myself that every time my brothers and Da have a barney.' He pulled up a feather-headed grass and began chewing on the stem. 'But *we're* still fine, you and me?'

'We'll always be best friends.'

His eyes slid from her and he studied the ground. 'I'll sign up today.'

Mary realised with a jolt that she didn't want him to leave. He had been so much part of her life for so long, as much a part as her own brother. 'Why don't ye wait until ye have to go, *if* ye have to go? Ye're learning a trade here. Ye're needed.'

'If things were different between us, I would. I had dreamed…'

Not wanting to hear any more or think about what unspeakable things he might have to face in this war, she could not shatter him further. 'I can't marry you right now, but who knows what the future holds.'

'I hoped ye'd change yer mind. We could still get wed.'

She shook her head. 'No, I'll no change my mind.'

His eyes became bright and she silently prayed he wouldn't cry. She'd never seen a grown-up lad cry and didn't know how she would act if she did.

Thankfully he seemed to catch himself, took a deep breath and said the words she didn't want to hear again.

'I love ye, Mary, I always will and seeing ye and not being with ye is purgatory. I'm sorry if I can't show it more, it's just that I want ye so much and I sometimes feel I couldn't control myself if we started to kiss and that.' His face turned red. 'I want ye, I want ye properly before I go, but I wanted a ring on yer finger before I laid a hand on ye. That's why I didn't say anything before, and … and it wasn't easy. But…but ye've got to want me too, and ye don't, do ye?'

She didn't answer straight away. 'I…I don't know what I want,' she said in a small voice.

'If it's that airman, ye'll probably never see him again.' Johnny pressed his lips together and his breaths were small and sharp, his nostrils tightening with every intake.

'It's nothing to do with him. Please don't make this hard,' she said, and wiped her eyes. She was breaking his heart and that in turn was breaking hers. He was right. She would never see Greg again, but she wanted to feel like that again and she now knew she never would with Johnny.

He stood and marched up the slope before she could say another word. She sucked in a trembling breath. Less than a month ago everything had seemed so straight forward. One month and she felt as if she had changed irrevocably.

Next day at work Johnny didn't as much as look her way.

'Aye,' said the miller coming up behind her. 'Have ye two had a falling out?'

Mary shook her head. 'Just a misunderstanding.'

'I'm going to join up,' said Johnny without looking at Mary.

Benjie stuttered as if searching for the right words, 'Ye daft wee laddie. They'll come for ye soon enough.' He looked at Mary. 'Hope ye're no thinking of volunteering as well. I've little enough staff left and folk still have to eat bread.'

'I've no been planning it,' said Mary. But something tugged at her heart. She knew she was needed here and probably would get an exemption. That is, if she decided to go after one. But her brother had gone, most of her friends were going and, maybe, her mother was only refusing Sinclair because of her and Peter.

73

Perhaps if she went they would get together, perhaps she was being more selfish by staying and that thought gave her hope.

Later that night, Rita came to her door. 'Hi Chrissie,' she said, waltzing into the living room. 'I've come to ask Mary to the dance. Why don't ye come too? There's no point in staying in because of the bomb. There'll be many more dropped before the war is over and we'll be off next week to do our bit.'

Mary looked at her mother. 'Will ye be alright on yer own, Mam?'

Chrissie laughed. 'For goodness sake, of course I will. What am I, ninety years old and dottled? Ye go on, lassie. There'll be little enough fun from now on. But mind what I said about the servicemen.'

'Don't ye worry.' Rita tossed her head. 'My Mam's already warned me that I'd better keep my hand on my ha'penny!'

Chrissie and Mary both laughed. 'Aye,' said Chrissie, 'Sound advice if ever I heard it.'

That night the hall was packed with servicemen. The local lassies flirted and the local lads hung around looking surly.

Mary went up to Johnny. 'This is daft ye avoiding me. Ye did want us still to be friends?'

'Aye, I do, but it's hard.'

'We don't know what this war will do to us, but I do care about ye.'

'Aye, so you said.' He looked around at a bunch of pilots standing together by the doorway. 'What's so great about them? I'll soon have a uniform too, ye know.' He lifted the mug to his mouth and took a long swallow.

'Please, Johnny. It's nothing to do with them.'

He wiped his mouth on his sleeve. 'Is it fair that they're posted here while the locals have to go elsewhere?'

'Everyone has to go where they're sent,' said Rita.

'I suppose so. But it's still no fair.' Johnny turned away and joined some of his pals.

'I wish he wouldn't be like that,' said Mary.

'What did ye expect? Ye broke his heart,' said Rita.

'Don't make me feel worse than I already do.' Mary pushed a stray lock of hair out of eyes that constantly scanned the hall, but didn't see any sign of Greg Cunningham. 'I didn't finish with him, just said I didn't want to marry him right now and he's acting like…well, he's different than he was. It's like…I don't really know him at all.'

Robert was dancing with Ellie and when she returned, she leaned close to Mary. 'He's been posted somewhere else,' she whispered.

'Who?' asked Mary.

'Greg of course. Don't think it's no obvious the way ye've been looking round the hall.'

'Posted where?'

Ellie shrugged. 'But don't be mooning over him or Johnny. Ye're too young to be so serious. Just look at all the lads here. A bonny lassie like ye could have her pick. I'm almost sorry I'm going now.'

'*I'm* sorry ye're going,' said Mary. 'I'll miss ye.'

Ellie was right. Mary didn't have to stand around for long. She was pulled up nearly every dance by eager young men. But each effort at getting closer was rebuffed. Not one affected her the way Greg had done and in any case, she didn't want to hurt Johnny any more than she already had.

By good luck there was a full moon to show her the way home as no lights were allowed, the headlights of cars were narrowed to mere slits and only the sound of the motors warned a pedestrian of approaching danger. Rita and Sally both had young men to see them down the road and she didn't know where Johnny had gone.

The day before Johnny left he came to see her. 'Take a walk with me,' he said. When she hesitated, he continued, 'I just want to say goodbye.'

'Goodbye? Have ye had the papers, then?'

He led her along the shore road. 'I'm going tomorrow.'

She turned to look at him. 'I…I didn't realise it would be so soon.'

'No going back now.' He gave an unhappy laugh.

'Just keep safe,' she said.

'Will ye worry about me?'

'Aye, of course I will.' And she meant it.

'That's the image I want to take with me. Ye standing here with the wind in yer hair and the sea behind ye.' He was looking at her with such fondness that she wanted to hug him.

He stared at his thumb, the nail blackened and yellowed where he'd struck it with something. 'And ye'll no marry anyone else while I'm gone?'

'There's no chance of that.' She paused. 'We'll be different people after the war. Who knows what'll happen, how we'll feel.' She didn't add that she was already a different person.

'Aye, ye said.'

'Do ye think *I* should join up? Everyone going, it's made me want to do my bit too.' She was eager to change the subject.

'Ye can help by keeping the home fires burning.'

'That's what my mam says. But it's no enough. There's no many young folk left.'

'But plenty servicemen.' He sounded resentful.

She offered him her hand. 'Goodbye, Johnny. I wish ye luck. Will ye write?'

He looked up at her. 'Will *ye*?'

'Write? Of course I will. I didn't mean to hurt ye.' They looked at each other for a long minute, before she turned to go.

He followed her up the path and back to the house. 'Ye've changed, Mary.'

'Everything's changed.'

'Can I have a photo of ye, to keep with me, like?'

'Yes. Just a minute.' She ran into the house and returned with a postcard sized studio portrait. 'Aunt Agatha took us all into Wick to have this taken. We've got a big one of us all together as well and one of her.'

'Thanks.' He took the photo and gazed at it for a heartbeat then tucked it into his inside pocket. 'Goodbye, Mary.'

She thought he might kiss her and got ready to offer her cheek, but instead of leaning towards her he nodded and turned on his heel. She watched his stiff back as he marched away.

Mary's feelings were jumbled as she returned indoors. Mixed with the sadness of losing Johnny, was a sense of freedom and she knew she had made the right decision. But oh, she hoped he'd return unscathed.

For a long time afterwards, she couldn't understand the emptiness she felt. But it wasn't just him. It was all her friends and the lads she'd known at school. She knew many might not come back, but she longed to be there too, not sitting here knitting socks or growing vegetables.

Chapter Thirteen

Mary

Mary saw him when he got off the bus and ran up the road to meet him. 'Peter,' she gasped as her brother released her from the hug. She stood back, holding him at arm's length. 'You're that bonny in your uniform. All the lassies are going to be after you.' She laughed. 'And look at ye, in a kilt no less!'

His grin lit up his face like it always did and he ruffled her hair, so like his own, soft, unruly and with golden highlights.

Mary's eyes travelled to his legs, thin but muscled too. She giggled and touched the rough material of his kilt. 'Is it true, do you no wear anything underneath?'

'Mary, stop it. That's classified information.' He picked up the kitbag he'd set down when she came running towards him. 'I'm no over fond of it, but it's the uniform of the Seaforth Highlanders. How's Mam?'

'Her usual. Worried about you. More so after what happened to Dad and all.'

'It's different this time,' he said. 'And I'm in the army, not the navy. I would've preferred the navy, but,' he shrugged, 'ye know.'

Mary's face grew solemn. 'I don't know what would happen to her if she lost you too. I don't know what I would do either. Have ye finished yer training? How long are ye home for? Do ye know where they're sending ye?"

'Yes, I've finished my training and no, they don't let on where we're being sent. I've only got the week. But what about you, how're ye doing at the mill?'

She immediately brightened. 'Fine. But I'm just passing the time till something better comes along.'

'There'll never be anything around here. Ye'd have better opportunity further south. Maybe ye should've gone with Aunt Agatha.'

'Are you wise? Aunt Agatha? Anyway, how could I leave Mam on her own?'

'Don't let her hear ye speaking about her as if she's disabled. She's plenty o' friends. How're ye getting on with Johnny – still keen on him?'

'No. He's joined up too. And…I'm no sure if what I feel for him's enough.'

'He'd have had to go sooner or later anyway. I'm glad ye're not getting too involved. He's a fine enough laddie, but I don't think he's right for a spirited lassie like ye.'

'Ye never said.'

'Ye'd just do the opposite if I did. Ye had to see it for yerself.'

She slipped her arm through his and hugged it to her. She'd missed her brother so much, especially the weekends in the half hour before bedtime, when he made her laugh at his tales of the coopering and the antics of the herring gutters. The work was hard and back-breaking, but it sounded like they had a great camaraderie.

'What about ye and Jess?'

'I'll talk to ye about that later,' he replied.

At that moment Chrissie appeared in the doorway of the cottage. Her face lit up with the sight of her much-loved son.

She ran to meet him. 'I'm so glad to see ye,' she said, grabbing his hand. 'Come away in, I've made all yer favourites. Tattie soup and rabbit pie, with rhubarb and custard for afters. Have they been feeding you alright? Ye've lost weight.'

79

'Ah, stop fussing, Mam. It's great being with the lads. We're all looking forward to doing our bit. I'll be home before you know it.' He stopped when her face creased.

'I pray for peace every night,' she said.

'Ye're no the only one. But don't worry over much. They're calling it the phoney war. Mightn't come to anything at all.' Peter hugged her and held out an arm to his sister.

'Have ye seen Jess?' asked Chrissie, afraid that after all, her son had left the first positive relationship he had ever had.

'That's the other thing.' He scratched his nose and looked uncomfortable. 'Me and Jess, we've decided to get married before I go back.'

In total surprise, Chrissie took a backward step. 'But ye're only home for the weekend. There's no much time. I'll need to get a new dress…'

'Stop, Mam. I'm sorry I didn't tell ye, but we're no having a wedding as such. We'll get married in the registrars. We set it all up before I left. Ye and Mary and Jess's mam and uncle will be there, but no one else.'

Chrissie looked at him in horror. 'No the kirk? What'll folk say?' Do ye have to, is that it?'

'She's no expecting if that's what ye mean, no. We just want to make it legal in case I don't come back. We love each other, is than no enough?'

'More than enough, but ye should have told us, given us time…'

'We didn't want a fuss. And her folks are fine with it.'

'It's up to yerselves of course.' Chrissie stared at her hands twisting before her. This was the opposite to what she'd feared, she *was* happy, but she had always hoped for a kirk wedding for her bairns, with friends and family and a feed later. Maybe even a wee bit music.

'Well, I think it's romantic,' said Mary. 'I can't wait to have a sister-in-law.'

'Come on, ye two,' he said. '*I* can't wait for that tattie soup.'

'When's the wedding?' asked Chrissie.

'Tomorrow, twelve o'clock.'

Chrissie gave a gasp. 'But what'll I wear?'

'Yer Sunday best. And don't worry about what folk say. Everything's different now.'

Mary squeezed her brother's arm. 'Did ye know it was love, the first time ye saw her?' she asked.

Peter laughed and ruffled her hair the way she hated. 'Let's just say we suit each other fine.'

That wasn't the answer she wanted, but nevertheless, she was overcome with excitement. 'Will there be a party afterwards to celebrate, like?'

'No, I told ye,' said Peter. 'We'll be married and then we'll both be off to Inverness where I've booked us into a hotel and we'll say goodbye in private. Don't look so disappointed, we'll have the celebration when the war is over and I'm back home.'

The wedding came and went all too soon. Both Mary and Chrissie were surprised to see that Jess looked nothing like her family. Her mother was a big beefy woman with a face that looked ready for a fight and her uncle, who lived with them, was a heavy man with vacant eyes and a mouth that hung open. Her father had been lost at sea, she told them.

When Mary and Chrissie waved them goodbye, they smiled, but in their hearts they cried.

'Ye'll come and see us?' she asked Jess.

'I will. Every week. Ye'll be fed up with me in the end.'

Aware that this could be the last time they saw Peter, they walked home in silence, lost in their own thoughts.

'Mam,' said Mary as they reached the door, 'I've been thinking…maybe I should join up.'

'No,' the word exploded from her. 'Ye don't need to.' The horror in her mother's voice was enough to banish her growing indecision. At least for now.

Chapter Fourteen

Mary

Mary missed Peter and her friends after they left. Much to her mam's despair, she began to keep company with Muriel, a lassie who worked in the hotel and had a wee girl. Her man was away in the navy, but being married didn't stop Muriel from having a good time with the many servicemen posted to the north.

'She's good fun and I like her,' said Mary, when her mother voiced her disapproval. 'And with all the single lassies gone, who else am I going to hang around with? I had a letter from Rita, seems like they're having a right laugh.' She knew she sounded regretful, but she didn't care. She wanted her mother to realise how she felt.

'They'll no be laughing once the training's over,' said Chrissie, who had her hands deep in flour as she made a batch of bannocks.

Mary understood it was hard going, but knowing the girls, they would be making light of the whole thing and building lots of memories, whereas she would only hear the stories second hand.

Last they heard, Johnny had been posted somewhere abroad and his letters had become less frequent. Mary prayed every night that he and Peter would be safe.

Determined to enjoy herself and forget about the war and its dangers for a while, Mary went out on a few dates and enjoyed laughing and flirting, but she would never see a young man more than once. She didn't want to get too attached to any of them when they might be gone a week later to God knew where, like Greg Cunningham, like Johnny, like Peter, like so many other lads she knew. Anyway, none of them interested her enough.

As time went on, Mary grew more and more restless. She hated the worry of it, the dwindling food supplies, the blackouts, the telegrams that arrived in the county too often, bringing heartache in every word, the waiting for every post and the sense of relief when another day ended without bombings, without bad news.

Since the blackout, it was difficult getting used to opening the door to utter darkness. No lights of passing steamers or fishing boats in the firth, no welcoming lights from the cottage windows.

Today it had been raining and the air smelled like damp tin. Mary picked her way around the cottage to the byre and only lit the lamp when the door was securely shut. She checked the cow and gave her more feed, before leaving her for the night. Away to her right the waves lapped against the shore, a three-quarter moon peeked out from behind a tattered cloud and bathed the bay in silver. She stopped and squinted. There was something unfamiliar in the line where the surf broke over the land. It looked like… it took a couple of minutes for Mary to realise what it could be. A boat? She dropped down out of sight behind the peat-stack. Nowhere in Britain was safe, not even this northern backwater.

For what seemed like an age, she watched the shape rise and fall with the swell, her heartbeat loud in her ears. Any minute she expected figures to spring from the craft and creep ashore. She longed to turn on the flashlight, but even the pencil slim beam from the dry-cell torch that Agatha had brought north was forbidden. Still, the path to the beach was as familiar to her as her own breathing. There was no sign of life and she dared to move closer. Curiosity would be her downfall, her mother often said, but she had to find out what was there. By morning, it might be gone, dragged back to sea by the ebbing tide.

She heard her heart thunder high up in her chest, she heard every careful footstep as, in the sporadic moonlight, she felt her way down the path, knowing exactly where it ended and the beach began. In spite of her fear, a sense of danger fuelled her adrenaline and drove her forward. There was no sound, no sign of any passing ship, no scuffle of bodies, only the deep breathing of the ocean and the mournful cry of seals. Mary pulled out her flashlight, kept her breath shallow and silent and waited, for what she didn't know. The muzzle of a gun in her back? Dark shapes materialising from rocks, taking her prisoner? When none of these things happened, she softly called out. 'Hello, is anybody there?' A creature of the night scuttled through the long grass by her side and she started. More seconds ticked by.

Mary took off her shoes and waded into the water until she reached the side of the craft. Once more she looked around, straining her ears. On hearing and seeing nothing out of the ordinary, she turned the flashlight on and scanned the inside of the boat. For a second, her heart seemed to stop. A young man in a dark coloured trench coat and wearing a beret with a badge the shape of a bird and the strange foreign word *Kriegsmarine* around the rim, lay motionless on the bottom.

Mary immediately switched off the torch and, turning around, splashed through the water and ran up the incline to the house. 'Mam, Mam,' She threw the door open. 'Come down to the beach. I've found something.'

'What, what is it?' Chrissie stumbled after her daughter. 'If ye've brought me down here for a dead seal, I'll…' As they approached the beach, she stopped and grabbed Mary's arm and

84

her voice became serious. 'Is it a boat? Don't go near it. It could be Germans.'

'It's alright, Mam. I've looked inside. It's a young man and he's hurt.'

'Tell me you didn't go up to a strange boat and look inside? What were you thinking?'

'I was careful.'

'Ye can't be careful enough. I don't know…'

'It's fine. Come on, Mam.'

Together they waded up to the craft and Mary turned on her flashlight, leaving it on only long enough for her mother to see the barely conscious figure lying there.

'Wha…, goodness… He's no more than a boy.' Chrissie grabbed the side of the boat. 'Let's get him ashore.'

'But… he's German, surely,' said Mary, not sure what she should feel. Her natural instincts to help a fellow creature in need battled with her hatred of the race who had devastated Bank Row. However, there was nothing else for it right now.

Together the women hauled the dinghy further up the beach. Chrissie laid her hand against the young man's neck. 'He's got a pulse,' she said. 'We need to get him inside out of the cold.'

The figure muttered something neither woman understood.

'What was that?' Chrissie put her ear close to his mouth.

'*Hilfe bitte*,' The words were barely decipherable and alien.

'Must be German. Let's get him into the warm.' She looked up at her daughter. 'What are ye waiting for?'

'He's the enemy.' Memories of the bombings were fresh in Mary's mind, the anger still burned. The initial thought was to upend the boat and leave him to the sea.

'Do you think German mothers don't cry as well?' asked Chrissie. 'I only see a lad in need of help.'

'He's maybe a spy. We should tell the authorities.'

'Aye, and he'll be dead before they come. What can he find out from us, eh? We'll get him to the house, get the warmth

85

back through him, then ye can run to the post office, knock Ethel up and get her to radio Wick.'

Mary still hesitated.

'What if Peter was hurt and found by a German family? They're not all Nazis, you know.'

Mary inched forward. Her natural instinct was always to help someone or something in need and this lad didn't look dangerous. She gave a brief nod. Between them, they supported the boy up the slope and into the house. He was slim and small and weighed very little. Once they got him into the light, his youthfulness became even more apparent. His face was small and smooth, almost elfin.

'Help me warm him up,' said Chrissie. 'His clothes are wet through. Come on, lassie, fetch me a towel and then hide your blushes; we need to get those wet clothes off him.'

The lad moaned, the eyes flickered, opened and filled with fear. The body stiffened. '*Bitte helfen.*'

'I'm no going to hurt ye,' said Chrissie. 'Ye're safe now.' She pulled him into a sitting position.

'Hold him, Mary, till I get the jacket off.'

'He's awful young,' said Mary as she bent down to support the quivering body, now making whimpering noises. 'He looks terrified. What'll they do with him?' Although she would remain on her guard, her heart had already softened.

'Prisoner of war camp somewhere I expect. There he can sit out the war in safety.' Chrissie eased off the sodden coat. The lad made a feeble attempt to stop her.

'What's wrong with ye? I'm trying to help ye.' Chrissie sounded as though her patience was growing thin. 'Come on Mary, get his shirt.' She looked down at the boy. 'I've got a son myself, laddie, I've seen it all before. This is no time for false modesty.'

Mary unbuttoned the shirt and Chrissie wrestled it open.'

'*Nein, nein,*' he cried in his falsetto voice.

86

Mary sat back on her heels, both her eyes and mouth open wide, a puff of air escaping from her lips. 'He's... it's ...'

The body fell limply back into Chrissie's arms fully exposing the small but full breasts. 'Oh my God in heaven, it's a lassie,' she gasped.

Mary was already on her feet. After pulling the quilt from the bed, she wrapped it round the shaking shoulders. She held the slight body against her as Chrissie pulled off the trousers.

'Oh, my goodness. I'd bet my reputation as a howdie, this lass is more than four months gone. Where did you come from, love?' Chrissie chafed the frozen limbs with a towel.

The girl shook her head. '*Nien, nien,*' she muttered.

'She should be in hospital. Best go to the post office, get them to call the police,' said Chrissie.

Mary stood up.

The girl looked at her with terrified, pleading eyes. '*Nein, keine Polizei,*' she whispered. '*Bite, Helen See Mir. Help me, please help me.*' Her huge, terror-filled eyes reminded Mary of the frightened deer she had seen, standing, unable to move, as one of the crofters levelled a gun at its head.

'Do ye speak English?' asked Chrissie.

The girl nodded.

'Where did you come from?'

'Help me.'

'Then tell us why we shouldn't call the authorities. Do you understand?'

Another nod. 'I run. I escape.' Her head fell forward. '*Bitte, helfen Sie mir,*' she whispered. 'Help me.'

Mary caught her mother's eye. 'What'll happen to her?'

'They'll incarcerate her, put her in a women's prison I expect.'

The girl started to gasp at air, shaking her head.

'Alright, alright,' said Chrissie putting her arms around her and rocking to and fro. '*No polizie.*' She lifted her eyes to

87

Mary's. 'Poor lamb's terrified,' she said. 'Make her a drink, Mary.'

The girl's breathing gradually returned to normal, but she continued to shake.

Mary warmed some milk, laced it with a wee drop of whisky and handed the mug to the girl.

'Thank you,' she whispered.

'We'll keep her till morning at least. Maybe she'll be able to tell us more. I've no got the heart to turn her away this night,' said Chrissie.

Mary looked at the slight body huddled in the folds of the quilt, the terrified eyes, the quivering lip and her heart melted. 'What if…' She couldn't think of anything else to say. The girl looked so young, younger than herself.

Chrissie continued to rub the limbs. 'I've nursed many a one with the cold through them before. This lassie needs help. I don't know how she came to be here, but the Lord brought her to our door this night for a reason.'

'Do ye think she's running away from the Nazis?' asked Mary.

'I don't know, but I do know this, she's going nowhere tonight. Come on, pet, we'll get you warmed up and something to eat, then get you to bed. Heat a piggy, Mary, and get a goon.'

Mary ran to the other room and returned with a flannelette nightgown and a stone hot water bottle, which she filled from the kettle.

The girl eagerly ate the paste sandwiches and drank the strong sweet tea that Chrissie served her.

'What's your name?' Mary knelt beside her.

The girl shrank back and stopped chewing.

'I'm Mary.' She pointed to Chrissie, 'Mam.'

Fear lessened in the girl's face. 'Liesel.' She pointed to Chrissie. 'Mam? *Mutter*?'

'Mutter? I'll be called worse for letting her stay,' said Chrissie. 'But she looks done in, poor thing. Put her in my bed tonight. We'll decide what to do in the morning.'

'You can come in with me, Ma,' said Mary.

'No, I'll keep watch. After all, we don't know who she is or why she was put ashore.'

'So you don't trust her?'

'I think she's somehow escaped from the Germans. I know you feel it too. But we can't be too careful. That's a German sailor's uniform if I'm not mistaken. Go get yer dad's shotgun from the shed and load it.'

'Ye don't think she…' What was her mother planning to do, hold Liesel at gunpoint?

'It's no for her. But someone might be looking for her. I'll keep my eye on the firth. Now I'm going to hide the dinghy.'

'I'll come with ye.'

'No. Stay with her. I'm being over careful, but we can't leave the dinghy for someone else to find.'

She came back half an hour later. 'It's in the small cave, well covered. No one'll know it ever came ashore.'

This was another side to Chrissie. She was so strong and decisive that Mary wondered why she had felt the need to stay with her to somehow protect her.

There was no need for concern. Once Liesel lay down she closed her eyes and slept for twelve hours straight.

When the clock struck midday, Liesel was sitting up in Chrissie's bed eating bread soaked in warm milk.

The night before, Chrissie had searched through the girl's clothes before burning them. In one pocket she found a photograph of a young man in a sailor's uniform and in another of a man and woman with two smiling children.

'*Familie.*' Liesel reached for the photo. '*Tot.*'

'Speak English if you can, please.'

'Sorry. My family. All dead.'

'Where did you learn your English?' Mary asked.

'My father was an English teacher. He taught his children English, also French.'

'What happened?' Mary sat beside her and took her hand in her own. 'Tell us how ye came to be in the Pentland Firth. Why were ye on that boat? And why are ye wearing a German uniform?'

Liesel said nothing, but looked at the hand that held hers. Mary felt the fingers tighten.

Chrissie met her daughter's eye. She shrugged and tried again. 'What happened to your family?'

'The Nazis, they kill us. We are Jews.'

Mary remembered what Sinclair had said about the Jews. This child looked nothing like a picture Mary had seen. She was pretty, petite and fair haired. The cartoon picture had depicted Jews as an ugly people with big, hooked noses. 'How did you get here?'

Liesel sniffed. 'I was on a warship. Gustav put me in the water for my safety. I am so tired. May I sleep, please?'

'No. Ye have to tell us more. Ye could be a spy. Why else would you be on a German ship?'

'No, no, no spy.' She shook her head with force. 'My lover, we were to get married, but he is German and Christian. He was taken to the forces. He joined the navy.' She stopped when her voice broke.

Chrissie pulled in a chair. 'Go on.'

'He dressed me in a sailor's uniform and smuggled me aboard his ship. I hid in the lifeboat until he think it safe to put me to sea.'

Safe? The Pentland Firth was one of the most treacherous stretches of water in the world. Mary remembered her primary teacher telling her this.

'I was nearly discovered. We would both be shot. I had to go.' She began to weep.

'And the baby?'

90

'Gustav's. He says I must live for the baby.' She leaned forward and grabbed Chrissie's hand. 'Please, help me. Gustav says there may be good people here.' Her eyes reflected her desperation.

Any doubts Mary may have had evaporated. She imagined how desperate Liesel and her Gustav must have been and wondered where he was now. Had he been discovered and put to death by his own people? Were they at this moment searching for Liesel, or had they given up, assuming the sea had already claimed her? Or were they still unaware of her presence and subsequent escape?

Mary studied Liesel. 'And the others, are ye sure they know nothing about ye?'

'They know nothing, I swear.' She shook her head and it fell forward as if it was too heavy for her neck. Tears dripped onto her hands.

'We have to let her stay here, Mam,' Mary said. 'I have clothes I can give her.'

'Do ye realise the trouble we'll be in if we don't report her? She'll be well treated, ye don't have to worry. It won't be prison as such. There are internment camps where she'll be a sight better off than in Germany.'

'But how can ye be sure? Look at her, she can't take much more. I'd say she was half starved. Will they care for her the way we would?'

In spite of her words, Chrissie looked sympathetic. 'I know. I feel the same. But we're going to have to do it, Mary.'

'The authorities might even return her to Germany. And Gustav, he'll be punished too.'

'They won't return her.' Nevertheless, doubt clouded Chrissie's face.

'But we don't know for sure. Look at her. She's terrified. Any more and she might lose the baby and at worst, she might die.'

'She's not a stray dog. If we did let her stay, how could we stop word from getting out? Furthermore, if there are German warships in the area, the authorities need to know.'

'Ye mean with all the planes flying overhead and all their new-fangled equipment and stuff they won't know? I'm sure we don't need to tell them. We have to let her stay.'

'Ye've changed yer tune.'

'That's before I knew she was a Jew. The Nazis are as much her enemy as they are ours. It would be the Christian thing to do.'

Chrissie sighed, but before she could argue further, the door opened and Sinclair Mackay strode in bringing with him the chill of the night.

Mary looked up and gasped. They should have locked the door, but that was something very few country people did.

'Who's this?' Sinclair raised his brow in question.

'Last night...' Chrissie began, but before she could say more, Mary interrupted her.

'This is my cousin from London. She arrived last night, came all the way up here to be safe. She's had a bad experience, so we're looking after her. Is that not so, Mam?'

'Mary,' Chrissie said, hesitated, stared at her daughter, then continued, 'Aye, that's so.'

'It'll be a big change here, compared to London,' Sinclair said, studying Liesel. Mary wasn't sure by his tone what was going on in his mind.

Liesel's terrified eyes flew from Chrissie to Mary.

'She's had a bad experience, like Mary said. Her name is Elisabeth Rosie and she's my cousin's lassie. She won't speak to strangers.' Chrissie rubbed Liesel's shoulder. 'Ye're alright, Lisbeth. No one's going to hurt ye now.'

'What cousin's that then?' Sinclair looked guarded. 'Ye've never mentioned having a cousin in London.'

'Ye've heard me talk of my Aunt Agatha, have ye not?'

'Ye don't know everything about my relations, Sinclair. Now I would ask ye to leave till I settle this girl.' She leaned close to him so that she could whisper in his ear. 'She's scared of men. Like I said, she's had a bad experience – know what I mean?'

'I think so.' Sinclair still didn't look convinced. He glanced once more at Liesel. 'I'll leave ye to it, then.' He touched Chrissie's arm. 'Are ye alright? Ye seem uneasy, is there something wrong?'

'I'm fine. Thanks for asking. I'll see ye the morn.'

Sinclair gave her another fond look before turning on his heel.

Once the door closed behind him, Liesel, still clinging to Mary's hand, collapsed back into the chair and burst into tears.

Chrissie knelt before her. 'Your name is Lisbeth Rosie. You have suffered a breakdown and you will stay in the other room if any of my friends come in. We will make excuses. Ye must not speak. Your English is good, but ye do have an accent.'

Once her tears subsided, Liesel, now Lisbeth, asked to lie down again and once more she fell asleep as if Sinclair's visit had drained her last ounce of strength.

Mary went outside and stared across the firth. There was no sign of any ships, German or otherwise. She only hoped the authorities did know the enemy fleet was somewhere in the north.

With Chrissie's careful nursing, Liesel soon put on weight and her skin took on a healthy glow. Her accent improved and her language became more Scottish. There were even incidents when she laughed.

Mary spent her spare time with Lisbeth, helping her to better her English and in return, learning all about her life. A happy life with loving parents, her brothers and lots of friends.

It seemed her family had a nice house and were well respected. Her best friend was a Christian but this never bothered them, as neither family were staunch in their religion. She did well at school and wanted to be a doctor. She could play the violin and the piano and did voluntary work in a local orphanage.

Then everything changed. First she was put out of grammar school. 'I was so unhappy to leave, but then I was enrolled in a special school just for Jews. I still remained best friends with Helle and I fell in love with Helle's brother Gustav,' she said. She told Mary how they walked hand in hand in the evenings among the trees by the river, how they did nothing more than kiss and exchange heartfelt declarations of love. Her eyes grew misty when she spoke of that time. 'We were so happy back then,' she said.

When she celebrated her birthday, there was another shock in store for Lisbeth. A new law had been passed, a law that forbade Jews from getting education beyond the age of sixteen and she had to give up on her dream, but, encouraged by her father, she believed it was not forever.

It seemed her father, a pacifist, was still optimistic. "It'll soon be over. Many of my students are Christians and they are good people. They won't stand for such a man as Hitler staying in power."

However, things grew steadily worse. Hitler "Aryanised" businesses, took them over and gave them to non-Jewish people. Lisbeth's family were forced out of their home and it was given to a German family. They managed to get a tiny flat outside town. Her brother slept on a board on top of the bath and she slept in the kitchen. By then she spent all her spare time queueing in shops for food. That was where she was the day they took her family.

Gustav came to find her and took her to his mother who hid her at great risk to herself. Within a week, Gustav received his papers to join the navy. Before he left, they made love for the first time. It was during his next leave she told him about the baby and he hatched the plan to get her out.

94

'It was madness, but I had to go,' she said. 'If I was found, not just me, but also his family would be killed. He is a very clever and a very brave man.'

Chapter Fifteen

Chrissie

Jess had been a regular visitor in the beginning, but Chrissie hadn't seen her for some time now. In one way she was pleased, as it saved any awkward explanations regarding Lisbeth, but in another way, she was worried. She hoped she hadn't done anything to offend the girl.

'I'm off to get some food,' she shouted to Lisbeth. 'Go into the ben room and don't answer the door.'

When Chrissie left the house the sky was pale grey and the autumn day was weakening towards dusk. Straggly trees whipped to and fro in an ever-strengthening wind. The wee shop that doubled as a post office was a half-hour's walk from her house and she was glad to reach the paraffin-scented warmth within its doors. There was one other customer in the shop, Alice Stewart, a woman from the south, married to a local farmer several years older than her. Since moving north, Alice, a buxom woman with a booming voice to match her stature, had become very active in local affairs and was a staunch pillar of the kirk.

'Any news from your Will?' Chrissie asked Myrtle, who was leaning on the counter, her chin cupped in her hands. Will was Myrtle's man.

She shook her head. 'They're maybe not in port. Even when he does write, they're not allowed to say much.' She nibbled her bottom lip and studied one of her fingernails where the red polish was beginning to chip.

'You're not to worry,' said Alice. 'The Lord is on our side. Of course,' she studied Myrtle, 'for those married women who go out dancing when their men are fighting for their country, the wrath will be swift and severe.'

Myrtle, who often went to the dances for a few hours free from loneliness, turned her eyes downwards.

'With due respect, that's a lot of nonsense,' said Chrissie, who knew Myrtle worshipped her Will and would never be unfaithful to him. 'There's many a God-fearing man has lost his life in the wars.' Chrissie pressed her lips together to stop from saying more. The woman's attitude was insufferable.

Although Chrissie went to the kirk every Sunday, read a passage from the bible and said her prayers every night, it was more because of upbringing and habit than any deep seated belief. She'd never pushed religion on her children, allowing them to make up their own minds. Mary always came to services with her, but Chrissie knew it was because it was the 'done thing'. Peter seldom ever went and didn't choose to get wed in the kirk.

'You mark my words.' Alice's voice continued, her face growing red.

'There's plenty who could do with the Lord's help right now and them good God-fearing folk and all,' said Chrissie. She found Alice to be both nosey and annoying. Myrtle caught her eye and an amused smile ghosted her features.

Alice Stewart blew out some air. 'Those who keep the commandments will have no need to worry,' she said, with her self-righteous air. 'If these Jews had been Christians they would have had no trouble. You can't deny that.'

'Is it the Christian thing to do throwing them out of their homes, locking them up in camps, killing them?' asked Chrissie, her anger rising.

Alice narrowed her eyes. 'You seem to know a lot about them. I hear you've got a girl staying with you. I've not seen her at the kirk. Where did she come from?'

'My cousin's lassie from London. And no ye've not seen her at the kirk because she's no very well.' Not that it's any of your business, she wanted to add.

Without staying for a chat with Myrtle, she made her purchases and left the shop. In this small community, any stranger on the bus would have been noticed and remarked upon. Chrissie knew it rankled Alice that she had not heard of the girl's arrival.

As she made her way to the door, she overheard Alice's loud whisper to Myrtle. 'What do you know about this girl who's staying with Chrissie? Funny no one saw her arrive.'

'How and when she came here is none of my business and I won't go sticking my nose in,' said Myrtle, loud enough for Chrissie to hear as the door swung shut behind her. She blessed Myrtle. The woman was a good friend and trustworthy. She must have noticed that Chrissie never had any ration coupons for Lisbeth, but if she had wondered why, she'd never remarked on it. It was as well Chrissie was pretty self-sufficient. She had hens and milk and grew her own vegetables, and there was aye a fresh fish or a rabbit from one of the locals.

Laden with two heavy shopping bags, Chrissie was struggling against a wind strong enough to blow her off her feet when Sinclair caught up with her.

'Let me,' he took the bags from her.

She flexed her sore fingers. 'Bye, it's a rough day,' he said, his face red with the wind that whistled across the Pentland Firth and turned the sea into white-tipped peaks. Chrissie's hair whipped and blew about her face until she removed her scarf from her pocket and placed it over her head, before tying it in a firm knot under her chin.

'By heck, that Alice Stewart has a mouth on her,' said Chrissie, still smarting.

'Aye, she's a right nosey besom. She's been asking a lot about the lassie who's staying with ye. Don't mind her though. She doesn't like anything to slip past her.'

'I know ye're right. She gets right up my nose though.'

'Talking about noses, where's your gas mask?'

'Och, clumsy great thing, can't be doing with it,' she replied.

'Nevertheless, it's for yer own safety.'

'Do ye no think I've enough to carry?' She nodded at the shopping bag. 'How was I to know ye were going to appear and help me up the road?' She smiled as she spoke to let him know she *was* glad to see him.

Sinclair took her arm. 'Come on, my love,' he said. 'This'll blow itself out by morning.'

Chrissie leaned into him, straining to catch his words above the whining of the wind. What was left of Sinclair's hair stood up, waving like sea anemones. He ran a hand over his head in a vain effort to tame the wayward locks.

'About yer cousin's girl. How long did you say she was staying?' Sinclair gave up on his hair and leaned down so that he was shouting in her ear.

'For the duration of the war, probably.'

'You know, if you ever want adult company or just to escape for a wee while, you could come and visit me.'

'Away with you, Sinclair.' She laughed, but something inside her stirred once more and she knew that she did want his company, all too much.

When they reached her front door and the shelter of the house, she thanked him and made to take the bags.

'Will ye no even invite me in?' he asked.

She hadn't intended to. The less he saw of Lisbeth the better it would be, but then, it *was* only being neighbourly, she told

99

herself. Furthermore, he'd always been welcome before. How she wished he'd never declared himself. It had changed the relationship and made her experience all sorts of feelings she'd imagined she'd never feel again. When he'd asked her to consider moving in with him, she'd been shocked. She knew he cared for her, but not that he was so serious. At first she hadn't known what to say. After all it was she who said she would never walk down the aisle with another man, but she'd been swithering, fighting arguments within her brain. The arrival of the girl from the sea had removed the choice. She couldn't risk him finding out who Lisbeth really was.

As soon as Sinclair entered the house, Lisbeth rose, grabbed her knitting and ran for the other room as she always did when any of the neighbours stopped by.

'Surely I'm not that bad,' he said, running his hand across his head once more.

'No, Sinclair, ye're not *that* bad.' Chrissie laughed, then gave him the explanation she gave everyone. 'She...she's bad with the nerves. She's had an awful time and can't face people. That's why she's here. That, and to be safe from the bombs.' Word had got round that Chrissie's guest was a bit 'touched in the head', but better that than to have them guess the truth.

'Safe, huh. A bomb fell on West Canisbay last night.'

'I didn't hear a thing.'

He gave a little laugh that sounded more like a snort. 'The ground was so soft after all that rain, the bomb sank into the bog and didn't explode. The disposal team were up all night.'

'Praise the Lord. I never thought I'd be thankful for seven days' rain.' She raised her hands and rolled her eyes upward.

'Maybe it's the case of the devil looking after his own,' said Sinclair, with a chuckle.

A look flicked between them and Chrissie, after a few nervous hiccuppy sounds, burst out laughing. Then Sinclair laughed too. Humour, no matter what the situation, was a defence against all that was happening around them. 'Aye, and

100

ye were a right devil in yer day, so I hear, Sinclair Mackay. I don't doubt ye'll be well looked after.'

Sinclair's smile slowly left his face. 'All the young chiels got into mischief. It took the first war to knock sense into us.'

'Why did ye never marry, Sinclair?'

'I could say I was waiting for the right woman.' He lifted his eyes and looked at her in a way that made her skin burn.

'Ye could say that, but there must've been someone. Don't tell me ye've never been tempted.'

'Not even close.' He took a deep breath. 'There was a lassie once, but that was a long time ago.'

'What happened?'

He gave a dry laugh. 'Like you say, I was a bit of a boy in those days. It was my fault. I broke her heart and she left, which broke mine. Anyway, enough of that, tell me more about this cousin of yers.'

'There's nothing to tell. The lassie had a bad time and I'm only too happy to help.' Lies never lay easy on her tongue and she could no longer look directly at him. 'Now for that tea. It's hard to get good flour now, especially with Benjie not doing so well, but I've managed a few pancakes. My hens are still good layers.' As she spooned the tea into the pot she could feel him watching her. 'How's the lamb sales this year?' she asked into the silence.

'No as good as usual, but considering there's a war on, fair I suppose. Look Chrissie, I don't want any awkwardness between us. If I spoke out of turn, I'm sorry, but I meant every word I said.'

'I'm flattered, I really am, but ye surprised me. Took me unawares, like.'

'Ye must have known how I felt.'

'I like ye too, but I'll never put anyone in Charlie's place.' And she wouldn't, ever. But she felt drawn to Sinclair and Lisbeth wouldn't always be here. Once she had gone, Sinclair, hopefully, would still be around and just maybe he would still

101

be interested. But, what if he wasn't? Suddenly she knew she didn't want to lose him.

'I wouldn't expect ye to. But do ye think he'd want you to be alone? Ye're still a young woman. I bided my time while the bairns were wee. But now they're all grown up. If ye really don't have any feelings for me, can we go back to the way we were, no awkwardness. It's up to you.'

Chrissie swallowed and cleared her throat. 'I do have feelings for ye, but I'm not ready. I need more time.'

'It's been eight years since your man died.'

'I'm sorry, I'm still not ready,' she whispered, as emotion churned within her. But was she? Would she have been so sure if it wasn't for Mary and Lisbeth?

'Do ye still grow that herbs that cure folk?' he asked.

'Aye, and folks still come for my cures, though the doctor hates me for it.'

'Do ye have anything for a broken heart?'

Chrissie giggled like a young girl. 'Bye, I wish I did.' The laughter died on her lips when she thought of all the young folk this war would claim. 'If only I did,' she added soberly.

'I'll need to get going.' Sinclair finished his tea and stood up. 'There's a hell of a lot more to do with half the workforce gone to war and, did I tell ye I'd joined the Home Guard?'

'No, ye didn't. Good for ye.' Home Guard indeed. She was doubly glad she hadn't confided in him about the girl from the sea.

He walked towards her and drew her into a long hug and the blood rushed to her head. It had been a long time since she'd been hugged. Peter sometimes put an arm around her shoulder and gave her a squeeze, but not like this and she suddenly wished it would go on and on.

'Well then, I'll see ye, Chrissie.' He released her, walked towards the door then stopped and faced her again. 'Mind, if ye ever feel the need of company…' With that he walked out, leaving Chrissie suffering the space where he'd been. The wind howled down the chimney and slammed the door after him.

Chapter Sixteen

Mary

That night Mary could not sleep. Her longing to see more of the world grew and she imagined herself in a WAAF uniform. Her neighbours would nod at each other and say, '*Doesn't she look smart*?' and '*She's really found her calling, hasn't she*?' If she learned to drive a truck like Rita was doing, then, when the war was over, she'd have skills she'd never learn here. It was even possible that she might meet up with Greg Cunningham again, although that seemed highly unlikely. Imagining her mother's opposition, she formed arguments in her head. She hated going against her mam, but Chrissie had Lisbeth to fuss over now and soon a new baby, so she wouldn't be alone. By the time morning crept over the horizon, Mary had almost decided.

'Liesel's story has got me thinking, Ma.' Mary had risen early, milked the cow and now helped Chrissie to lay the table for breakfast.

Lisbeth, call her Lisbeth. Thinking what, pet?

'When I'm eighteen, I *am* going to join up.' As soon as the words left her mouth, she disappeared into the closet, every nerve in her body tense as she waited for her mother's reaction. She returned with a jug of fresh milk thick with cream and gave Chrissie a tentative look. *Please don't say no*, she prayed silently.

Chrissie shook her head, disbelief on her face. 'Is it no enough that your brother's gone?'

Mary crossed to the stove where the porridge simmered and took a careful breath. 'Everything's getting worse. They bombed Wick again last night. I'm sorry, Mam, but I'll like as not be called up eventually any way.'

'You can do your bit here.' Chrissie took the serving spoon and began to fill the bowls, not looking at her daughter. 'Growing food's as important as anything. With the men gone, we need young hands on the land. They're already recruiting girls for the land army. You won't have to go to war.'

But Chrissie's words fell on deaf ears.

'I don't like working on the land. I want to do more.' She didn't say she wanted to wear a uniform, learn to drive a truck, experience the things her friends were experiencing. She missed Rita and Sally more than she thought possible and every letter made her more unsettled.

Chrissie's face had flushed. 'Aw, lassie, ye're young and ye don't know the ways of the world. It's not just the war, it's...it's everything. Ye can just forget about it. I won't give my blessing.'

'I've got to leave home sometime and I won't be in the front line or anything like that. I want to join the WAAF. But don't worry over much, they mightn't want me.' She couldn't deny this turmoil within her which grew worse with every day.

'I never expected ye to leave me, Mary. A few years ago, ye wouldn't even go and visit yer aunt in Raumsey unless I went with ye. It's those letters from Rita that's made it sound exciting. I tell ye, it'll no be the truth she's coming with. And I know what like ye are, Mary, ye're a home bird if ever there was one. Ye'll be crying to come back within the week. It'll be too much for ye, a country lassie never away from the north.'

That was probably true, but hearing it from her mother's lips made her bristle, made her feel useless and childish and fired her determination. 'I really want to go. Please, Mam. If I go as a volunteer, I can leave if it doesn't suit me. If I wait till I'm called up, I'll have no choice. Ye must see the sense in it.'

'Yer Uncle Angus died and yer dad was left badly injured after the last war. Peter's in the thick of it. And ye're going too?' All the previous colour had left Chrissie's face except for two pink dots which appeared high up on her cheekbones.

'There's whole families gone to fight. Everybody has to pull together.'

But it was no use. Chrissie was adamant.

Mary said no more about it then. She understood Chrissie's fear, but wasn't it the same for every mother? She wouldn't be called up until she was nineteen and maybe her mam would be able to get her a dispensation, but staying here all her life, something that once had seemed her preordained destiny, was no longer the only option.

She wished Mam would get together with Sinclair Mackay. It was obvious they liked each other. Although Mary did not relish the idea of another man in Dad's place, she sometimes felt stifled by responsibility and although the thought of another war filled her with dread, she hoped she would be called up. That would remove the choice and her mam would have no argument.

When she turned up at work, she found Benjie in poor spirits. 'I'm going to give up the bakery,' he told her. 'I need Daisy's help in the mill and with so many of our young folk going away, I can't get the workers. Johnny was almost finished his apprenticeship, a young boy just out of school could never fill his shoes. I'm getting no younger and that's a fact.' He took another bout of coughing that turned his face red and made his eyes water.

Mary should have felt upset at the prospect of being laid off, but this might work to her advantage. If she had no job, it was another argument to convince her mother.

'So ye'll no be needing me?' she asked.

'I'm so sorry, lassie, the money's no in it,' said Benjie.

'Don't be sorry. I understand.' She laid her hand on his arm and tried not to smile.

Chapter Seventeen

Chrissie

Snowflakes whirled around the house leaving a thick silence. Chrissie set her knitting to one side and turned on the wireless. The signal was poor tonight and the reception was crackling too much for her to get any significant news about the war. With Peter gone and Mary champing at the bit to be off, worry was Chrissie's constant companion. Thank goodness for good friends and neighbours although she had been finding their visits a bit of a strain since Lisbeth had come on the scene,

Betsy sat in the chair next to the stove, cradling her youngest, Matthew, a hefty lad who seemed to be permanently hungry and now guzzled noisily at her enormous breast. Betsy had no qualms about feeding in public. She had six lads and every name began with the letter M.

Daisy, looking weary, sat by the table, sipping her tea. Lisbeth no longer rushed away when any of Chrissie's friends came by, but neither did she talk further than giving one word answers.

Since she'd no long given birth herself, Betsy claimed an affinity with the girl, now in her ninth month, and constantly gave out advice, regaling her audience with harrowing tales of the many births she'd endured. Thankfully she never expected an answer and any direct questions she addressed to Chrissie.

'How's she been keeping, any swelling o' the hands and feet? I was a martyr.'

'She's young and healthy,' replied Chrissie. 'I don't see any problems, so don't ye go scaring the lass.'

'Ye'll be in no better hands than here with Chrissie,' she said, nodding at Lisbeth before adjusting her baby's weight and pulling her jersey down over her bosom. 'I'd best get away up the road. My boys will be tearing the house apart by now. I really don't know why I keep producing them. I'll soon run out of names.' She laughed, her many rolls of fat wobbling and rose from the chair.

'I'd better be off too. With Johnny gone, Benjie expects me to do twice the work,' said Daisy, pushing herself to her feet, it seemed, with difficulty. She nodded at Lisbeth. 'Ye've done wonders with that girl, Chrissie. Mind when she first came, ran away as if we were going to eat her!'

Chrissie saw them to the door. Much as she enjoyed their visits, she took a deep breath of relief when they left. She had preferred it when Lisbeth *had* run to her room.

Later that night, Lisbeth sat knitting yet another multi-coloured baby jacket from oddments of wool donated by Chrissie and her neighbours. Mary was curled up in the far chair, her nose stuck in a book. There had been no news from Peter apart from one letter saying he was doing well, but he'd warned her before he left that they were not allowed to say much.

The dog lifted his head and gave a sharp bark. The door opened and Sinclair Mackay came in stamping the snow from his boots and dragging the breath of winter in behind him. With a nod of acknowledgement, he closed the door. 'I came to see if ye were alright. There's news of a blizzard. We'll be snowed in by morning. Have ye everything ye need?'

She *was* glad to see him. Sinclair radiated a sense of strength and security missing in her life since Charlie died. The worry about her children, the strain of keeping Lisbeth's secret had brought on an acute bout of despair that dampened her naturally cheerful nature. But much as she wanted him to stay, she could not risk him questioning the girl from the sea.

Sinclair nodded at Lisbeth. 'You settled in, lass?'

'Aye, thanks.' She smiled shyly and turned her eyes back down to the pattern she'd been following.

'Some tea, Sinclair?' asked Chrissie. 'I couldn't get enough flour to bake today, but I do have some tattie soup.'

'I don't have time. I've been in the lookout watching the firth. After the Royal Oak was sunk, we have to be on our guard. If a German submarine could creep in through Kirk Sound once, they could do it again.'

He looked at Lisbeth and appeared to be about to speak again.

'I thought the home fleet didn't anchor in Scapa for very long now.' Chrissie was determined to divert his attention. There was nothing Sinclair liked better than to show off his knowledge about the war.

He shrugged. 'Scapa is a still a prime target. It's the base for the Arctic convoy escort ships that sail to north Russia with war supplies and now the hunt for *the Bismark* and her sister ship *Tirpitz* has started from there.'

'What about the barrage balloons? Are they a help?'

'Aye,' he gave a laugh. 'As long as there's no too much wind. The last gale on Cava uprooted a balloon's winch, dragged it across the moor, right over the cliff and into the sea.'

Mary giggled.

Although she saw the humour in it, Chrissie shot her a sharp look. 'It'll no be fun for the folk who live on Orkney. I've still got family there, ye know. I can't even go and visit unless I get a permit.'

'It's all about security, Chrissie.' Sinclair stopped for a breath. 'But there's something much more worrying. We found a dinghy hidden in a cave not far from here. Seems like it's been there for some time as well.'

Ice shards froze Chrissie's blood.

Mary, sitting behind Sinclair's line of vision, lifted her book to cover her face.

Lisbeth gave a cry and her knitting slipped from her hand.

Sinclair stared at her. 'Something wrong, lass?'

Lisbeth shook her head, but her face had gone white. She reached for her knitting with a trembling hand.

'Where was it ye said ye came from?' asked Sinclair.

Lisbeth turned terrified eyes to Chrissie.

'Do ye have a pain? Is it the bairn?' Mary sprung to her feet.

'Yes … yes a pain.' Lisbeth set her hand on her stomach.

'Come away through to the ben end. I'll have a look at ye. It's maybe the labour started.' Chrissie glanced over her shoulder at Sinclair. 'I'm sorry, ye'll have to go.'

'Do ye want me to fetch the midwife?'

Mary grabbed his arm and steered him towards the door. 'My mam's a howdie, remember? She's delivered more bairns than ye've clapped eyes on, long before the days of district nurses.'

'There's going to be a storm. If something goes wrong…' By the tone of his voice, Chrissie guessed he wasn't completely convinced that everything here was as it should be.

'We'll be fine.' Mary hesitated, worried eyes searching out her mother's.

'Go to the ben end and wait for me, Lisbeth.' Not to ask about the dinghy might raise his suspicion. With one hand still on the bedroom door, Chrissie turned to Sinclair. 'What was that ye were ye saying before about a dinghy?'

'Seems odd. Why would someone hide a dinghy? And what's more it isn't one of ours.'

'It's probably some young lads found it and hid it, maybe they stole it even,' said Mary.

'Hmm. It's not like anything I've seen round here. It is a cause for concern. Ye haven't seen any strangers have ye?'

'We'd tell ye if we did,' said Mary. 'Now go, I have to help my mam with Lisbeth.'

He seemed reluctant to leave. 'Look, anyone could have come ashore in that boat. Spies even, blending with the locals, pretending to be something they're not.'

Surely, Chrissie thought, he couldn't see a slightly-built, pregnant girl as a spy coming ashore in a boat? 'We've not seen any strangers,' she said.

'Just keep all yer doors locked. I'll check on ye tomorrow.' With another long look towards the ben room, he took his leave.

Mary leaned against the door and puffed out some air. 'Do ye think he suspects anything?'

'How can he? But that was close,' whispered Chrissie. 'I hate lying to him. He's been such a good friend.'

Mary nodded. 'But he's no daft.'

'Thon Alice has been asking questions as well. Lisbeth can't stay here. I doubt if she could stand up to questioning if it came to the bit. Then we'll all be in the midden and it might even mean prison.'

'Sinclair likes ye, Mam, more than likes ye. He wouldn't do anything to get ye into trouble,' said Mary.

'I can't be sure of that. He's awfully patriotic.' Sinclair would be horrified and even if, for her sake, he kept his mouth shut, it would be totally unfair to put him in that position. Not for the first time, Chrissie doubted her wisdom in not reporting Lisbeth's arrival. It was too late now, they were all involved. It would be best to get the girl away from here, then everything could go back to normal, but where could she go? Chrissie didn't have long to contemplate the problem. A sudden scream from the ben end pulled them to attention. Lisbeth was no longer acting. That was real.

'The shock probably brought it on.' Chrissie bathed the girl's face as she arched in agony. 'But don't ye worry, lassie, everything seems just fine.'

The labour was hard and long but by the following evening, a small, angry baby boy made his way into the world.

'What are ye going to call him?' asked Chrissie cuddling the precious bundle against her breast. It had been a long time since she'd held a newly born infant and she'd missed it. Almost reluctantly, she parted with him, laying him in his mother's arms.

'Gustav, after his dad.'

'Then we'll have to call him Gussy,' said Chrissie. 'Sounds more Scottish.' She gazed at the infant and touched his cheek. It felt soft and velvety. 'He's just beautiful,' she whispered.

Much as she would have loved to keep the baby and Lisbeth with her, she was overcome by a fearful desire to get the girl away from here at any cost. That night she wrote a letter to Aunt Agatha who had already moved to her bungalow in Aberdare.

Dear Aunt Agatha,

I hope this letter finds you well. I was thinking about the offer you made to our Mary. We've a young girl here who got herself into trouble. She needs to get away. If you could see your way clear to put her up for a bit, we'd be very grateful. Mary will come with her of course. Lisbeth is painfully shy and very nervous, so don't expect her to be sociable. I know that you will help us out at this time of trouble.

Your loving niece, Christina.'

It was more than likely Agatha would assume it was Peter's baby and wouldn't pry into the whys and wherefores. She would agree, Chrissie was sure of that, especially if Mary was going too.

'She'll have to go as soon as she's fit to travel,' Chrissie said to Mary. 'We can't hide her forever. Ye'll have to go with her. I've too much to do to keep the croft going.' She had strong

113

reservations about letting the girls go alone, but she couldn't think of any alternative.

'Do ye think she'll let anything slip to Agatha?' asked Mary.

'Do ye think she'll get a word in edgeways?'

In spite of the situation, the women laughed.

Mary welcomed the suggestion. If Chrissie got used to being without her, she might be more agreeable to her joining the forces. The while apart would do them both good. At the same time she shivered with both excitement and disquiet.

'Ye're going now?' Benjie's eyes opened wide. 'I've work for at least another month!'

'My cousin had her baby and her mother has moved to Wales. Somewhere there anyway. So I'm taking Lisbeth home. I'm seriously thinking of joining the WAAF.'

'Why on earth would ye want to do that? It's the airmen I suppose. Coming up here turning young girls' heads. Might as well close my doors.'

'Ach, away. Ye'll get someone else. A lot of women are looking to make a penny with their men gone.'

'Ye just take good care of yerself, lassie. I want both ye and Johnny back in one piece. Has he written?'

'Aye. He seems to be enjoying it. Just out of his basic training.'

'Good luck, lassie. Me and the wife, we'll say a wee prayer for ye.'

Chapter Eighteen

Mary

Chrissie went with them to Wick railway station constantly reminding them to take care, not to talk to strange men and telephone the post office the minute they arrived. She hugged both girls. 'Remember and write as well,' she said as the train came in, chuffing and hissing and belching steam.

'As if I could forget,' whispered Mary, a lump rising in her throat. If only Chrissie were coming too. What was wrong with her? This was what she wanted, yearned for and yet, faced with the prospect of taking this step into the unknown, she was overcome with unease. She was not only responsible for herself now, but for Lisbeth and the baby as well.

'Remember everything I told you,' said Chrissie, for what had to be the hundredth time.

'Yes, Mam. I'll be fine.' Her voice was small.

'I'm sure you will, lassie.' Chrissie patted her arm, her smile just wide enough to make the dimples appear on her cheeks, but her eyes held a wealth of worry.

'Lisbeth, ye'd better have this. Make life easier for ye.' Almost like an afterthought, Chrissie removed her wedding ring and pressed it into Lisbeth's hand. 'It means a lot to me, be sure and bring it back one day.'

With misty eyes, Lisbeth nodded. 'Thank you. I will take good care of it, I promise.'

'Mam, ye can't,' said Mary. 'Dad gave ye that.'

'It'll make her story more believable. Yer dad would have approved. Remember, if anyone asks ye, the bairn's name is Angus Rosie and yer man's away at the war.'

Lisbeth held little Gussy tightly and kept her head lowered as she slipped the ring onto her finger. It was a bit too large and she closed her fist to keep it safe. 'I will miss you,' she said to Chrissie, then added, 'Mam.'

The platform was crowded, mostly with young men planning to join up and also servicemen returning from leave, all going to fight in a war they scarcely understood. There were tears as loved ones hugged, before being left, ashen faced, not knowing if they would ever meet again in this life. Once on board, the lads' demeanour changed. It was as if, facing an uncertain future, laughter and banter was the best option.

'Ye coming on, hen?' A young soldier raised his eyebrows at Mary and picked up her case when she nodded. His companion grabbed Lisbeth's. 'Don't ye be worrying about the lassies,' he said to Chrissie. 'We'll see they get there safe and sound.' He turned to Mary. 'Where ye lassies going?'

'Aberdare eventually,' said Mary.

'Isn't that in Wales? There'll be a fair few train changes before then, but me and the lads will take care of ye as far as Perth.' He twisted his head around and yelled down the corridor, 'Hey, Dougie, Acky, ye're going over the border aren't ye? Come and get to know these wee lassies, here.'

Mary looked back at her mother's worried face and gave a little wave, relieved to have the boys to support them. Another two privates squeezed their way into their carriage. 'Why are ye leaving Wick?' one asked.

'My cousin's family have moved out of London. It's safe where they are now and they want her and the baby back. I'm

116

joining the WAAFs, but I'll stop with Lisbeth till I get my papers.'

'Great. A wee bit of female company. I'm sure ye'll be better companions than that lot back there. Now ye mind yer mouth, Dougie.'

Mary laughed, her earlier fear replaced by a measure of excitement. 'I've heard many a curse word, don't ye fear. Where are ye boys going?'

The smile didn't slip from Acky's face. 'We've done our training. We're ready now to take on the Jerries.'

'Aren't ye scared?'

'Scared is not a word we say.'

Then the engine snorted and the wheels squealed against the rail and, with a jerk, they were off.

Acky looked around and pulled a flask from his rucksack. 'Anyone for a wee bit of the best home-brewed whisky this side of the Ord?'

There were cheers and hoots. Acky held out the flask to Mary. She took a long swallow and gasped as the rough liquid burnt her throat. 'Where was that brewed? In a pile of pig muck?' She wiped at eyes that had started to water.

Acky held it out to Lisbeth who shook her head, her pale hair falling forward and covering her face.

'She's feeding a bairn. Can't have a drunk baby,' Mary explained.

'Where's yer man stationed, love?' Acky looked at Lisbeth.

'He…he was lost..' she stammered, her face reddening.

Terrified of her being questioned further and slipping up, Mary shoved her hand beneath the shawl and nipped wee Gussy's leg. He screamed.

'He'll be needing fed,' she said as the baby continued to cry. 'We'll need privacy for that.' The lads in the compartment toned down the noise.

'Aw, I get what ye mean,' Dougie said, his cheeks turning pink. 'Come on lads, out till the lady's finished.'

'Take the flask,' someone shouted and they crowded into the already packed corridor. Mary pulled down the blinds.

'They are nice boys,' said Lisbeth as she undid her blouse. 'But I think I mustn't speak with them.'

'Aye, they're a great laugh. But from now on ye're too upset to speak about yer man. I want ye to pretend to sleep a lot as well. Let me do the talking.'

Lisbeth had picked up the local dialect well, but not well enough to fool someone who'd lived in these parts all their lives. Furthermore she was very nervous.

'I will do what you say.'

Mary relaxed. She was beginning to enjoy her new independence.

Once Gussy was fed, Mary called the lads back.

It wasn't long before they were involved in a singalong and strains of *Pack Up Your Troubles*, *Oh You Beautiful Doll*, and *Hands Knees and Boomps-a-daisy* echoed through the carriage.

Gussy was a good baby and slept most of the way, his small starfish hand covering his nose, his thumb finding its way into his mouth. Lisbeth seldom took her eyes from him and often pressed her lips to his downy head.

In Perth they said goodbye to some of the lads. As she wished them well, Mary wondered how many would come back in one piece, how many would come back at all.

Acky and Dougie accompanied them through the train changes, all the way to Birmingham, and left them with strict instructions of how to complete the journey.

Every platform teemed with uniformed bodies; smartly dressed soldiers, pilots and sailors with their bell-bottoms flapping and their big white collars blowing up against the backs of their heads. They all carried kitbags on their shoulders and cigarettes dangled from most mouths. Some stopped and smiled at the baby, some gave him a silver coin for luck.

Mary thanked Acky and Dougie and though it was not the Highland way, she hugged them in turn. 'Ye made that journey pass so much easier. I don't know what we'd have done without ye. I've never been on a train before.' The tears that gathered in her eyes were genuine, as if she were saying goodbye to lifelong friends.

The trains were crowded, mostly with young servicemen, and a trip to the lavatory was more of an expedition, involving clamouring over kitbags, rifles, tin helmets and various other pieces of gear. The accents around them were varied, some unrecognisable. Two young soldiers offered to help them and rescued their luggage from among the pile as they changed trains for the last time and Mary wondered why she had been so scared before she left the north. They'd had so much help and support on this journey.

Chapter Nineteen

Mary

At Aberdare station, the girls alighted, tired and bedraggled. Totally mesmerised, Mary looked around the platform, wishing Dougie and Acky were still with them. Then she saw a small twinkling man wearing an untidy suit and a bowler hat. He was waving a large card with her name scrawled across the surface.

She took Lisbeth's arm and they made their way over to stand before him. 'I'm Mary Rosie,' she said.

The small man's face broke into a myriad of tiny lines as a smile split his face. 'Ah, the girls from Scotland. Your Aunt Agatha's gardener, George Jones, at your service. I'd bring the car, but petrol's difficult to get, so instead I brought faithful old Neddie here with his cart.'

Mary immediately liked this little man. 'As long as we don't have to walk,' she said nodding towards the two cases. 'Not carrying this lot.'

'We'll not need to go through the town and you'll be safe enough in your aunt's home. Is this the little fella?' He peered down at Gussy who was stretching in his mother's arms, his lips forming a perfect circle as his head turned from side to side.

'He's hungry again,' said Lisbeth.

There was a rug in the cart and Mary draped it around Lisbeth's shoulders to give her privacy to feed her bairn.

An hour later they turned down a country lane to where Aunt Agatha's sizeable bungalow sat. It had been raining and large globs of mud clung to the cart wheels and fell off making splattering sounds.

Aunt Agatha met them at the door her arms open. 'So glad to see you again, Mary.' She eyed Lisbeth. 'And this is... Mrs Rosie, I believe. Any relation?'

'Different Rosie's,' said Mary quickly.

Agatha's eyes told them that she didn't believe it for a minute, but Agatha was forward thinking and seemed genuinely happy to welcome them.

She let go of Mary and extended her hand to Lisbeth.

Lisbeth adjusted the baby so that she held him one-armed and allowed Agatha to grasp her free hand. 'Excuse me, I have to see to him.'

'Of course,' said Agatha, parting the shawl to look at Gussy who was beginning to grizzle. 'Pretty little thing. Was your man killed, dear?'

'He was a sailor. But please, I don't want to talk about it.' Lisbeth spoke confidently enough and cleverly used the Caithness dialect, which was good, Mary thought.

'Of course. I hope you enjoy your stay,' said Agatha with a knowing look. 'Once you've unpacked, come directly downstairs into the lounge. I'll have cook bring tea and scones.'

Lisbeth made to follow George, but Agatha stopped her with a raised hand. 'You know, you must try to lose that Scottish tongue. English is the thing if you want to get on. Didn't they tell you that at school?'

Lisbeth nodded and turned away.

Mary stifled a giggle. 'Aye, Auntie,' she said. 'We've been practising the English. So if she ever sounds a wee bit funny, that'll be what it is.'

Agatha frowned after the girl's retreating back. She bent down to pick up an enormous white and grey cat that was weaving round her ankles.

'Like Mam said, after her man was killed she needed to get away. She's awful nervous. Ye'll no be hard on her will ye, Auntie? She doesn't say much.' Mary spoke quickly. She knew her aunt would think Lisbeth's hasty retreat was rather bad mannered.

'She looks like a frightened mouse. I assume she'll be able to help my cook in the kitchen?'

'I'm sure she will.' Mary hoped that Lisbeth would remember everything about the life they had concocted for her. She reached out and stroked the cat, now purring contentedly.

'This is Sheba,' said her aunt. 'I've had her for almost thirteen years now. Come and meet her children, Cleopatra and Brutus. Then you can have a chat with my cook.'

As Mary fussed with the cats, Lisbeth returned and sat in silence, nursing her baby.

Cook bustled in carrying a tray which she set on the small table. She was a hefty, pleasant lady called Katrine McGill from Edinburgh. She wore a skirt to her ankles and what looked like a man's shirt, covered by a hand-knitted cardigan in several different colours that reached to her knees. Her pepper and salt hair was cut as short as a man's. 'Great to see you, dears,' she said in a whispery voice, her round red face beaming. Your great aunt has been beyond excited.' She leaned forward and looked at Gussy, fed and changed and sleeping now, small fists half-closed. 'What a wee darling. He'll be a great comfort to you, dear.'

'That will be all, Katrine,' said Agatha.

Katrine winked at Mary. 'Likes to pretend she's a dragon, but she's no a bad old body, but you'll know that already, dear.'

'Really, Katrine, don't be so familiar. I don't know why I've put up with you all those years.' Agatha's mouth pursed.

122

'Ha, it's because no one else will put up with *you,* dear.'
Katrine waddled out, grinning.

Agatha shook her head. 'You can't get the staff since the
Great War. Gave women ideas above their station. It'll be
worse this time, mark my words.' But she'd seemed to take the
exchange in good form and the look she'd given Katrine was
quite affectionate. Mary surmised that maybe her aunt wasn't so
difficult to get on with after all.

'I'm thinking of joining the WAAF,' Mary said as she
sipped her tea the following morning. 'My mam's no for it, but
now that I'm no at home, she'll maybe get used to doing
without me.' Already she missed home, but coupled with that
was the excitement brought by each new experience.

'It's admirable that you want to do that,' was the surprising
reply. 'If I was your age I'd do the same.'

Mary had expected Aunt Agatha to take her mam's side, try
to talk her out of it. Say it was no job for a girl.

'Will ye write to my mam? I need all the support I can get.
She thinks I'm no up to it.'

'Of course I will. Don't know why your mother thinks you'll
be safer up north. And the town, full of servicemen, the young
girls will be led astray, wait and see. There'll be a lot of
unwanted babies before this war's over. No, you'll be better
employed doing something useful and you're as up to it as any
other young inexperienced girl. Tomorrow you must go to the
recruiting office in Cardiff. They'll welcome you with open
arms. But Lisbeth, I assume she'll be staying with me for a little
while? She is a mother when all is said and done.'

'As long as ye'll have her, Auntie. It's awful kind of ye.'

'We'll welcome the company. But she's a strange girl.
Hardly speaks.'

'I told you, Auntie, she's very shy.'

'Hmph, affected, my mother would say. Still it's little I can
do to help and I will do my duty.'

Though her lips pursed, her eyes softened when she gazed at Gussy and Mary knew she was already secretly in love with the baby. 'Black clouds may hang over Europe, Mary,' she said, tenderly, 'but there's always a wind that will blow them away and let the sun shine through again. Every new soul brings hope for the future. Let's pray that this child grows up in a free world.'

That night sleep didn't claim Mary. She understood why Chrissie was so anxious, why she wanted to cling onto her younger child. If only her dad were still alive he would know the right thing to say. 'Oh Dad,' she whispered, 'What would ye tell me to do?'

As she lay in that half-world, not quite awake, but not asleep, she slipped back to the realm of her childhood and the day Charlie Rosie had left them forever. She had blocked that memory, afraid to relive it until this moment. Why her subconscious chose to revive it now, she had no idea, but it was as clear in her mind as if it had been yesterday.

Chrissie had taken Mary's hand in hers.' Come away outside till Mam talks to the doctor.' She'd opened the door and shouted, 'Peter, take your sister down to the beach like a good laddie.'

Peter reached towards her. 'Come away, love, we'll go and look for crabs.'

Mary lifted her hot face. 'Will Dad be alright?'

'I'm going to talk to the doctor,' Chrissie said, her breaking voice heightening the child's anxiety.

Mary trotted reluctantly after her brother, occasionally looking back over her shoulder.

'Mrs. Rosie.' The doctor called to Chrissie from inside. His face was sad. 'I'm sorry. Charlie's lungs won't take any more...'

Peter dragged her away before she could hear whatever else was said.

She refused to listen to her brother, refused to be drawn into the world of make-believe they so often enjoyed. She instinctively knew that her da was bad this time, otherwise her mam would never have sent her away.

Before long Peter gave up trying to tempt her out of her mood and sat on a rock staring over the firth towards the island where they both had been born. She could recall everything about that day, how the sea was quiet, barely trickling over the shingle and between the rocks, how the seagulls circled above their heads, how porpoises arched and played in the firth, how several seals basked on distant rocks.

'Please Jesus,' whispered the child clasping her small hands together and closing her eyes, 'make my daddy better. I promise to never be bad again. I'll go to Sunday School and I'll pay attention to what my teacher says. I will.'

When she opened her eyes, Peter wasn't staring over the firth any more. He was looking inland, up the slight rise. She followed the line of his vision. Chrissie stood there silhouetted against the pale sky, her hands hanging by her side. It was as if a dark cloud hung around her shoulders, blotting the sun from where she stood and Mary knew. She ran up the slope and threw her arms around her mother, burying her face in the folds of the wide skirt.

From that day on, Chrissie had devoted herself to her children to the extent of blotting out everything else. Oh, her door was always open and the kettle always on the boil ready to make a cup of tea for her many friends, but it had been as if the light had gone from her life. In spite of her youth, Mary felt it, like a black fog that had infiltrated their home and nothing had ever been the same again.

It was a month before Mary got the call to report for duty. A month in which, to her dismay, she became aware that her great aunt's health was far from good. Agatha spent the first half of each day in bed and lay down again after dinner every night. She had a cough that had grown noticeably worse since her visit north. It was Mary's excuse for not coming directly home as Chrissie wanted.

She's really no well, Mam. And Lisbeth's no settling in as good as we hoped. Mary wrote although that wasn't quite the truth. Katrine was a pleasant, motherly soul who took Lisbeth under her wing and fussed over little Gussy every moment when she wasn't fussing over Agatha. Mary quickly became aware of something else too, that a close bond existed between her aunt and Katrine, something much closer than mistress and servant. They would often take a trip into the past, telling stories of how it was in London when they were young, Agatha, the bride of a fledgling lawyer, and Katrine, a domestic servant. Yet despite the divide, they would look at each other tenderly while remembering past times.

Gussy thrived under the attention heaped on him by all four women. Mary couldn't help but be captivated when his lips stretched in his first smile, or the way his legs kicked and grew fat and the way he stared at his fingers as if he'd discovered something new and exciting.

The day the letter arrived she was simultaneously filled with excitement and apprehension. She had to tell her mother the news she'd been putting off. At the appointed time she waited for her mother to ring.

'How are ye doing, pet?' said Chrissie, and the familiar accent touched Mary's heart as it never failed to do.

'I'm fine. Ye should see little Gussy. He's smiling all the time now.'

'Are ye thinking about coming home? Ye're sorely missed around here.'

Mary took a deep breath. It had to be now. She couldn't carry on with this deception any longer. 'I've joined up, Mam,' she said, and closed her eyes at the quick intake of breath on the other end.

'Mam, be happy for me.' In her mind's eye, Mary saw her mother's tightened lips and the way she screwed down her brows when she was angry.

'No, ye can't. We agreed on it.'

'I didn't agree, Mam. I don't want to hurt ye, I don't want us to be bad friends. Please, Mam. I can't bear it if ye're angry.'

'Of course I'm angry. I should have gone with Lisbeth myself. Ye're so thrawn.'

'I'd still have done it. Ye brought me up to fight for what I believe in, to know my own mind. Is that being thrawn?'

'So, ye've really done it – after all I said?'

'Yes, Mam. I'm sorry to go against ye, but ye know I have to do it.'

Chrissie's voice changed, became resigned. 'Where will ye be stationed?'

'I don't know. But I'll no be near the fighting and I'll learn a trade. That'll be good for afterwards. Better than working in a mill all my life. Ye always said I had a brain.'

'Ye have that and ye've also got my own stubborn streak. Ye're sure about this aren't ye?'

'I am and I am homesick already, but I would never have let up till I went.'

There was another long pause before the bleeps went, telling them their time was up, then, in the few remaining moments, Chrissie said, 'Just come back safe. I am proud of ye. I'll pray for ye every night.' The line went dead.

127

Chapter Twenty

Chrissie

10th April 1940.

'Ye know,' Chrissie said to Myrtle as they sat before the stove sipping tea and the leaden skies outside wept their misery on Caithness, 'I haven't heard from Peter for some time, nor seen sight nor sign of Jess.' Her mood was uncharacteristically low. Since Mary's revelation she had the irrevocable feeling that she'd lost her daughter for good.

'Why don't ye go and see Jess yerself?' asked Myrtle. 'She's maybe no coping very well either.'

'I will,' said Chrissie. She had been thinking along those lines too. 'I'll go this very afternoon.'

'I'd best go and open the shop; although it's less and less I have to sell. Thanks for the eggs.'

'Ach, it's fine. I don't need many now with the bairns gone. And I've still got a puckle left for his Majesty's forces,' she gave a sly grin.

When Jess got off her shift, Chrissie was standing at the door of her lodgings.

'Oh… Chrissie, hello,' Jess said, then her eyes opened wide. 'Nothing's wrong is there? Peter?' Her hand flew to her chest.

'No we've had no word. It's just that I haven't seen ye for so long. Have I done something to offend ye?'

'Oh, no, no.' Jess shook her head. There was a nervousness about her that Chrissie hadn't seen before. 'It's been so busy and I've been away with the herring. I've no seen much of my own folks either.'

'I thought I'd come and call on ye, ask how ye were getting on, like. Ye're part of our family now. I miss ye, especially with Mary gone. Did ye know she'd joined up?'

'No, I didn't know. I'm fine. Like I say, busy. I'll have to go to the wash house, get rid of these stinking clothes. It was nice to see ye.'

'I'll come with ye,' said Chrissie, determined not to be brushed aside. She had the impression that Jess wanted rid of her.

'Aye, alright.' Jess led the way up the side entry and round to the back of her lodging house, where she stripped off her overall and filled the basin with water from a ewer at the side.

'Have ye heard anything from Peter?' asked Chrissie, although she knew it was unlikely that Peter would have written to one and not the other.

Jess shook her head and her eyes grew watery. 'I worry so much about him,' she said and sniffed. 'I write every day and I don't even know if he's getting my mail. It's so lonely with him gone. I'm sorry I've not been out. I will try to come more often.'

Chrissie softened and her heart went out to the girl. 'See you do. Come on Sunday. I'll make yer tea.'

Jess gave a small smile. 'I will. Thanks Chrissie. It's good to see ye again.'

There was an awkwardness between them that had never been there before. 'Good to see ye too,' Chrissie said. 'See ye Sunday.' But in her heart she had a feeling that she'd lost Jess as well.

Sunday came and Jess had not appeared. The night was still with a misshapen moon illuminating the countryside. Chrissie sighed. Now everyone had gone, she felt the emptiness of the house more acutely than she could have ever thought possible and the nights became unbearably lonely. She'd cried the night Mary told her that she joined up, but deep down she had to admit to a certain admiration. Mary was growing into a strong, independent young woman and isn't that what she wanted for her?

As she emptied the dishwater outside, she was dimly aware of a deep drone that seemed to fill the air around her. The all too common sound of a distant siren travelled over the waters from Orkney. Suddenly the sky above grew dark and only flashes of the moon could be seen between the enemy planes that filled the air like a swarm of bats, too many to estimate the number. Within minutes, the sound of gunfire echoed from Scapa Flow and the sky over the islands was lit up by shellfire and the probing rays of searchlights. The barrage balloons could be clearly seen in the terrible beauty of the explosions.

No sooner had the deadly wave of bombers departed the scene, either shot down or heading towards Norway, than another swarm, larger than the first came from the south. It seemed they were determined to annihilate Scapa. Chrissie wondered how long the base could hold out. And what then? Would the enemy move in from the north, occupy Shetland and Orkney like they did the Channel Islands and then move on to Caithness? It was unthinkable.

It was not the first attack she'd witnessed, but was by far the most intensive. She stood, transfixed until the planes had gone and although many miles across the water, the fires left in their wake were clearly visible and she wondered how much of the island had been destroyed, how many had been killed.

'Sixty bombers in all attack Scapa in a succession of relays,' said Sinclair, when he made his nightly visit. She looked forward to these visits and felt the emptiness once he had left.

Tonight she was particularly glad of his company. During the daylight hours her other friends still came round, but most had young families or ageing parents to look after and could not stay too long.

'It must have been young lads who found that dinghy and hid it,' Sinclair said and scratched his chin. 'There's been no sign of anything since. They're no likely to own up, but I still wonder where they got it.' His shrewd eyes scanned her face and she wondered once more whether he suspected that she knew more than she was letting on.

Chrissie shook her head. 'Why are ye looking at me like that? Surely ye don't think I had anything to do with it?' She instantly wished she'd kept her mouth shut. Her sudden denial might have made her sound guilty.

'Na, ye would have told me if ye knew anything, wouldn't ye, Chrissie?'

'I don't go to the beach anymore.' Chrissie couldn't give a direct answer. She had never found lying easy. Sinclair was a stickler for the truth. He'd wasted so much of his precious time looking for an answer, if he found out she'd known all along, surely he would never forgive her.

'Why's that?' he said.

She pushed her cup of tea to one side and raised her eyes to his. 'I'm scared I'll find a body washed up. I read about that, bodies on the beach.'

'Didn't think ye were scared of anything, Chrissie.' He held her with his eyes. 'Except maybe a relationship.'

She was glad he'd stopped talking about the dinghy.

'I'm not scared, not any more. With the bairns gone it's different...' As she said the words, she knew it was – different. Sinclair drew back, slowly moved his hand up to her chin and raised it, before touching her lips with his, no more than a fairy touch and when she didn't pull away, he kissed her fully.

Her heart thudding, she allowed the kiss, slipped her arms around his neck and pulled him tightly against her. She was

131

fooling herself if she imagined this was just to divert his attention away from the dinghy. Every nerve-ending in her body exploded to life. It had been so long since she'd been kissed like this. Not that she hadn't had offers. Since Charlie, she never thought she would welcome another man's lips, till now.

When Sinclair's hand strayed to her breast, she pushed him away, afraid to look at him. How could she allow herself to love again? How could she explain that she found him unbearably attractive, but that there would always be a barrier — one that protected her from further pain. And the other one, the one that stopped her from being honest about Lisbeth. She would tell him, but after the war when knowing the truth would no longer compromise his position with the authorities. Then he could forgive her or not.

'I'm sorry. I shouldn't have let ye do that.' She kept her head low,

'Why?' he said with a low groan. 'What are you doing to me?'

'I don't mean to lead ye on, but there's things ye don't know about me.'

'What things?' said Sinclair. 'There's nothing ye can say that'll make me feel different. Let's face it, there's things ye don't know about me either. We could swop tales of our past, or we could just draw a line and move on from here.'

'It's not that simple,' she said.

'It is exactly that simple. I didn't imagine that kiss. Say what ye like, ye feel the same as I do. Why are ye fighting it?'

'I don't know.' Her hands twisted in a nervous knot.

He looked as if he was going to say more, then changed his mind. 'I'll be off, then, if that's what ye really want.' He sounded hurt.

'See you tomorrow,' she called after his retreating back, already suffering the pain of parting.

Once the door closed after him she crossed to the window and watched as he went down the path, drinking in his broad shoulders and the long legs that gave him a loping way of walking.

Whatever the outcome, she wasn't sorry she'd helped the girl from the sea. Anyway, it wasn't just about Lisbeth. She hadn't always been the virtuous woman Sinclair believed her to be. She thought of the men she had loved and lost because of the lies that damaged their relationships. Davie Reid, who had left her for another. He had been her first, but she went to his brother's bed pretending to be a virgin. It was only on learning the truth that Jack Reid began to hate her. Sinclair didn't know about Jack. No one from her new life on the mainland did.

Then there was the lie that she'd kept to herself all the years she spent with Charlie and the one great lie she still lived with. That she didn't know who Peter's father really was. Had she been wrong to let the lad live his life believing that the murdering Jack had fathered him, or would he have been more at peace knowing that the loving, caring Charlie Rosie who he'd looked up to all his life, might have been his father? Fear of her children finding out that she'd been sleeping with someone else while still married had stopped her from being honest.

Peter had been a good son, but he had moods where he would sink into himself for long periods of time, sink into a place where Chrissie couldn't reach him. If he died without ever knowing the truth, how would she ever forgive herself?

When she was a child, the boys would climb down the cliffs to collect eggs. Holding her breath, she watched them, never knowing if they would slip and tumble into the icy water or hit the rocks below. That was how she felt now – never knowing at what moment the unthinkable would happen. That's the way it would continue to be if she went to another man while living a lie.

The next morning as Chrissie stirred her porridge, Betsy waddled into the kitchen, baby Matthew, now Matty, supported on one ample hip. 'Aye, Chrissie. I brought ye some bits of wool for yer socks.' As well as growing more vegetables than they needed, most of the women knitted socks for the servicemen.

Betsy set the wool and a letter on the table. 'Met the post on the way. This is for ye. Was that Sinclair I saw leaving late last night?' She gave Chrissie a knowing look.

'Sinclair aye drops in. Ye know that fine.' She tickled Matty's tummy. 'Hello, pet, how's my wee man?'

Matty removed his thumb from his mouth and rewarded her with a gummy smile.

'Why do ye no let the man stay? Half a glass eye could see the way ye feel about each other. Ye're both single,' said Betsy.

'Aye, and be the talk of the whole county? There's nothing between us and there's no likely to be either. I'll just put the kettle on.'

'Don't know how ye can live without a man. I couldn't.' Betsy laughed so that her chins and her stomach wobbled. 'Why do ye think I keep having bairns? It's no because I want any more.'

'I'm well used to doing without. Have ye had word from yer laddies?' Chrissie lifted the letter and, after glancing at the postmark, set it on the table. It was from Agatha. She would read it later.

'There's no been much from Martin. Had a letter from Murdo though. He's somewhere in the Middle East. Did ye hear about Frankie Cooper?'

'No, what?'

'Killed in action.'

'Oh, no. not Frankie too.' Frankie was the same age as Mary and Martin, the only son of a widowed mother. Chrissie thought of him as she had last seen him, his bonny face serious as he said, 'Cheerio, see ye when I get back.' And then he had smiled

134

and he looked once more like the little laddie she'd known all his life.

'This is a terrible time. When will this madness ever end?' she said.

'How's yer Peter?' asked Betsy.

'I don't know.' Chrissie shook her head. She'd had no news of Peter for over four weeks, but no news was good news, so her granny used to say. She pulled the kettle over the flames and measured two teaspoonfuls of tea into the pot then threw in an extra one for luck.

'And how's wee Mary getting on?' asked Betsy.

Chrissie sat down and looked at her friend. 'Ye know, I always thought Mary was young for her age, a bit giggly. I was frightened to let her go, but she went anyway. She's grown up so fast. By, but she's a big miss.'

'She's a fine lassie. I'm sure she'll know the right thing to do. Ye can be right proud of her, of both yer bairns.'

'Thanks Betsy.' She was silent for a minute, then stood up. 'Would ye like a wee drop of the craitur in that tea? I've a half bottle put by for the animals when they take bad.'

'Ye're an awful woman,' said Betsy holding out her cup, 'but I'll no say no. Now, when are ye going to make an honest man out of that Sinclair Mackay?'

'Will ye stop going on about it,' said Chrissie. 'Why do folk always think the worst?'

'I've known Sinclair since he was a wee boy and I'm right fond of him and all. The man needs a wife. I don't like to see the way ye keep him dangling, I'll tell ye that.'

Chrissie forced a laugh. 'When it's time for ye to buy a hat, ye'll be first to know.'

Before the end of the week, Mary received a letter from her mother. It started off with all the news of home and then the cryptic message,

Sinclair has been round a lot.

135

Sinclair always had been round a lot. Mary hoped that by writing it, Chrissie was trying to convey that they were growing closer. Chrissie ended the letter with the words…

Sorry I can't be more enthusiastic about you joining up. Your dad and I never thought we would have a bairn after the war, never thought it possible with his injuries. You were a miracle and every day since, I've thanked God for your birth.

Mary swallowed against a lump in her throat. Although they had always been close, it was highly unusual for Chrissie to lay her feelings bare like this. She read on.

Although I miss you, I'm proud that you are sticking to your beliefs and growing into a wonderful young woman. Just stay safe and come home after this terrible war is over. I love you.

Love Mam.

Mary wiped a moist eye. Chrissie had committed to paper what she could never say in words. She rose, brushed her hair, rouged her cheeks and wished she had some lipstick. It was with a lighter heart that she set out for her interview.

Chapter Twenty-One

Mary

When Mary exited the train, there were at least another fifteen girls gathering round a uniformed woman holding a clipboard. Some were excited and chattering to their neighbours, others looking as lost as she felt. Controlling the nerves that danced in her stomach, she approached the small group.

'Excuse me,' she said to the nearest, a thin, tall girl, 'Is this where we wait for transport to RAF headquarters?'

'Yes, it is. Don't look so scared, love, it can't be that bad.' The girl held out her hand. 'Bethany Cooper. Just call me Beth.' Her hair was long and black, her face narrow and her eyes blue and twinkling. Mary liked her at once.

'Mary Rosie. Where are ye from, then?'

'Nottingham. My father's a vicar there, but don't let that put you off. I'm a rebel.' She laughed.

'How are yer folks about ye joining up?' asked Mary.

'They believe in accepting what can't be changed. I'm sure they'll pray every night for my safety as well as my soul — and all the others of course. It would be the Christian thing to do. How are yours?'

'There's only Mam. My brother's already gone overseas. Mam's worried sick, but she'll cope a lot better than she's letting on. I only hope I'm accepted.' Her stomach gave another little shudder of excitement. She was looking forward to this new adventure, but at the same time she was beyond nervous.

When her name was called, she felt her heart beat all the way up to her mouth. The uniformed woman carrying a clipboard directed them towards a truck with a rope hanging out of the back. The girls looked at each other, a question in their eyes.

The woman with the clipboard introduced herself as Corporal Danes. 'Go on girls,' she said, 'climb up the rope.'

Beth shrugged, gave a whoop and pulled herself up. The others followed. 'This is a hoot,' she shouted.

Used to hoisting herself up a rope into the hayloft at home, Mary followed her. She smiled a greeting at the other girls as they climbed up too, many a lot less fit than herself. One girl, short and a bit on the heavy side tried several times without success.

'Grab my hand, love' said Beth. 'You take one too, Mary.'

Several other girls got behind her and between them they hoisted her up.

'Thank you,' she said. Mary could see she was near to tears. 'My mammy said I wouldn't be up to this and she was right.' She drew her hand across her nostrils and sniffed.

'I'm sure ye'll get used to it. My mam said that about me too.' Mary introduced herself and held out her hand.

'Agnes MacLeish,' said the girl. 'I'm from Paisley.'

The drive into town was short, but the driver had no thought for his passengers. The jeep swung round corners and stopped suddenly at junctions and the girls, who were seated on narrow wooden benches, were flung against each other which caused a lot of laughter and even swearing.

Once at their destination, an old, high building, the girls were ushered into a dark lobby, told to sit on wooden chairs and remain quiet until they were called.

'You will have a medical first,' explained Corporal Danes, who had followed in a jeep. 'No point wasting time if you are unfit. Now, no talking please.' The girls looked at each other and some covered their mouths in silent, nervous mirth.

One by one the girls were taken through a door in the hallway and up a flight of stairs.

Eventually it was Mary's turn. The surgery was a large room with a high, narrow window and a dark-oak desk. An elderly man with a stethoscope round his neck rose from behind the desk and approached her. 'I'm Doctor Andrews,' he said. 'This is Nurse Brown.' He nodded at a white-clad figure standing to one side. She barely returned Mary's smile. Mary thought she looked tired and more than a little bored.

For what seemed an age, Mary suffered all sorts of indignities before she was pronounced fit and then led into another room. Here she had to sign papers and answer questions until her head swam. Finally she was shown into yet another office, again a fair-sized room with the same narrow windows and filled with heavy, dark furniture.

Two interviewing officers, one male, one female raised their eyes as she entered, but gave no word of welcome. The woman, broad-set with a formidable face, glanced at paperwork on the desk. 'Mary Rosie?'

Mary nodded and clasped her hands in front of her, not sure what to do next.

'Take a seat will you.' The woman shuffled papers. 'I see you've no qualifications.' Her voice was as dour as her appearance.

Mary's spirits dropped. She hadn't realised she needed qualifications to do her bit for her country. She was desperate for a drink of water, but was too afraid to ask. Ungluing her tongue from the roof of her mouth, she said, 'I was good at my lessons, but my dad died when I was young and I had to get a job and help at home. I learn quick, like.' She snapped her mouth closed, least her runaway tongue did more damage than good.

'Nevertheless, I think we'll have to use you in a non-professional post. A cleaner or something in the kitchen would suit you best, I think.'

'Something in the kitchen?'

The woman gave a deep sigh and Mary sensed a mental rolling of the eyes.

'You really don't have much of an education,' said the man.

Her expectations tumbled. Being some skivvy wasn't what she had envisaged for herself.

'Would that appeal to you?'

Mary detected a slightly sneering twitch to the female officer's lips. She shook her head. 'Isn't there anything else?'

'What did you have in mind?' asked the man. He had a soft voice and kind brown eyes and Mary guessed she had an ally.

'I want to fly a plane.' Where did that come from? She'd never meant to say anything so ambitious.

The officers looked at each other and exchanged a slight stretching of the lips.

'I'm afraid that won't be possible, my dear.' said the man, barely hiding amusement. 'You'd have to have a pilot's licence for one thing.'

Blood rushed to her face. Why was she acting like this? Neither Rita nor Sally would ever have said anything so ridiculous, they would be all knowledgeable and cool. Her mother had been right; she was much too naive for the WAAF. She took a deep breath and said the next thing that came into her head. 'Then I'll drive a truck.' She would like to learn to drive. It's what Rita was learning to do. And she needed to learn something other than being a maidservant.

'Have you any experience?' asked the woman.

Even her ears were hot now. She tried to swallow and her dry throat closed in on itself. 'I can drive a tractor and see to it when it goes wrong and all.' It wasn't exactly a lie. Sinclair *had* let her drive the tractor up the road a few times and she *had*

140

held the tools for him and asked questions while he fixed something or other.

'I don't know about MT. Maybe some other kind of domestic work?' The woman looked at her colleague, then said in a condescending tone, 'She's from the Highlands,' as if she wasn't fit for anything more taxing.

Mary bristled and indignation killed her nerves. 'That doesn't make me stupid,' she snapped and immediately regretted her sharp answer. 'I'm...I'm sorry,' she stammered convinced that she'd ruined her chances of getting in.

'I'm sure it doesn't.' The man seemed to have taken to her. There was a slight twinkle in eyes that never left her face.

'I don't...' began the woman. The man stopped her with a raised hand.

'We're short of candidates for the trucks,' he said. 'I'd like to give her a try.'

'Hmmph, That's it then,' replied the woman with a disapproving sniff.

'How did you get on, love?' asked Beth when they met outside.

'I've been accepted!'

Beth gave a little whoop. 'Me too. Hopefully we'll be posted to the same place. What did you say you wanted to do?'

'I said I wanted to fly a plane.' Mary stifled a fit of giggles. 'Don't think they were impressed.'

Beth burst out laughing. 'Girl, you are a tonic!'

'I was serious.' Mary chuckled, the relief of having that interview over made her spirits rise. 'They turned me down, but at least I'm going to learn to drive.'

'Me too. That's great, love.' Beth giggled. 'That woman, wasn't she scary? Reminded me of a schoolteacher I once had, except the schoolteacher was quite pretty, whereas that officer looked like a garden gnome!'

At that both girls erupted with laughter, Mary holding her stomach till her sides ached.

She was still excited when she returned to Aunt Agatha's, dying to tell everyone about her day. She burst through the door. There was only Katrine and the baby in the kitchen. 'I'm in the WAAF,' she said, her voice high-pitched. She picked up baby Gussy who was lying in his pram kicking his fat little legs and blowing bubbles. 'How's my wee man been doing?' She blew a raspberry on his stomach and he giggled and shrieked.

'He's a wee angel,' said Katrine with an indulgent smile. 'I've seen a difference in your aunt too. She won't admit it, but she loves having him and Lisbeth. I take it the interview went well?'

'It started off bad. I was so nervous, but when she implied in her posh, plummy voice, that I was ignorant because I came from the Highlands, that did it. I forgot all about my nerves then. Is there tea in the pot? I'm as dry as a cork.'

'Good for you, dear. I'll make some tea fresh. You deserve it.'

'Where are Lisbeth and Aunt?'

'Your Aunt is having a lie down. Lisbeth's in her room, she takes to her room a lot, like a wee mouse, she is. Hardly says a word. I'm beginning to think she's a bit soft in the head.'

'She's just shy,' said Mary, mentally crossing her fingers.

It was another three weeks before Mary got the call to report for duty. Three weeks during which she watched Lisbeth grow in confidence, but her aunt grow ever weaker. So much so that Mary was less enthusiastic about leaving than she would have been. 'What's wrong with Aunt Agatha?' she asked Katrine once.

'It's her lungs. Her cough's been getting worse for a few years now.'

'She's lucky to have you.'

'Ah, lass, we've been together for a long time. We've both had our three score years and ten. I'll never leave her now.'

'I'm glad,' replied Mary. And she was. Glad that Agatha wasn't someone else who was going to make her feel guilty about abandoning them.

She wished she could have gone home to see her mother before joining up, but apart from the cost and distance, she feared Chrissie would once again try to dissuade her.

Chapter Twenty-two

Mary

The atmosphere on the platform was emotional as passengers, most of them servicemen and women, exited the train and others surged forward to take their places. There were moving reunions and tearful goodbyes. After stepping onto the platform, Mary squeezed through the crowds. Among the throng she saw someone she recognised.

'Beth,' she squealed.

Beth turned around. 'Oh, my giddy aunt, Mary!' The girls hugged each other. 'Over here, love. We're being picked up.'

Together they joined another group of girls, some of whom Mary recognised from the interviewing office.

The girls greeted each other, introduced themselves to those they did not know and chatted away, some animated, the realities of war not yet having confronted them. Others had already suffered the effects of a bombing, but still found that laughter was the best way to cover their disquiet.

At last a uniformed, middle-aged man marched onto the platform, raised his eyebrows at them and checked the clipboard he was holding. 'You all for the RAF camp?'

'Yes,' the girls chorused in unison.

'Follow me.' He turned and marched to where a lorry was parked. He opened a flap at the back and pulled down a rope attached to something inside. 'Climb aboard.'

'Something tells me we ain't half going to be experts at this,' said Thelma, a girl who'd introduced herself earlier, before hoisting herself up.

The lorry rattled along. Once more the girls sat on two hard benches, one on either side, and were tossed together at every bend. Mary giggled and clung to Beth.

Finally the lorry stopped. The driver came round the back and opened the flap. 'All out,' he shouted. They tumbled onto the ground, stretched their cramped muscles and looked about them. The camp was little more than a collection of Nissen huts.

'Over there,' said the gruff-voiced driver pointing at a hut with the sign, RECEPTION, on the wall.

'Enter,' directed a voice from inside when Beth tapped on the door.

Inside was warmed by an odorous paraffin heater. On the wall was a large poster that read, *Homesickness is like sea sickness, it soon wears off*. Behind a desk sat a woman in the WAAF uniform, who took their names and checked them against a list she held. After signing each girl in, she stood up. 'Right next door are the stores. Pick up your pillows and blankets there and someone will direct you to your billets.'

After being used to a puffy, feather-filled pillow and her mother's home made quilt, Mary was dismayed at the flat pad and two rough blankets issued to each girl along with the number of her hut.

'Stay together, love. Take the bed up here, next to me.' whispered Beth, grabbing her arm as they came through the door. The sleeping quarters held twenty beds apiece and were heated by an antique boiler in the middle of the room. The beds were iron framed with a mattress which was flat and hard and folded in three. 'What's this?' said Thelma. 'Garibaldi biscuits without the currants?'

The girl who took the next bed along picked up the pads and wrinkled her nose. 'How the hell are we supposed to sleep on this?' She reached over to Mary and offered her hand. 'I'm

Patricia, by the way. You can call me Trish.' Trish was a clumpish girl, with a pleasant but plain face and springy red hair.

'Mary.' They shook hands.

'You unfold them,' said yet another girl who introduced herself as Anna and she demonstrated. 'I've been here over a week. By the end of the day, you'll be so tired you'll not notice how hard they are.' Anna had a face that was unlikely to turn heads, yet her personality shone forth as soon as she spoke.

'Where do you come from?' Mary asked.

'I'm from Liverpool. And you're Scottish by your voice. They're from everywhere here.'

'Scotland? Me too. I'm Ella from Glasgow.' Yet another girl, fair-haired with a ready smile was reaching towards Mary. 'Sorry, I couldn't help overhearing ye.'

'Caithness,' said Mary.

'Manchester,' said Trish. 'I worked in a hotel. But I want a change from cooking. Told them I wanted to do something mechanical. I'm going for driving. You?'

'Me too,' said Anna.

'And me,' said Agnes.

Mary was delighted. There was a chance they would be kept together.

'And you?' Anna raised her eyebrows at Beth.

'I want to learn to drive, too. My father would never let me do that. He thought there was no need for women to drive a car. I know war is bad and all, but it is kind of an adventure, don't you think?'

They'd no sooner made up their beds than a voice came over the tannoy instructing them to line up at the cookhouse for cocoa and buns, then report to the NAAFI.

'It's where we eat,' explained Anna. 'Come on, I'll show you.'

'Thank goodness. I could eat a horse,' said Mary who hadn't eaten anything since breakfast.

146

The cocoa was weak and unsweetened and the bun was dry, but after so long without food, it tasted like manna. Still ravenous, Mary licked the last of the crumbs from her fingers.

They had barely finished before they were ushered to yet another building where they were kitted out with two uniforms, a heavy coat and what Anna called 'blackouts'. These were the officially-issued, thick, black knickers.

'How are these for a pair of passion killers?' said Trish.

'Most of us save up our clothes rations to buy nice underwear for when we go out,' said Anna.

'Are we allowed?' asked Mary.

Anna let out a hoot. 'How are they to know?' she said.

The uniform jackets and coat had brass buttons and the cap had a brass badge. Mary thought they looked very smart.

'These have to be cleaned every night with Brasso polish and a brush. Your shoes have to be shining bright and the space around your bed needs to be washed and polished every day. You'll find this will use up most the spare time in the evenings,' said the officer in charge with a clipped, no-nonsense voice and without once smiling at any of the girls.

By the time they returned to their berths, the bell rang summoning them to dinner.

'If you join the queue for the NAAFI, over there, you'll get your knife and fork,' Anna told them.

When they finally reached the counter, they were each presented with a knife, fork, spoon and a mug. 'Welcome to paradise,' said the officer in charge and chuckled at his own joke. 'Keep these grand pieces throughout your time in the forces. If you lose them, you'll not get any more.' They moved on as he greeted the next two girls in the same way, a broad grin never leaving his round, cheery face.

Anna led them into the dining area where they formed a line where each girl was served with two sausages, a scoop of soggy mashed potato and a mug of weak tea. They carried their food to long trestle tables where they took a seat on wooden benches.

147

At the first mouthful of tasteless sausage, Mary wrinkled her nose. It was doubtful if there was any meat in there at all.

'Not exactly the Ritz,' muttered Trish.

'Trust me,' said Anna, 'this is a treat.'

By the time they had finished eating it was late and the girls were sent straight back to their billets. Mary was horrified as Trish stripped off her clothes and, still naked, folded them before donning her night attire. She had never stood naked in front of anyone, even her mother, since she was six years old. Looking round the hut, she was shocked to see many other girls doing the same.

Beth was more modest and undressed discreetly, pulling her gown over her head before removing her underclothes.

Anna took one look at Mary's pink face. 'We've all got the same bits and pieces,' she whispered. 'You'll soon get rid of your false modesty here. No one'll look at you, but watch her at the very end bunk. She's one of them, you know?'

'One of what?' asked Mary.

'You know, them that likes other women.'

Mary was mystified. 'What do you mean?'

Anna stared at her. 'Are you serious? Do you really not know what I'm talking about?'

Mary shook her head.

'She likes women the way we like boys.'

Mary had never heard the like. 'You're joking.'

'Oh, Mary, you're such an innocent. I can see I'll have to take you in hand.'

Thelma let out a hoot. 'Bloody Nora, she'll not look at me then, not with my two poached eggs. She'll probably think I'm a boy in disguise. Now you, Mary,' she nodded at Mary's generous curves, 'You'll be fair game.'

The others giggled.

'Anything else you want to warn us about, Anna?' asked Beth.

'Well, watch out for the fly boys. There's still those who act like the WAAFs are only here to service the men.'

'In what way?' asked Mary, although she had a suspicion she knew.

Anna rolled her eyes. 'Where have you been brought up? In a convent?'

The others roared with laughter.

Although the mirth was good natured, Mary's face grew hot.

'Never mind,' said Trish putting an arm around Mary's shoulders. 'We'll soon have her as bad as the rest of us.'

Once the lights went out, Mary pulled the blankets around her chin. The hut was icy and her breath hung before her. She thought of her cosy bedroom above the kitchen back home. What she would give for her mother's stone hot water bottle and her chaff mattress right now. The beds here were as solid as a wooden floor and the tick pillow might not have been there at all for all the support it gave her head. The muffled sound of sobs came from further up the hut and someone else coughed continuously. A bout of homesickness swept through Mary and she felt like weeping herself, but she was so tired that sleep soon overtook her, blotting out everything else for a few blessed hours.

When they were wakened at five o'clock the next morning she was stiff and cold and it felt as though she'd never slept at all. The stove had gone out in the night and they had no hot water to wash in. The girls shivered as they struggled into their clothes.

'Come on,' said Anna, 'hurry up. It'll be warmer in the NAAFI.'

'Bleeding well hope it is. It's colder in here than a whore's heart in winter!' said Thelma.

The girls raced across the compound and stood shivering in line in the marginally warmer hut.

'Is this it? Where's the bacon and egg?' said Trish, staring at her plate with the jam and toast.

149

'What's bacon and egg?' asked the NAAFI girl who splashed weak tea into her mug. 'Suppose it doesn't hurt to dream.'

Mary accepted her ration with a wan smile and thought of a fine plate of porridge and cream topped with a spoonful of honey. Like the girl said, it didn't hurt to dream.

After breakfast, the new recruits were given a few hours off.

'Do you think we could go to the town?' said Trish. 'I don't want to spend any more time than we have to in that awful hut.'

'Of course we can,' said Anna. 'A bus stops at the end of the road every hour.'

'What do you think, Mary?'

'Yes please.' Mary was excited to see the town and she did feel grand in her uniform. Unlike many of the others, her body filled it out perfectly. The only down side was the ill-fitting shoes which chafed her heels and would soon cause blisters. She was still tired and the meagre breakfast had done nothing to satisfy her appetite, but each new experience brought its own surge of adrenaline.

Linking arms, they walked to the end of the road and caught a bus into town, where they marched along the waterfront with their shoulders back, feeling sure they looked impressive. She briefly wondered where Rita and the girls were and whether they would ever bump into each other.

'There's a café,' said Beth. I've got a few pennies. Let's go and see what they've got to eat.'

'I'm not hungry,' Mary lied. She didn't have any money.

'I can afford to treat you,' said Trish, as if guessing her reasons. 'Come on girls, you can pay me back later.'

The café, too, was suffering from rationing, the tea was weak and the scones floury and dry, but the girls devoured them none the less. Afterwards they walked round the shops, before catching the bus back to barracks. Once there, the new recruits were sent off to clean the ablution-blocks and spent the rest of the day doing other menial tasks.

Chapter Twenty-Three

Mary

A week later, Mary and her new friends had grown used to the diet. The new world they had entered was strange and regimented, but whatever was asked of her, Mary embraced with enthusiasm. She was determined to make a success of this.

After life in the country and working at the mill, Mary had thought herself fit, but the drill followed by aching muscles and utter fatigue told a different story. When training began in earnest, the girls were directed to a freezing hangar, where an RAF sergeant put them through their paces and shouted at them constantly. Within a few days Mary had learned how to salute officers and recognise the different ranks. She learned how to march, how to pass a kit inspection and other Air Force requirements.

But not all the girls learned as quickly.

'Get those arms higher,' the sergeant yelled at them.

His main target seemed to be Agnes MacLeish from Paisley. She was overweight and clumsy and often reduced to tears which seemed to anger the sergeant even more. 'Arms up, I said.'

Agnes's arms were already shaking as she fought to raise them higher. Her face was red and her eyes pooling. Mary longed to say something kind, but they had been forbidden to talk. They had just been vaccinated and found raising their left arms especially difficult.

Finally, unable to stand Agnes's discomfort a moment longer, Mary opened her mouth to explain. 'Sir…' she said, but before she could utter another word, the sergeant glared at her. 'Silence.' And he whacked her with his baton where the needle had entered her arm which was now slightly swollen. The pain shot to her teeth and she cried out.

The sergeant sneered. If you can't stand a little bit of pain, you'll never be good enough to become a WAAF.'

'Yes, sir.' Every nerve in her body seemed to shiver. Mary swore to herself she would never show such weakness again, she would grit her teeth and take whatever that bully dished out.

He turned once more to Agnes who now had beads of sweat running down her temples in spite of the frigid air. 'Up, I said. You lot are rubbish. I have never had such a lily-livered batch of recruits in my life.' With that he struck Agnes's arm even harder than he'd struck Mary's. With a screech, Agnes crumpled to the floor.

When she regained consciousness it was to the sergeant's voice telling her she should go home. 'Get her out of here,' he shouted. Mary and Anna took an arm each and helped her to her feet. They half carried her to the Nissen hut, laid her on her bed and covered her with her blanket.

'Don't mind him,' said Anna. 'He does that all the time. And you're not the only one to faint. It happens every day. I think he's a sadist.'

'That was cruel, just cruel.' Mary, who had no idea what a sadist was, agreed anyway.

She took the blanket off her own bed and tucked it around Agnes.

'I'm so cold I can't feel my feet or my hands,' said Agnes.

'At least it got us some time off.' Anna gave a little laugh. 'We've always got to be thankful for something, don't we? I'll nip to the NAAFI and see if I can rustle up a cup of tea, or at least a cup of hot water to warm you up.'

Mary chafed Agnes's hands. 'Are ye a wee bit warmer?' she asked. 'I'll get ye my coat.'

'No, no,' said Agnes through chattering teeth. 'Ye'll get into trouble. It's my arm, it's awful sore, so it is.'

'Hush, it'll be better by the morn.' Mary stroked the girl's hair back from her face.

'I've had enough.' Agnes stifled a sob. 'I'm leaving.' She wiped a tear from her cheek.

'Don't give up, pet. We're nearly there. Just a couple more weeks,' said Mary.

'I'm a volunteer and I'm only seventeen, I can go when I want. They all hate me. I try my best, but I'm too slow at washing up, my uniform isn't neat enough, my bed area hasn't been washed, my buttons don't shine. I'm sick of it. I'm no cut out for it. I'll try and get a job in a munition factory or something. Can't be any worse.'

'It's the same for all of us,' said Mary. 'Please don't give up now.'

'It's no just that,' Agnes replied. 'I miss my mammy and my bed and if I don't leave now I'll no be able to get out. It's no what I thought it was.' With that she started to cry in earnest. 'I've tried, I have tried. The food's awful and I can't sleep. Ye've been kind to me, Mary, but I just want to go home.'

Mary sympathised. She too longed for the home comforts, the warm kitchen, her mam, her friends' banter. And, especially after a hard day, there were nights when she fell onto the solid surface of her bed and would have given anything to be back home or even at Aunt Agatha's. But she'd come this far and sheer determination drove her onwards.

'Ye might feel different after a wee sleep. Look, here's Anna with a cup of something for ye. Don't be hasty.'

'I've made up my mind. I can't take it.' Agnes sat up and took the cup from Anna's hand.

153

'I'll be right sorry to see ye go,' Mary said. 'I'll miss ye.' And she would. She felt closer to home with another Scottish voice in her hut, albeit a different accent from the north.

'You're going? I don't blame you,' said Anna. 'Wish I could. And if I get whacked by that bloody man one more time, I'll not be able to keep my temper, I'll not. I'll grab his baton and shove it where the sun doesn't shine. That'll get me out!'

'It'll get ye court martialled!' Mary laughed and, in spite of her misery, Agnes joined in, but feebly.

The girls soon found out that saying goodbye was part of life in the forces. Agnes was not the only volunteer to give up and go home.

Although she tried her best, with Agnes gone, Mary became the main whipping girl, always at the wrong end of the sergeant's tongue. She didn't pick her feet up properly, she didn't swing her arms the right way, she wasn't keeping in line. Every day he almost reduced her to tears. The one thing that stopped her from feeling a complete failure was the knowledge that her companions were going through similar beratings, although not as severe, and that every day took her nearer to completion.

Three weeks in, the square bashing became easier. Both her body and her nerve grew ever more resilient. By the end of the training, Mary's muscles were harder, her sleep deeper and her homesickness less acute. Eventually, along with the others who had stuck it out, she could march to the satisfaction of the commanding officer. At the passing out parade her heart was filled with pride in her achievement and there were no more tears.

Chapter Twenty-Four

Mary

The recruits were then broken up and sent to various parts of Britain for their respective training. Drivers were sent to Morecambe and billeted in guest houses along the sea front. Once more there were tearful goodbyes to friends with whom, in spite of their short acquaintance, Mary had built a strong bond. However, she was delighted to discover that Beth, Thelma and Trish were going to be her billet mates.

'Oh my giddy aunt,' said Thelma, when they saw the grand house that was to become their home for the foreseeable future.

'No more freezing hut and hard bed,' said Mary, hugging herself with glee.

'Posh, innit?' said Thelma in awe.

The door was open by a dour faced woman who greeted them with a brief nod.

'My name is Mrs Whitely,' she said, and indicated that they should follow her. 'This is a respectable house.' She spoke as they walked along the wide, airy hallway and up the stairs. 'There will be no smoking inside, no coming home drunk and no young men. You have to share a room, but there will be no chatter after ten p.m. You will keep your room clean and tidy at all times.'

She stopped and opened a door, one of four on the first landing. The room had two beds, a double and a single, one wardrobe and a chest of drawers. A large bay window looked out on to the esplanade granting them a spectacular view. The only thing not in in the room's favour was that the air was as frigid as it was outside.

'On your day off you may use the kitchen to cook in, but you will leave it as you find it. You'll have to bring your own food, I have little enough rations.' Mrs Whitely stood with her hand on the door knob.

The girls nodded in unison. 'We will,' said Trish, her eyes shining.

'The bathroom is at the end of the corridor. You will have no more than one bath a week and you will not put more than four inches of water in the bath.'

'Yes of course, Mrs Whitely,' said Mary with a smile which was not returned.

'I'll leave you to settle in.' Without making any eye contact and with a sniff, she turned and left.

As soon as she was out of earshot, the girls looked at each other and raised their eyebrows. 'I imagine she's not happy at having WAAFS forced upon her,' whispered Beth. 'She didn't give us a ruler. Do you think we should ask for one?'

'Why would you need a ruler? asked Mary.

'To make sure we have exactly four inches of bath water, silly.'

'Oh, aye, we'll need one.' Mary giggled and the other three joined her.

'Do you suppose she ever supplies a heater?' said Beth with a shiver.

Mary shrugged. 'I doubt it.' The room was cold, but that was little discomfort compared with what they had already endured.

'I'm off to check out the lav,' said Thelma. She came back a moment later. 'A real bathroom,' she breathed. 'Let's pray the water's hot.'

'This is pure luxury,' sighed Trish who had thrown herself on the double bed. 'Who's going to share with me?'

'I don't mind,' said Mary.

156

'Then you can sleep with me. Beth snores.'

'Suits me,' said Beth. 'I prefer my own space anyway.'

'What about me?' said Thelma. 'I'm the fattest. I should have the single bed and I fart.'

'She's right,' said Trish holding her nose. 'You'd best come in with us, Beth. But I'm not going in the middle.'

'I will,' said Beth. 'I'm used to sleeping three in a bed. I've two older sisters and they always put me in the middle when we were growing up.'

'Let's get unpacked and do a bit of sightseeing. I'm going to find a shop that sells hot water bottles, since I won't have you lot to keep me warm,' said Thelma.

In the operational RAF station, life was very different — here the girls really knew there was a war on. There were people everywhere, all rushing about looking important, engineers, technicians and armourers, aircrew, as well as the cooks, cleaners and office workers who helped to keep the station running. Here they ate in the Mess. The NAAFI was where they could buy items such as toothpaste, soap, shampoo and hair combs. It also doubled as an entertainment hall.

The girls were amazed at the airfield and the hundreds of aircraft: taking off, landing or being maintained, being repaired, re-armed or refuelled.

Every day they went out, four girls to a vehicle with an instructor, driving through the lovely Lancashire countryside, deep into the Lake District. Mary found there was little time to take in the scenery as she struggled with gear changing, double declutching and stopping and starting on the steepest of hills. A different vehicle was allocated to them each day. They never knew whether it would be a luxurious staff car, an ambulance with the accelerator where the clutch usually was, or a fifteen or thirty hundredweight truck. Beth had absolutely no road sense and they were all terrified when it was her turn to take the wheel. She was eventually taken out alone with the instructor, who she flirted with on every opportunity, which was, Mary suspected, what she'd been angling for all along. Especially since, once she got to know him better, she no longer found him attractive and her driving immediately improved.

They were taught how to maintain an engine, how to grease a chassis, how to change a wheel.

Mary loved driving from the minute she first got behind a wheel and she loved the camaraderie with the other girls. She put up with the rigid discipline and regimentation, finding it easier with every passing week. She was one cog in a well-oiled machine and together they were going to show Hitler what was what! Thoughts of home, Lisbeth and Aunt Agatha retreated to a place far from her mind.

Chapter Twenty-Five

Mary

When the results of the final tests came through, Mary was delighted to discover that she had done much better than she'd expected. Nothing could erase the smile from her face that day. She was a real WAAF, and she could drive and maintain a truck!

Training completed, she was posted to Marham, a bomber station, and here she was back in a Nissen hut. She was upset because Beth would not be joining her, but they had already been told that there was every chance they would be split up. The girls had to go where they were sent, no special requests allowed. They exchanged home addresses and hugged. 'You will keep in touch, love?' asked a tearful Beth.

'Of course I will,' Mary replied.

The first night in Marham, Mary was wakened by an ear-numbing blast, a wailing roar that filled her ears. All the girls sprung out of their beds.

'What the hell is that?' asked Mary grabbing the arm of the girl who stood beside her, a girl who'd introduced herself as Janet.

'Sounds like a low flying Beaufort. Don't worry, duck, there was no siren. It'll be ours back from a sortie.' Janet had been here for some time and appeared very knowledgeable. Knowing there was no immediate danger didn't still the thunder of Mary's heart. 'It scared me,' she said, setting her hand on her chest as she fought to control her breathing.

'You'll get used to it.' Janet lit a cigarette and took a long draw before handing it to Mary. 'It'll settle your nerves, duck,' she said when Mary shook her head.

'I could never afford to buy cigarettes,' said Mary. 'So there's little point in starting.'

Janet shrugged her shoulders. 'Suit yourself.'

The plane landed with a squeal of brakes that caused Mary to jump and cover her ears.

When the noise finally abated, she followed the other girls as they crept to the door and tumbled out into the dawn. Mary's earlier fear was replaced by a sense of excitement. People were everywhere, running around or cycling unsteadily along the track. Voices shouted orders, vehicles, their lights subdued, travelled along the road, metallic doors ground open and crashed shut.

'Is this normal?' she asked.

'Pretty much every night,' replied another girl who had introduced herself as Gloria.

More low flying planes with a less threatening purr came in like a swarm of bees, dark shapes through the semi-night. 'Spitfires,' explained Janet.

Now knowing what they were, the new girls no longer cowered against the noise, although Mary wondered how they were ever going to get a night's sleep if this happened on a regular basis. Gloria, Janet and several others who had been here a while counted the Spitfires as they landed.

'Two missing,' said someone.

'Missing?' asked Mary.

'Probably shot down. You'll get used to well-known faces disappearing and new ones arriving.'

'I have to go, find out if Rob made it,' said Janet. She stubbed out what remained of her cigarette, returned to the hut long enough to bundle herself into her clothes and raced towards the airfield.

'She's been seeing a pilot,' Gloria explained. 'If you take my advice you'll have fun, but you won't fall in love. Chances are you're heading up for heartbreak if you do.'

Mary was finally slipping into sleep when the door opened and Janet came in. She gave a stifled sob and put her hand over her face. Mary sprang up. 'Are ye alright?' she whispered.

'He...he didn't make it.' Janet's whole body was shaking. Knowing there was nothing she could say to make it better, Mary hugged her, led her to her bed and tucked her blankets round her. Her sobs grew louder and before long other girls were clustering around the bed, hugging her, muttering words of condolence.

'See what I mean?' said Gloria. 'Janet'll be fit for nothing come daybreak, but a broken heart is seen as no excuse for slacking.' She gave a sigh. 'Tomorrow'll be another day and another broken heart.'

For the few hours left of the night, Mary lay staring into the darkness, her adrenaline still pumping too much for sleep.

The next day, Mary was provided with a small standard van and her main duty was to fetch and carry pilots from the mess to flight headquarters, pick up drogues when they were shot down and generally be at the beck and call of anyone who needed transport. A drogue, she soon found out, was a cylindrical target towed behind an aircraft and used for firing practice.

It was here she met Dermot, a young man who she liked immediately. He wasn't much taller than her, slightly overweight with a round, cheery face, and he winked at her whenever they met. The first time she drove him to base he asked her about her life and told her a little about his. He was

161

from Belfast, an only child, he said, born when his parents were already middle-aged, and he told her he was a Lizzie pilot.

'What's a Lizzie pilot?' she asked, not sure if he was joking.

'We Lizzies tow the drogues and the Wimpy pilots manoeuvre the planes for the gunners. Most of us have either done a tour of ops and are resting, or we're waiting to be posted to an operational unit.'

'Which are you?'

His normally jovial face became serious. 'I'll be back doing the serious stuff soon.' He scratched his arm. 'I'm resting. I was exhausted. I've already done more than my share of sorties before curtains, so I have.' He pulled a packet of cigarettes from his pocket and lit one.

'Curtains?'

'Yes. By the law of averages, I shouldn't be alive. I've lived longer than the standard life of a pilot.'

'But they're sending you back?'

'If I'm lucky a few more times, they'll put me onto training the new pilots.'

Then the smile was back. He winked. 'I'm fighting fit, can't wait.' He sounded confident, but Mary could sense the stress behind his bonhomie.

He drew deeply on his cigarette and allowed the smoke to escape in a dribble. 'Fancy the pictures in Kings Lynn on Saturday night? It's a Fred Astaire and Ginger Rogers. Supposed to be good.'

'I would love that. Is Kings Lynn easy to get to?' The base was miles from any town.

'You and the girls come round the back of the NAAFI after tea. There's a lorry going. The lads are good for hitching a lift. There *is* a bus, but the times often don't fit in.'

Mary, Gloria and Trish were excited to get out of camp. They had tried unsuccessfully to persuade Janet to come too, but she convinced them that she'd be better left alone.

'I'll lend you my silk stockings,' said Gloria.

'And you can have some of my make-up, you've practically had most of it anyway,' said Trish.

But Janet, lying face down on her bed, just covered her head with her arms and refused to speak.

'Maybe we shouldn't leave her,' said Mary, wishing she could do something to comfort the girl.

'You heard her, she doesn't want us,' said Gloria. She took Mary's arm. 'Really, do as she asks.'

The boys in the lorry were great company and they laughed all the way to Kings Lynn. By the time they reached the picture house, the girls knew all about Tow-target flights, about Lysanders, Martinets, Defiants and Hurricanes.

Afterwards the boys took them to a pub where Dermot bought a round and Mary tasted gin and tonic for the first time. When he bought her a second one she protested. She hadn't brought much money with her. 'I can't buy you one back,' she said.

'Sure, and you've not to worry your wee head about that. You can pay me back some other time.' And he bought her a double.

Now and then she would remember Janet and the smile would slip. 'I still feel bad about leaving her,' she said.

'Don't let it affect you too much,' whispered Gloria. 'Happens every day. Life goes on.'

'Aye,' said Mary, still uneasy.

'Don't drink too much,' Gloria warned as Mary tossed the gin back. 'You'll be use for nothing in the morning.' But she had begun to relax. After yet another drink, she felt merry and just wanted to laugh.

By the time they returned to camp, the stresses of the war were forgotten for a few hours. She even let Dermot kiss her goodnight and, giggling at her daring, kissed him back.

Lying in bed, still high on the excitement of the evening, she listened to the sound of bombs and air fire. So far the airfield

163

hadn't been hit and the fighting had become as common as the cry of the seals back home and she fell asleep to the sounds of conflict.

'Goodness me,' she said to Trish as they washed next morning. 'I hope I've not encouraged Dermot. I like him a lot, but not in that way.' Actually she remembered very little about the kisses, only that she'd let it happen and even enjoyed it.

'Don't worry,' was the reply. 'I'd a fumble in the back of the lorry myself and I don't even know who with!'

'Oh, Trish, how could you no know? Did you no ask his name?' Mary was shocked.

'I didn't even see his face. It was dark in there. Oh, come on Mary, he probably didn't know who I was either. It was just a bit of fun.' She giggled and before long, Mary joined her.

The first pick-up she had the next day was Dermot. 'Sore head this morning?' he asked.

Was his smile wider than ever this morning? She felt his eyes appraising her. She lowered her head, her cheeks burning. Raising one hand, she covered her face. 'Never again,' she muttered.

'Good night, though, wasn't it?'

'Aye, Dermot… we…uh…that kiss…' She had to explain.

'Don't you worry your wee head about it. Sure, for I know it was the gin. It was grand though.' His grin suddenly seemed forced, or was it her imagination?

'I'm sorry…'

'Don't be. Hey, I'm back in action.'

'You mean you're going to fight again?'

He nodded. 'I'll be protecting you girls from the enemy, so you'd better treat me well.'

'You're a good friend, Dermot. The best.' She felt a rush of affection for this fresh-faced lad with the ready smile, who was once more going out on missions from which he might never return.

'Maybe you'll come out with me again some time,' he said.

164

'I'd like that, but only if you let me pay my share.' She knew her meagre wages would not support too many nights out. That was a luxury and they had few enough of them, except for when the girls got parcels from home, which they would share. The things Mary particularly looked forward to was a jar of rhubarb jam and her mam's home-baked treacle scones. Now she could add a gin and tonic and a night out with the lads to that list.

Chapter Twenty-Six

Mary

On her first leave she travelled to Great Aunt Agatha's full of stories about her time in the WAAF. She found Lisbeth looking healthier and happier and the baby had won the hearts of everyone, especially Katrine.

'Lisbeth's a good girl,' said Aunt Agatha. 'But she doesn't say much. And she's very reluctant to come to church, something I insist on. Will you have a word with her? She always seems to have a sore head and must take to her bed on a Sunday.'

'I'll have a word, Auntie,' promised Mary.

'It's part of your cover, Lisbeth.' They walked in the gardens around the bungalow pushing Gussy in a pram Katrine had borrowed from someone in the village. 'Your God will understand.'

'Agatha's been kind, but strict. I try my best, but she says dreadful things about Jews and she doesn't believe the stories that are coming out of Europe. It is hard to remain quiet. I have to, how do you say, *bite my lip*.'

'But you must.'

'I know this.' A tear trickled down her cheek. 'I miss my family so much. I don't know if they're alive or dead and I wish they could see little Gustav. I wish his father could too. I don't know if he's still alive even. He *is* a good man, Mary. There are many good Germans.'

'How can you say that after what they did to your family?'

'If it wasn't for Gustav's parents I too would have been captured. They hated what was happening and they could have been shot themselves for helping me.'

The baby started to grizzle. 'Hush little Gustav,' she whispered.

Mary experienced an uncharacteristic surge of irritation. 'Stop calling your child that. Why did you even give him a German name? You escaped from Germany.' Mary's experiences in the war had already tainted her opinion of all Germans.

'I *am* German,' declared Lisbeth. 'Most young men are ordered to go to war, they have no choice. Their mothers and sweethearts cry as well. It is Hitler and his followers who are the Satan.'

Mary said nothing. She thought about the young pilots who risked their lives every night and how many did not come back. She thought of Peter and Johnny and all her friends, many of whom had already lost lives and limbs. She thought of the danger she was in every time the RAF station was bombed, she especially thought of the first bomb that dropped on Bank Row, the vision of the small body on the stretcher forever ingrained on her mind and she found it impossible to sympathise with German servicemen.

'I'm sorry, I can't listen to this. Let's go back.' She suddenly had no patience with the girl before her. She would never regret helping her but she was sticking up for the enemy, for the very people who had killed her family, who were trying to kill Mary and her friends. In battle she could understand as this was war, but they were bombing innocent people in towns and cities, civilians who were just trying to survive.

'Have you heard from your brother?' Lisbeth asked as they retraced their footsteps.

'Not much.' In her mam's last letter she said he sounded fine, but they both knew the reality could be very different.

'I hope he's well,' said Lisbeth.

'If he can dodge a German bullet,' muttered Mary.

That night, as Mary got undressed, Katrine came into her bedroom holding a folded newspaper. She sat down on the end of the bed and the springs creaked with her weight. 'Sorry to disturb you, dear, but who is Lisbeth really?' she asked, her voice low.

'I told you,' answered Mary.

'Why is she so secretive, dear, and why has she not got a ration book?'

Mary froze. Neither she nor Chrissie had even thought about the absence of a ration book.

'We forgot to bring it with the rush and everything.'

'I'm no a fool, dear. I lied to yer aunt and told her I had it. Now what's really going on? It's hard feeding three on two lots of rations, dear. It's lucky I have friends who do a little trading on the side.'

A cold hand closed around Mary's heart. The well-known line of a poem by Robert Burns flashed through her mind. *The best-laid schemes of mice and men gang aft agley.*' Everything was in danger of being blown apart. What would it do to her career in the WAAF if they found out that she'd helped someone who might have been a spy, unlikely as that was. 'I'll give you some of my coupons if you say nothing. Trust me, it's better ye don't know. Please God this war'll be over before the bairn needs solid food.'

'Is this something that'll get us all in trouble, dear?' Katrine's head tilted a little to one side.

Mary came to a decision. Katrine wasn't going to stop until she had an explanation she could believe. She was shrewd and no nonsense and Mary felt she could trust her. It was as well she was sitting down. 'This story'll take a wee while to tell,' she said.

'Ye should have never put us in this situation, dear,' said Katrine when Mary finished.

'She came from a German war ship. She'd have been interrogated and incarcerated,' said Mary.

'Would that be so bad?' Katrine's voice took on a sterner edge.

'With hindsight, maybe not, but if you could have seen her that night. She was terrified and like a drowned rat. She needed help and we gave it without a thought. Please Katrine, you would have done the same. Will you cover up for her till this war's over?'

'We're right fond of her and I've seen a real difference in Agatha since she came. I'm trusting you, dear, but if this backfires...'

'I'm sorry. Please say nothing. Aunt Agatha can be very unreasonable sometimes and if she finds out Lisbeth's a Jew....'

'I'll keep quiet for now, dear. You do realise that your aunt is very ill? Something like this might accelerate her symptoms.'

'Aye, I do realise. I am sorry; we didn't know what to do.'

'It's only for her sake that I'm saying nothing, dear. She thinks a great deal of you and your family and she'd be very hurt if she knew you'd lied to her.'

'I'll try and find somewhere else for Lisbeth.'

'Well, you'd have to think of a plausible excuse, one that your aunt would believe. Ye should read this, dear.' She opened the newspaper she held in her hand.

The Daily Mail. On the front page the headline screamed, **German Jews pouring into this country.**

Mary read the article out loud.

"The way stateless Jews and Germans are pouring in from every port of this country is becoming an outrage. I intend to enforce the law to the fullest."

In these words, Mr Herbert Metcalfe, the Old Street Magistrate yesterday referred to the number of aliens entering this country through the 'back door' — a problem to which The Daily Mail has repeatedly pointed.

The number of aliens entering this country can be seen by the number of prosecutions in recent months. It is very difficult for the alien to escape the increasing vigilance of the police and port authorities.

Even if aliens manage to break through the defences, it is not long before they are caught and deported.

'It's not only that, people have been arrested for harbouring them. I'm no hard woman, dear, I've no wish to see the lass harmed...' Katrine stopped for a moment. 'I know the law has changed and Jews are allowed in now, but I don't know what the truth would do to your aunt or your career. And then you and your mam, you broke the law, dear.'

Neither woman had seen Lisbeth in the doorway, or heard her as she slipped away.

The next day as she and Lisbeth walked down the lane, Mary stopped her with a hand on her arm. 'Katrine knows the truth,' she said at last.

Lisbeth's face paled. 'I understand,' she said in a small voice. 'I have to leave. I'll not put them in danger.'

'Maybe it won't come to that. But as long as you're here you must go to church with my aunt.'

Although her feelings for Lisbeth were no longer as warm, Mary hoped the relationships would work out. Aunt Agatha was clearly fond of the girl and the baby and both were blossoming under Katrine's care. No one questioned the shadow that often crossed Lisbeth's face or the sorrow behind her eyes. There were many such shadows up and down the country. Mary wondered what they would say if they knew it was partly for a German sailor.

170

Lisbeth nodded. 'I will do as you say.'

'Good,' Mary said.

Once her leave was up, Mary went to bid her aunt goodbye.
Agatha had had a bad night and was still in bed. She held out
her hand and Mary grasped it, noticing how wrinkled it was,
how the blue veins bulged under the skin. Agatha was nothing
like the woman who breezed into Chrissie's cottage two years
ago.

'I'm so pleased you came and gave me these few months,'
she said, in a broken voice. 'And having Lisbeth and Gussy
around, you've made an old woman's last days very happy.'
She clutched Mary's hand. 'God go with you my child. I fear
I'll not see you in this world again.'

'Don't say that, Auntie. I'll be back on my next leave.' She
had been hoping to go home to Caithness, but with Agatha so
ill, that might not be the best option.

Agatha closed her eyes. A thin smile played around her lips.
'Say goodbye to your mother and brother from me.'

Mary bent down and kissed the papery cheek, wishing she
could stay a bit longer. She hadn't realised before how much
this woman meant to her. 'I have to go,' she whispered.

'You have to do your duty. Go win the war for me, girl.' It
was as if saying these words sapped the last of her strength and
she sank into a breathy sleep.

When Mary left the room, Katrine met her by the door.
'Goodbye, dear,' she said. 'Give them hell. I'll see to yer aunt.'

Mary hugged Gussy loving the feel of his plump little body
and milky smell. 'See you both on my next leave,' she said,
looking over the baby's head at Lisbeth, little knowing she
would never see either of them again.

Chapter Twenty-Seven

Lisbeth

Lisbeth had heard Mary read out the article, especially the bit about deporting Germans. She had no way of knowing that the address had been made on the 20th of August, 1938, before Britain declared war on Germany and, as she had left immediately, she had no way of knowing Jews were allowed into Britain now, even welcomed. She went to her bedroom and packed her belongings in the bag that Chrissie had given her. Early next day she told Katrine and Agatha that she was going for a walk.

'Don't go too far, then,' said Agatha who liked to see Gussy before his midday nap.

'I won't,' said Lisbeth, and kissed the old woman on the cheek. Then she hugged Katrine. This display of affection surprised both women.

'You be careful, dear,' said Katrine.

Lisbeth left the pram around the corner behind a hedge where it couldn't be seen from the road and, with Gussy in her arms, she waited for a bus into Aberdare. Swallowing the ever rising lump in her throat, she clutched the baby to her and mounted the bus. Ever since Hitler had declared his aim of ridding the continent of Jews, she had carried a fear deep inside. A fear that whatever fate had befallen her family would one day claim her too. She had met with kindness, Chrissie and Mary, Agatha and Katrine, and the words Lisbeth overheard had been a cruel blow. She would miss them all terribly. For a while she had almost believed that she would, after all, survive this war, maybe even meet Gustav again, but she had been fooling herself. It was as if for the second time she'd lost a family.

'You okay, love?' asked a round woman in the seat next to her.

Lisbeth jumped and clutched the baby tighter to her chest. 'Thank you, I'm fine.' She pressed her lips together to stop the tremble and looked out the window hoping the woman would understand she'd no wish to talk.

The woman stroked the baby's head.

'Bad news, love?' she asked.

Lisbeth nodded and could no longer stem the tears that trickled down her cheeks.

The woman patted her arm and fell silent, undoubtedly assuming that Lisbeth had just lost someone in the war.

She left the bus in the main street without knowing what to do next. She wanted to ask directions to the nearest synagogue where she was sure to get help but, after what she had overheard, she was afraid to let anyone know she was Jewish. Was there even a synagogue in the town? Walking along, looking this way and that, she eventually found a newsagents where she purchased a map.

By the time she reached the synagogue, her legs were aching, the baby grizzling and growing more demanding with every step. The sky spitting rain that threatened to get heavier lowered her spirits even further. Finally, hungry and footsore, she pulled herself up the steps of the building, yanked the heavy door open and walked inside. There she was greeted by the rabbi, a fresh-faced man with a thick white beard and kindly brown eyes.

'*Shabbat Shalom*,' he said.

'*Shabbat Shalom*,' she replied, almost fainting with relief. Memories of the childhood greeting made her feel instantly at home.

'Come and sit with me, child.' The Rabbi took her arm and led her to a seat. 'I'll fetch my wife and she will care for the child.'

He returned carrying a glass of water, a fresh-faced woman by his side.

'I'm Rabbi Hyman, by the way, and this is my Lisa.' His handshake was firm and reassuring.

Lisa smiled and took the child from Lisbeth's arms. 'I will get him some milk,' she said and made soothing noises.

'Now, how can we help you?' the rabbi asked.

Lisbeth sobbed for some minutes and then controlled herself. 'I've been living with a Christian family, but the lady of the house will hate me once she knows I'm a Jew. I have been found out. I ran away. I'm afraid I'll be deported.'

'Whatever made you think that? You will not be deported, of that I'm sure.'

She looked into his kindly eyes and most of the story tumbled out. It was such a relief to be honest once again, to be with people who would not judge her, her own kind.

'I'm tired of pretending to be what I'm not, of going to a Christian church to keep up the lie.'

'Many English help us. Why don't you tell the truth?'

'Miss Agatha is kind, but you should hear what she says about our faith. And I'm not just a Jew, I'm German. Even if I'm allowed to stay, Chrissie and Mary may get into trouble for hiding me, they all might. It's better I just run away.'

'Ah.' He folded his hands together. 'The worst that could happen is that, as a German, you might be interned. It would be better if you claimed to be Belgian.'

'That wouldn't be a lie exactly. My mother was Belgian and my parents were married there. They moved to Germany before I was born. My father had the offer of a good job you see.'

The rabbi scratched his ear. 'I know a family in Cardiff who will take you in. They themselves fled Europe. I can take you there in a couple of weeks. What's your name?'

'Liesel,' she said. 'And this is Angus. I gave him a British name.' She would keep one secret. That little Gussy's father was a German serviceman with whom she was still in love.

However, in the synagogue, in the presence of the rabbi, she felt a sense of belonging that she hadn't realised she missed.

She resolved to write Agatha and Katrine a letter thanking them for what they had done, but not giving them her reasons for leaving. She didn't want to cause any bad feeling between Agatha and her family. In spite of Rabbi Hyman's assurances that she would be safe in Britain, she spent each day on edge. The Hymans had many visitors and Liesel held her breath until she knew they had not come for her.

One afternoon, when the rabbi and his wife were both out, she put Gussy down to sleep. A knock came to the door. She shrank behind the curtains, from where she could peer without being seen. A young, bearded man dressed in a suit and wearing the Jewish skullcap, stood there. Breathing deeply in relief, she opened the door. A pair of deep brown eyes drank her in. 'And who are you?' he asked in a velvet voice.

'I'm Liesel Hirsch.' She waited for him to explain why he was here.

'I'm Josh,' he replied.

She raised her eyebrows in question.

'The rabbi's son. Is he in?'

Any lingering fear she may have had evaporated. This man was the image of Rabbi Hyman, or how he would have looked when he was young. She relaxed. 'I've only been here a few days. The rabbi didn't tell me he had a son. And no, neither of them are in. Were they expecting you?'

Josh gave a low chuckle. 'They never know when to expect me.'

She suddenly remembered her manners. 'Come in, come in. I'll make coffee.' He followed her into the kitchen.

'Have you been in the country long?' he asked.

'About a year. How did you know I'm a stranger?'

'I assumed so since my father has taken you in. You're not the first. Your English is excellent, by the way. Where did you come from?'

'Belgium. My father was an English teacher. I also speak French, German and Italian.'

His eyes sparked with interest. 'Fluently?'

'Yes.'

'Interesting.' He took the coffee cup from her hands.

'How long are you staying?' she asked.

'I only have the weekend.' He leaned forward and studied her in a way that made her skin grow hot. 'Tell me all about yourself, Liesel.'

About an hour later, they were deep in conversation when the insistent cries of Gussy wafted down the stairs.

'Oh, my baby's awake.' She leapt to her feet.

Josh's face changed. 'I didn't know you had a baby.'

'Sorry, does it matter?'

He looked down at his hands, then, as if coming to a decision, he spoke. 'I work for the government. I thought perhaps you might be able to help the war effort. The Home Office needs interpreters. But a baby...' He shrugged.

She went upstairs and returned a few minutes later with Gussy in her arms, just as Rabbi Hyman and his wife came in.

'Ah, Joshua!' The couple greeted their son with wide grins and hugged him in turn.

'I see you have already met our guests,' said the rabbi. 'Has Liesel been entertaining you?'

'Very well,' replied Josh.

That night, long after she retired, Liesel could hear the voices of Josh and his father. She couldn't forget his words, *The Home*

Office needs interpreters. This country had been good to her and she hated the Nazis. She would love to help in any way she could, but she had to put little Gustav first.

Next morning over breakfast, she brought the subject up. 'This help you spoke about, what would it entail?'

'You would have to come to Buckinghamshire, but leave the child behind. The work is quite time consuming.'

'I would have liked to help, but I can't leave my baby. He's all I have left of my family.'

'I understand,' said Josh.

'If you ever change your mind, Lisa and I are willing to care for Gussy until the war is over,' said the Rabbi.

'Thank you, that's kind. But I can't be separated from him.'

Before he left, Josh shook Liesel's hand. 'I'm very glad to have met you. Take care of yourself and the boy.' Then he slipped a sixpenny piece into her palm. 'Buy him something.'

'Thank you,' she muttered, sorry to see him go.

It took another week for the rabbi to make all the arrangements to move Liesel and Gussy somewhere else.

'We'll be sorry to see you leave,' he said, 'but I must keep an extra room for other Jews seeking lodgings. We'll go and meet the couple I told you about later today. I've been saving my petrol ration and I have just about enough.'

The couple, a Mr and Mrs Goldberg, lived in a small flat in a tenement near the river in Cardiff.

'*Baruch haba.*' Mr Goldberg, a heavy set man with short-cut, crinkly, greying hair and sparkling blue eyes, greeted her in Hebrew. 'We are Renata and Walter and this is our daughter, Eva.' Renata clasped her hand in both of hers and Eva, a girl of about ten, grabbed Gussy's fingers and smiled up at him in obvious delight. Eva favoured her mother in looks. They were both petite and shared the same dark brown hair and small, heart-shaped faces that made their brown eyes look enormous.

'Eva loves babies, as do we all. You will be very welcome here,' said Renata. 'The room we have for you is small, but we've made it comfortable.'

'It's lovely.' Liesel looked around. The room was white-washed with a wooden floor and a rag rug. It held a wardrobe, a writing desk and a narrow single bed covered by a faded patchwork quilt. Against the foot of the bed was a wooden cot. There were no curtains, but a black-out blind which could be drawn down at night.

In spite of the warmth of the family, Liesel suffered a sense of isolation. Too many goodbyes, too many new people in her life, but she would survive and give her son the life he deserved, hopefully in a free country. She closed her hand and felt the outline of Chrissie's ring which she kept secure by winding a thickness of wool around her finger. One day she would make good her promise and return this ring to its rightful owner.

Chapter Twenty-Eight

Liesel

Once Gussy was asleep, Liesel sat at her desk and wrote four letters, one each to Agatha, Katrine, Mary and Chrissie. She explained to Mary, Chrissie and Katrine her reasons for leaving and promised never to forget them. She thanked Agatha for all her help and said she left as she was a drain on their resources. She explained that she was living happily with a family in Cardiff, but did not reveal her address.

Less than a week later, as she lay on her narrow bed staring at the moon through the oblong window, her thoughts went once more to Gustav, the young man who was never far from her heart. She saw him on the deck of the warship gazing at that same moon, thinking of her.

'I'm safe, my love,' she whispered, trying to reach him with her mind and heart. Once again she visualised them walking hand in hand along the banks of the Isar. Then they stopped and he bent forward and gently kissed her. She raised her fingers to her lips as she remembered the moment, the magic, the way her heart had soared and suddenly she was back in that time of innocence. She had been so happy, so much to look forward to. The sound of water, birds in the trees, the scent of spring in the air, their futures and dreams ahead of them. The biggest problem in her life was how to tell her parents she was in love with a Christian.

The sudden, harsh screech of sirens tore the air and jolted her from her dreams. She pulled her coat over her nightdress and grabbed Gussy from his cot. She met Renata and Eva on the landing and together they hurried downstairs. Walter, a member of the Home Guard, was away on night duty. By the time she reached the ground floor and flung the door open, she could hear the drone of the bombers overhead, an eerie, unnerving sound.

'It's too late to reach the shelter.' Renata shouted over the noise of whistling bombs and exploding buildings. 'Under the staircase, quick.'

Liesel slammed the door shut on the hell outside. They huddled under the staircase where another family had already taken refuge. All of a sudden the whole building shook and pieces of masonry crashed around them. Liesel was pitched forward, still clinging to the screaming baby. Her head jarred against the concrete floor. Gussy's screams abruptly stopped. In that moment she lost consciousness.

When she next opened her eyes it was to a throbbing pain in her head. She was lying on her back staring into the sky. As the dust cleared, she saw that most of the building around her had gone and the sky over the city had taken on a strange red glow. The colour seemed to rise and fall and it took her a while to realize that it was the reflection from fires blazing all around them. Overhead the searchlights were tracking one of the German bombers. Once they had it pinpointed, it looked like no more than a silver fly. How could a fly inflict such damage, she thought as the ante-aircraft guns burst into life. It wasn't long before the sound of the bomber engines changed. The drone became a high pitched scream as a plane plunged downwards.

Liesel watched the swirling colour above her head and felt no pain. Then another piece of the building crashed towards her

180

and she watched it as if in slow motion. It hit a mish-mash of beams to her right where it was arrested and balanced precariously. Dust and small bits of masonry fell, filling the air and cutting off her breath, as more of the building tumbled inwards entombing her. She tried to swallow, but her mouth was full of dust.

The house has gone, she thought. She felt the weight of Gussy on her breast and knew there was something important that she should do, but couldn't fathom what. Then the weight had gone and someone stood above her surrounded by a bright light and in his arms he held her smiling baby. At that moment she thought she recognised Gustav. She tried to speak, to say his name, but as she fought to hold onto consciousness, she slipped once more into nothingness.

The next time she woke it was to a white light. She tried to move her head but pain swept through it. Things gradually became clear and realisation crept in. She was in a hospital bed.

'Gustav? My baby?' she cried, but only a croak came from her dry throat. A nurse bent over her. 'You're awake. You're safe now.'

'Thank God you're alright,' came a voice she recognised. Slowly, she turned her head and Walter was sitting by the bed, his craggy face streaked with tears. He still wore the uniform of the Home Guard.

'Mr Goldberg's been here all night,' the nurse told her. 'I'll leave you now.'

'The others?'

'There were a few survivors,' his voice broke and he covered his face. 'Renata and Eva…' Deep painful sobs tore his body.

'And Gussy?' Her heart seemed to swell painfully until she was sure it would explode.

'I'm…so… sorry. He…he … would have died instantly.'

At first she experienced disbelief. Gussy dead, no, it wasn't possible. She'd seen him and he had been smiling up at his father. His father? She was dreaming. None of this was real. A

181

coldness claimed her. A pain so deep it defied an outward display of grief. She turned her eyes and stared at the far wall. 'Why are you lying?' she whispered. 'I saw them.'

The only answer was Walter's big paw of a hand closing on her shoulder.

Several days later the rabbi and his wife came to collect her. She had not spoken since the devastating news of her son's death. The Nazis had taken everything from her leaving her numb, her only emotion, a burning desire for revenge.

Chapter Twenty-Nine

Liesel

'Can I get you anything?' Rabbi Hyman looked tired, dark circles under his eyes, sad testament to the fact that he had had very little sleep for several days.

Liesel said nothing for a long minute, then nodded. 'Let me use your telephone. Have you got your son's number?'

He studied her for a minute, then nodded slowly. 'I'll call him for you.'

Josh came up from Buckinghamshire to pick her up. 'I'm so sorry for your loss,' he said, and clasped her hand in both of his. His dark brown eyes were full of sympathy. 'Are you sure you want to do this?'

She felt nothing. Her body and mind had become numb – it was the only way she could function. Staring straight ahead, her white face as still and as expressionless as if it had been carved from ice, she spoke in a monotone. 'I will do whatever you ask. I have nothing and no one left to live for. Whatever happens to me now, I must accept it as God's will.' In spite of his attempts to draw her into conversation, she said nothing more until they reached their destination.

'We're here,' he said. 'Would you like some refreshments before your interview?'

Eager to get it over with, she shook her head. Neither hunger nor thirst had plagued her since she had woken up in hospital. She had eaten and drunk barely enough to keep her alive and then only at the Hymans' insistence.

Josh took her to an office, where two uniformed men sat behind a desk and he took a seat beside them. Then began an hour long interrogation about how she came to Britain, who her parents were, what had she been doing since. She used Renata's story of how she had come in legally as a refugee. She would not tell them she came on a German warship.

'Are you sure you can do this?'

She nodded. 'I'm sure. I hate the Nazis.' Her eyes narrowed, showing the only signs of emotion since Josh had picked her up.

'It's like a university here, you will be taught to break codes. How does that sound?'

'I will do what I can to help.' She spoke with resolution.

'You understand that the work you'll be doing is top secret, if you ever mention it to anyone, you'll be shot.' Josh gave a laugh, then looked embarrassed so that she wasn't sure whether he was joking or not. It did not matter. Who would she tell?

'You need have no worries,' she replied.

'You'll be working in Hut 8 with other women.'

She nodded. 'I am ready.'

'You must never talk to your colleagues about what they are doing, nor must you divulge your own work,' Josh explained. 'And you must never enter another person's hut. Churchill describes the code breakers as '*golden geese who lay the golden eggs and never cackle.*'

'I'm not here to make friends.'

Once they left the building, Josh took her arm. 'I know how hard this is on you, but the work you're going to do is very important.'

She glanced up at him and saw that the concern on his face matched the kindness in his voice. 'I won't let you down.'

Hut 8 turned out to be a long, low, wooden building, run by two middle-aged men, both solemn and stern-looking. The conditions appeared smoky and suffocating.

Josh continued to explain. 'Like the others, you will work shifts – morning, afternoon, evening. Convoys of buses bring the code breakers in from their lodgings, but I've got you a billet nearby, so we'll give you a bike. You can ride a bike I assume?'

She nodded.

'It's only two miles away with an elderly couple. You'll like them.'

She didn't want to like them. She wanted somewhere that she was left in peace, only wanting to work and sleep. With no appetite for food, she would eat only to keep her strength up in order to do the best job she could.

She was introduced to Mr and Mrs Hillman, both in their seventies, the man tall and spare, the woman short and round and motherly. 'Call us Jean and Fred,' she said, clasping Liesel's hand.

'I'm pleased to meet you,' said Liesel. 'I'll stay out of your way as much as possible.'

'No need for that,' said Fred, clapping her shoulder. 'Make yourself at home.'

Liesel nodded and gave a small smile.

'I'll leave you now,' said Josh. 'I'll see you at eight o'clock tomorrow morning.'

Liesel nodded again. Josh had said that all the couple knew about her was that she had recently lost her baby and she might need time to herself. They had had boarders from the camp before and knew not to ask questions.

The room was pretty. There were floral curtains on the windows and a patchwork quilt over the bed. There was a small wardrobe and a chest of drawers.

'I hope it will be alright for you,' said Jean, a worried look crossing her face.

Realising how her lack of enthusiasm might be interpreted, Liesel said, 'It's lovely,' and forced a smile. She didn't care one way or the other. After all, it would be just a place to sleep.

Fred and Jean were kind, but she was no more than polite, pleading tiredness after a day's work when they invited her to sit with them in the best room.

To escape the pressure and the boredom, the young people of Bletchley would go to the local cinema or the hotel for drinks and socialising, but Liesel never joined them. She sat in the canteen alone and did what she had to do to get through the day. It was monotonous work, but she learned the codes quickly. Josh often came in to see her and in spite of herself she began to look forward to his visits.

Chapter Thirty

Chrissie

As she sat staring into the fire Chrissie thought of Charlie. Once again she pictured the bonny laddie with his cheeky grin walking up her path to nervously knock on her door. That's the way she remembered him, the way he always appeared to her in her dreams, not the broken man with the dreadful scars that the Great War had inflicted on him both physically and mentally. Once more she imagined Charlie when he first came home, his spirit broken. Her love had brought him back to life, but the fun-loving, mischievous young man she had fallen in love with had gone forever. Peter had been born before the war and Charlie had always loved him like his own and when Mary was born, their little miracle, he held her in his arms and cried.

She took the framed snapshot from the mantelpiece. Charlie and Angus, his twin brother, dressed in their sailor's uniforms, smiling, confident, two young lads about to set out on what they saw as an adventure. Little did they know what was in store. 'Oh Charlie,' she whispered into the dusk. Her body and heart still yearned for him, even after all this time. But Sinclair was right, Charlie always wanted what was best for her. He would have never wanted her to be alone and, no matter what happened in the future, she would always have her memories.

When Sinclair walked through her door, Chrissie shot to her feet and turned her back to him, hiding the tears she didn't want him to see. She hadn't expected a visitor tonight and grabbed the kettle out of habit. 'Cup of tea?'

'I would love a cup of tea. But… is something wrong?'

Embarrassed at being caught at such a moment, Chrissie sniffed and wiped her cheeks. 'Nothing, don't mind me.'

'Come on, love, I know you too well.' He moved forward and laid his hand on her arm. His concern released something in her and loosened her tightly reined-in emotions.

'I…I just had a phone call from Mary.'

'What's happened?' Concern filled his face.

'Nothing. It's just me being maudlin,' she said with a small, forced laugh. 'Miss her, that's all. Daft, am I not? She's fine.'

He shook his head. 'I'd never think ye daft. I'm sure you do miss her, the place seems empty without her. What's her news?' His eyes searched her face and she had the unsettling feeling that he could read her mind.

'I worry about her in the WAAF.' Chrissie shrugged. 'I know I'm being selfish, but both my bairns…' Her voice failed and she bit her lip.

He set his free hand on her shoulder and, looking deeply into her tear-filled eyes, he whispered, 'They'll come back safe. Ye have to believe that.'

There's every chance they won't, she thought, but nodded. After all, she wasn't the only mother wracked with worry. 'I do try, but it's hard.'

'Maybe sometimes ye should stop trying and lean on someone else. Ye're only human. I'm the one who's doom and gloom on legs, remember?'

She took a deep breath. 'Ye're right. We've all got to take our chances in this war. But I hate it,' she said, her voice rising, no longer pretending that she was coping well.

He pulled her into a hug and she laid her head on his shoulder, appreciating the strength of his arms, his muscular chest pressing against her breasts. This time he held her longer than he ever had before and she allowed it, needing his reassurance and his strength. He returned his hands to her shoulders and moved a little way from her. 'Ye're all alone in this house now, bonny lassie. Is that really what ye want?' His voice was slightly ragged.

She wanted to say, no, no, it's not what I want at all. I want Mary and Peter back and yes, I want you. 'Stop being daft,' she said, pushing him away with her little laugh that covered a wealth of emotion. The moment of vulnerability had almost passed.

'Do you want me to go?'

'No...' The thought of being enclosed alone in the same four walls for another night was too much to bear. She had been strong for too long.

'I could stay,' he said.

She fought the urge to turn away from his burning gaze, knowing that if she refused him she would regret it once the door had closed behind him. What was the matter with her? One minute she wanted to keep him at bay and the next she wanted nothing more than the feel of his arms around her, yes, that and more.

'Do you want a ring? I'm all too keen to put one on yer finger.'

She shook her head. 'No. I'll never wear another man's ring.'

'That's it then?' Their eyes met and held, their breath mingled and for a moment the air was fraught with possibilities. If he had kissed her then she would not have resisted, but he hesitated that moment too long.

She felt her body slump. 'It has to be that way.' She lowered her eyes and the spell was broken.

The place where his hands had been cooled. He turned as if to go and suddenly she couldn't bear to see him walk away. What was wrong with her? There was a time when she had cared little for the wagging tongues. What had happened to her over the years? When had Chrissie Rosie become afraid to take

189

a chance? For years she had lived a celibate life for the sake of her children. But they weren't bairns anymore; they were adults with minds and lives of their own. Maybe now was the time to think about herself. Glancing once more at Charlie's photograph, she had the feeling he was smiling at her, giving her his blessing. It was time to let him go.

'Sinclair,' she said.

He turned to face her.

'I want you to stay.'

In a rush of bravado, she grabbed his hand and pulled him back against her, holding up her face for his kiss. He looked surprised, then grinned and his lips found hers. The thirst that she had hidden for so many years surfaced, the heat filled her up and she didn't care about the gossips any more. What was happening here, right at this moment was much more important. Let them talk, at least she wasn't going out with a serviceman like so many others she'd heard tell of and their men away fighting for a cause they barely understood.

'Ye're right,' she whispered. 'I've been alone too long. I don't want to be alone tonight.'

Grinning like a schoolboy, Sinclair did not release his hold.

Her heart raced, blood seemed to fill her as if she might burst and she gave herself up to his lips, his hands, her own urgency no less than his.

'Lock the door,' she said through hurried breaths. He left her only long enough to turn the heavy, iron key, then he lifted her as if she weighed nothing at all and carried her to the bed.

'How do you feel?' he asked, much later, as they lay warm in the aftermath of love-making.

She sighed and snuggled against him. She'd forgotten how good it was to lie in a man's arms. 'As if I've woken up after a long sleep.' And her body stirred again. After years of neglect, all her dormant desires, now released, demanded even more satisfaction.

He groaned. 'Oh, my God, Chrissie, I never realised...' his voice drained away and turned into a whimper as her hand made small circling motions down his body until she found the centre of his desire and coaxed it back to life.

'Will ye be back tonight?' she asked while he struggled into his clothes.

He turned and studied her, his expression tender. 'Wild horses wouldn't keep me away. Ye can't get rid of me now. But whether I manage back this night depends on the workload.' He leaned over and kissed her cheek, quickly, dismissively, and then he was gone, the door opening and closing only long enough to permit the chill of a new day. She lay back and let her hand fall into the dent on the pillow where his head had been and she thought about the night just passed. Had she done the right thing? Whether she had or not, there was no going back now.

Chapter Thirty-One

Mary

Meanwhile, Mary sat in her truck waiting to pick up yet another pilot. When he stepped off the train, her heart rose to her mouth. Something like a bolt of lightning jolted inside her. It couldn't be, yet it was. A few easy strides took him up to the truck and, for a heartbeat, he looked straight into her eyes.

'The drivers get prettier,' he said, with a light laugh.

She stared back at him. 'You don't remember me, do you?' she asked, blushing furiously.

He screwed up his eyes and studied her. 'You do look familiar. Remind me, where did we meet?'

'At the dance in John O'Groats.' She could hear the blood pounding in her head.

'John O'Groats? Oh, Caithness. I was barely any time there.' He leaned forward and took off her hat. 'Of course, Mary. It is Mary, isn't it?'

She nodded, glad he had recognised her, hurt that he hadn't right away. 'It's the uniform and the haircut,' he said. 'But you're still as lovely as ever. I say, this is a surprise.' He climbed in beside her. 'How long have you been in the WAAF?'

'Almost six months now.'

'Really? Only six months? You look as if you belong. Pleased to meet you again.' He held onto her hand that moment too long. Locked in the gaze of those dark eyes everything inside her melted. It was as if she'd only seen him yesterday and all the feelings that first night had kindled flared and burned as brightly as ever.

'What's it like here?'

'Good,' said Mary. 'I'm enjoying it. Well,' she gave her giggly little laugh, 'if you can call anything about the war enjoyable.'

As she drove back to base, she was shaking so much inside it was surprising she drove so well. She let him off at the guardroom.

'Maybe I'll see you again?' he said, as he collected his kitbag.

'Maybe,' she replied with her most winning smile while her heart sang, *yes please.*

'What's up with you, sunshine?' asked Gloria. 'You're going around with a stupid grin on your face and God only knows where your mind is. I don't think you've heard a word I've said.'

'I'm sorry, what?'

'They're talking about holding a concert and we're all expected to do something.'

'That's nice,' Mary said. 'Oh, Gloria, you'll never guess. I met someone I knew back home. What are the chances of that?'

'Tell me more.' Both Gloria and Janet leaned towards her and Mary poured out the story of meeting Greg, that fateful dance, and Johnny.

'Just don't get in too deep,' Janet warned.

'Don't worry about that,' said Mary.

That night as she fought for sleep, she couldn't get him out of her mind. First thing in the morning, he was back there again, the smile that lit up his face, his deep blue eyes, his soft voice and he was here, somewhere on this camp and he had mentioned seeing her again.

193

They had some free time next afternoon and Gloria persuaded her to go shopping. She often got a postal order from home and when she did, she would treat her friends to something in the café. They enjoyed watching the airmen, sailors and soldiers who passed by, and flirting with those who stopped for a drink.

'I mean to have fun,' Gloria told Mary and the more serious Trish. 'But I will never get so involved that losing someone breaks my heart. It's not worth it.' She shot a glance at Mary.

'Me neither,' said Mary, but her voice lacked conviction.

'Even the pilot you picked up yesterday?' asked Trish.

'Especially him,' she said, knowing that falling for him would be too easy and knowing that perhaps it was already too late.

Then she saw him through the window on the other side of the road. Her breath caught and her heart plummeted. Greg Cunningham, walking along with a pretty, blonde woman on his arm. He was laughing down at her as if she'd said something funny.

'What's wrong?' asked Gloria following Mary's line of vision.

'That's him,' said Mary.

'What? Him with the blonde?' asked Trish. 'He's absolutely gorgeous, but looks like he's spoken for.'

Mary tore her eyes away. Just as well. It could only lead to heartache anyway, she thought, but her stomach contracted with disappointment. Since meeting Greg again her dreams had taken flight in spite of her convictions and all the warnings from her friends.

She felt Gloria's hand on her arm. 'Plenty more fish in the sea,' she said.

'Of course.' The normally enlivening trip to town had lost its magic and, finding the effort to remain cheery difficult, Mary was glad when it was time to return to base.

Mary took a seat on the bus and stared through the dust encrusted window hoping to catch a glance of *him* again.

'Mary!' Trish elbowed her in the ribs.

She looked up, at the enquiring face of the conductress.

'I said, where to, luv, the base?'

'Yes, yes.' Mary rifled in her pocket until her fingers found the change she had put there for her fare. The machine tinged as the conductress turned the handle and she handed the ticket to Mary.

'Honestly, you were miles away,' said Trish.

The engine revved. The bus turned into the traffic.

The sudden, alarming shriek of sirens rent the air. The bus speeded up throwing them backwards in their seats, then, just as suddenly, the driver rammed on the brakes. 'Quick,' he shouted. 'There's a shelter down that street.' He pointed at an alleyway to his left.

The girls joined the other passengers as they ran to the stone building and downstairs into a basement-like construction. They had no sooner crowded into the airless space than the explosions outside shook the foundations.

'Just our luck,' muttered Gloria, with as little emphasis as if she had been complaining about the rain.

Mary briefly wondered about Greg and the pretty blonde, wondered whether they had managed to get to safety.

When the all-clear eventually sounded, they emerged to a rubble strewn street that, when they had arrived, had been neat and orderly. Everything smelt different — smoke and gas and sewage and air filled with sirens and screams and shouts. Fire engines and ambulances were already in attendance and men were carrying stretchers while others used their bare hands to search among the rubble. Long hoses snaked and curled across the pavements. Some of the buildings were on fire.

'We have to help,' cried Mary. 'There's bound to be people trapped.'

'Come on then,' said Trish. 'What are we waiting for?'

Gloria looked dazed. But she followed the others. They joined the searchers, ruining their hands and carefully painted nails. When the injured were pulled out, the girls attended to the less serious cases while the medics were hard at work with others. After a couple of hours, dirty, sore and tired, someone called to them. 'Come on girls, you've done well, but you have to get back to base now.'

Mary stood up and dusted her hands together. Her back and shoulders were aching and her fingers were cut and bleeding.

Dermot and a young airman with a sallow, haunted look were standing beside a truck. 'I've been sent to collect any of the unit still in town,' he said.

'Thank you, girls,' said one of the firemen. 'You've been a great help.'

'Glad to do something,' replied Mary. She looked around, but Greg and the pretty woman were nowhere to be seen.

'There's a dance on tomorrow night. You going?' shouted the driver, as they jolted along in the back of the truck.

'A dance. Of course we're going.' Gloria elbowed Mary and she was sharply reminded that life goes on and giving in to the agony around her helped no one.

Although it remained at the back of their minds, they didn't speak about the raid or the carnage they had witnessed. Instead the conversation was all about the dance.

'Hope the band is good,' said Gloria. The others murmured in agreement.

'I've been saving up my clothes coupons. Going to get a new pair of cami knickers,' whispered Trish.

Gloria gave a hoot. 'Another pair? Good God, girl, what are you doing with them eating them?'

'I like nice underwear. Hate those blackouts. Proper passion killers them,' said Trish.

'Hear, hear,' shouted Dermot, who'd obviously heard every word.

'*You'll* not be getting your hands on them anyway,' Janet retorted.

The others laughed, and Mary found herself laughing with them, the earlier horror relocated to the background of her mind. She decided that she, too, would feel better wearing nice underwear and decided to use her clothing coupons the next time she went to town.

There was no band. Music that night was provided by a young airman playing the piano, yet the atmosphere was good and the girls were soon in high spirits. Mary was popular with many of the young pilots, but she always turned down their advances. In spite of seeing him with the blonde the day before, her eyes constantly strayed to the door just in case Greg came in. She had not heard if he had escaped the raid.

Afraid of giving encouragement, she did not dance more than once with the same man, except for Dermot who appeared to be his usual, cheery self in spite of having been out on a couple of sorties from which a few of his colleagues had not returned. The dance lifted her spirits and she went to bed that night giggling with her friends about things that had happened and the young men who had made passes at them. No one mentioned the bombing in the underlying hope that they would have a peaceful night.

Chapter Thirty-Two

Liesel

'Goodnight. See you tomorrow.' Liesel replied to the farewells from a bunch of her colleagues who all left together. She knew they thought her strange and unfriendly, but she didn't care. The wind had a sharp nip in it and she knotted her headscarf beneath her chin, picked up her bicycle and was about to mount when Josh drew up in his car.

She smiled a welcome and gave a little wave.

He exited the car, walked round to the passenger side and opened the door. 'Leave the bicycle for now. Come with me, I'll treat you to tea in the local tearooms.' He looked so serious it worried her.

He guided her to a seat in the far corner. 'What'll you have?'

As they waited for their food, she asked, 'Is something wrong?'

He glanced around, then leaned across the table. Although the café was almost empty, he dropped his voice, barely above a whisper. 'I have two colleagues who would like to speak to you.'

She stared at him. Had they checked on her story? Found out that she had lied about coming into the country with the Goldmans?'

'Am I in trouble?' She held her breath as she waited for his answer.

'No. Not at all.' He reached across and covered her hand with his in a reassuring gesture.

Their food arrived and they fell silent until the waitress had gone.

Liesel ignored the sandwich before her. 'What…what is it then?'

He nodded at the snack. 'Eat up, then I'll take you to the office where we'll explain. But don't worry, you're not in trouble. Everyone is highly impressed with your work here.'

He waited while she chewed the dry bread and fish paste, washing it down with chicory coffee, while trying hard not to gag. Finally she pushed the plate away from her. 'I can't eat anymore until I know what's going on.'

He stood up and took her arm. 'Come on then. There are two warrant officers who want to talk to you.'

'Ah Liesel Hirsch. Take a seat, please,' one officer said. Neither introduced themselves.

She sat down and swallowed, but with a dry mouth, there was nothing to swallow.

'It has been brought to our notice that you have worked very well here,' said the other lacing his fingers together and leaning slightly forward.

'Thank you,' she said.

'We also believe that you speak fluent French, is that so?'

To demonstrate she answered in French.

'I'm afraid you have the advantage on us, Miss Hirsch. You'll have to speak English,' said the one who had asked the question.

'Yes. My mother was Belgian. As a young child, I learned it simultaneously with German.'

'We believe your language skills can be better used elsewhere.' He leaned back and steepled his fingers.

She glanced from one to the other and then at Josh, who was smiling at her encouragingly.

'How would you feel about parachuting into France?'

She gasped, speechless for a moment and then unstuck her tongue from the roof of her mouth and spoke without hesitation. 'I would be very happy to,' and for the first time since her baby's death, she experienced a spark of life. At last she could take an active part of bringing Hitler down and to that end, she would gladly give her life.

'We plan to parachute you into the area around Bordeaux. You will masquerade as a French peasant girl. It will be dangerous work. Are you sure you want to do this?'

'Yes.' With a glance at Josh's worried face, she continued, 'please don't try to persuade me otherwise.'

'Would that be possible?' he said. 'Remember, what you're doing *now* is worthwhile. You'll be going in as a spy and if you're caught you'll be tortured and possibly shot.'

She shook her head. 'I don't care. I want to take a more active role.' She turned and looked at the two officers. 'When do you want me to go?'

Chapter Thirty-Three

Johnny

For the soldiers in France, the news was worse than ever. The Germans had crossed the Meuse, the capitulation of Holland was announced on the radio, tanks were pouring into Sedan and the road to Paris was open.

Johnny's company were already advancing south when the news reached them and they were ordered to prepare for an encounter with the enemy. His stomach clenched. The thought of having to take someone else's life horrified him, enemy or not. What he dreaded most of all was hand to hand combat. The thought of impaling another human being with his bayonet, like they had been trained to do using bags of straw, horrified him as much as thought of an enemy bayonet ripping his own guts open.

It wasn't long before they heard the distant drone of planes. Although it was cold, he had begun to sweat. He looked upwards and swallowed bile. 'My God,' he gasped, 'there must be hundreds.' They spread across the sky like symbols on a pale grey slate, symbols of death. The soldiers had been told that the German troops were approaching from the front. This was it. This was the real thing. There was every possibility he would die today. In that moment he wanted to vomit.

Within minutes the British convoy was under attack from both ground and air.

Johnny closed his eyes and suddenly there was no more fear. Each man became devoid of emotion as the training kicked in. It was kill or be killed. Anti-aircraft guns were already engaged, too late, but despite the speed and expertise of the soldiers, they were spinning, screaming, falling with hardly a shot being fired from their side.

When the gunner in the tank before him fell, Johnny, acting on pure instinct, leapt up and grabbed the controls. Screaming, he fired at will into the flock of airborne, killing machines. The sky was filled with fuzzy black dots like ink spreading on blotting paper, but more and more came, a plague of locusts. Then the shelling began. The platoon was desperately outnumbered.

'Retreat to the forest,' came the shouted order.

But Johnny didn't move. Still screaming his defiance, he was frozen to his gun.

'For God's sake man, retreat. It's an order.' Someone was pulling his arm, dragging him from the tank. Then he found himself running for his life, tripping and falling between the trees. His stomach hit the ground and then his face. Winded, he manoeuvred himself around so that he could see the road. One by one each and every truck flew up in bits and the air was filled with the dreadful scent of smoke and death. One man was running towards him, his terrible screams filling the forest, his clothes on fire. An arc of flame seemed to rise from his side and Johnny realised it was his arm with a gun clutched in his hand. With one shot to the head he took his own life and ended the unbearable agony. Driven by the momentum, the burning body continued forward, collapsed and, finally still, lay in a silent heap, yet the screams echoed in Johnny's mind and the dreadful smell of roasting human flesh clung within his nostrils. Had he waited a second longer, he would have suffered the same fate. At that moment he stopped being a human and believed himself to be an automatic creature programmed only to obey his commanding officer's orders. Surviving this war and going home was no longer an option.

The remaining men dug in and waited for the attack to stop. It seemed to last forever. Every now and then, Johnny touched the pocket where he kept Mary's photograph and in a whispering, shaking voice he chanted the Lord's Prayer.

After it was over and silence reigned, the men slowly emerged to inspect the carnage. All their trucks had been hit and damaged beyond repair if not destroyed totally.

'We'll withdraw to the Brussels-Charleroi Canal,' said the sergeant major. 'Now fall in.' Clutching their weapons, the men regrouped and waited silently.

With no transport, they had to march. They passed bands of civilian refugees with their possessions laden on carts of all shapes and sizes, old horses pulling farm carts, dogs pulling dog carts, bicycles piled high with possessions, adults carrying loads on their backs, children plodding along behind them. Old people, labouring under heavy, anonymous bundles, often collapsed on the road and had to be loaded onto a cart among remains of a once happy life. The lines of pathetic humanity seemed to go on for miles. A Persian cat, grooming its coat, sat in an armchair, part of a mish-mash of possessions piled on a cart. Something about that cat, its act of normality, released something in Johnny and silent tears began to trickle down his cheeks.

In order to avoid the stream of human misery, the company had to break ranks and march in single file, often being stopped by a desperate refugee pleading for help the soldiers were unable to give. They filled the roads, mile after mile.

Eventually the sergeant ordered the men to take to the fields to avoid them. They had no sooner left the road than the now familiar drone of enemy planes filled the sky like a swarm of bees. The planes swooped low. The refugees ran for the ditches. The planes opened fire. From the safety of their hiding places, the soldiers watched in horrifying fascination. Horses, carts and bodies were blown sky high. Women, children and old men thrown up in the air, falling back down in pieces.

Once the planes had gone, the soldiers ran back across the field to offer what help they could, but apart from shooting badly wounded animals there was little they could do. They could not offer the wounded first aid or food. They had nothing themselves. A horse lay screaming by the side of the road, his stomach torn open, his entrails lying in the dust. It was then that Johnny's numb horror disintegrated and his gorge rose.

A cold anger worse than before, now seethed within him. All those people, hungry and tired with fear on their faces, fleeing the enemy, shot down for no reason, unless it was simple sport.

'What kind of mentality do these people have,' shouted Johnny, tears growing cold on his skin. 'Why did they need to shoot innocent people? Children, old men and women?'

'It's not just propaganda, the stuff we heard back home. This is pure murder,' said Matt Wilson, who served with him.

A baby still wrapped in its dead mother's arms started crying. Johnny picked it up. He felt the small body squirm against him, the mouth opening like a baby bird as it searched for food.

'Leave it,' said Matt. 'There's nothing we can do.'

'I can't just leave it.' He looked around desperately for someone who would take the child, but all he saw were the seriously wounded, broken bodies and pieces of limbs.

A few survivors clambered out of the ditch. A young woman stared at the scene before her, her face vacant with shock. She turned slowly until she saw Johnny. The first thing he noticed was the amazing colour of her eyes. They were so pale, like water to which one drop of blue ink had been added.

'Can't you help us? Where are *your* planes?' She spoke perfect English.

'We've no transport, barely enough food for ourselves.' Johnny handed the baby to her. 'Where are you going?'

'We're trying to get to the coast. They say there are boats that will take us out of Europe to the Middle East. I have friends who have settled in Syria. But before we get there I am afraid that, even if the Germans don't kill us, we'll die of hunger. All we have is hope and that's fading fast. Every town we come to has already been destroyed.' She looked down at the whimpering child in her arms. 'I'm afraid he'll die soon. We've no milk for him. We've nothing for ourselves. The first wave of the German Army destroyed everything they couldn't eat. Crops are rotting on ground covered by abandoned corpses of men and animals. France is a land of the dead.'

Johnny could hardly bear the despair on her face.

'Private Allan,' fall in,' shouted his sergeant.

'What's your name?' he asked quickly.

'Suzanne.'

'I won't forget you. You speak good English.'

'I am English.'

Surprised, he opened his mouth to reply, but she had turned away.

'Come on,' Matt grabbed his arm. 'We need to move.'

Together, the regiment began to march again.

Three days later, with very little sleep, they were still marching. They marched until their feet were blistered and stinging; they marched past forests where all the trees were uprooted blasted and dead; they marched past many more bands of starving refugees, all trying to reach the coast where they hoped to find boats that would take them to safety.

Johnny discovered that despite blistered feet and empty stomachs it was possible for men to fall asleep while marching. The only time they woke up was when they bumped into the man in front or the man behind bumped into them. At times he imagined he'd died. He envisaged an army of dead men, still marching on, because that was what they had been ordered to do.

Finally they saw buildings in the distance, a town or village, smoke rising possibly from a recent attack. Nevertheless, there had to be food, a place to sleep, a few hours to rest. The French people always welcomed them and shared what little they had with the allies. It gave them hope, hope that they might see tomorrow after all.

As they drew closer, that hope died. They marched down a street of ruined buildings, fires still burning, smoke and dust choking them, water flooding the streets. And over all of that, was the terrible, unforgettable stench of death.

If anyone had been left alive in this town they had recently vacated it leaving the bodies of their loved ones behind.

'I doubt if there's anything here for us, lads,' said the commanding officer. 'But search the cellars, see what you can find.' Many French used their cellars to cure meat. The men didn't need to be told twice, the instinct for survival outdid the overpowering stench of rotting flesh.

The cellars were empty. Either the fleeing survivors or the German army had taken everything with them.

Johnny covered his face with his hands. 'Nothing, there's nothing.'

'Come on, man. Let's take to the fields,' another soldier jolted his elbow. 'We'll find more than we'll find here.'

The rest of the platoon followed.

'Neeps, tatties,' shouted Johnny, then, in case he wasn't understood, he used the English words. 'Turnips. Potatoes.' When he was a boy the lads would pull them from the fields on their way home from school and eat them raw. Now they were too hungry to do anything else. The only water they could find was from the ditches and boiling it was essential. Back among the still smoking debris, they built a fire and made tea.

'I can't stand the smell here,' said Johnny.

Another soldier lay on his side, his head propped up on his hand. 'Dear God,' he whispered as if praying. 'Neither can I.'

The sergeant said, 'It is pretty bad. We'll retreat to the woods. Find some sort of shelter and get a few hours' sleep.'

The platoon needed no second telling. They stumbled into what was left of a shattered forest nearby where the smell was of charred wood and damp ash. They took turns at sitting guard and Johnny fell immediately into a deep sleep. He woke when the sentry prodded him with his foot. 'They're coming back.'

The men leapt to action, grabbing their guns and, throwing themselves flat on the ground, crawled into the undergrowth. The earth and vegetation suddenly gave way under Johnny and found himself tumbling down into a gully. He trapped a scream in his throat – to cry out would be suicide. At that same moment, bullets showered around them as German guns strafed the forest. Once he stopped his downward slide, Johnny lay for a minute, too stunned to move, and that saved his life. Once he recovered enough, he crept upwards and peered out through the foliage to a vision of hell. His comrades were falling like skittles. This was it. He closed his eyes and waited for death.

Finally the shooting stopped and Johnny realised he had not been hit. He slowly lifted his head. Those of his regiment who were still alive were throwing down their rifles and holding their hands in the air. Silently they waited for capture.

One German officer raised his pistol and shot them anyway. Germans began picking up rifles, pushing bodies over with their feet. Horrified, Johnny didn't move. Couldn't move. He would rather die of starvation out here, than by an enemy bullet.

Once the coast was clear he stood up, unable even to cry. A rustle from behind him made him spin around, rifle at the ready. His legs buckled with relief when another two of his outfit crawled out. Matt and Ozzie.

'Fuck sake, I nearly killed you,' he said.

Matt stood up, but Ozzie dragged one leg which was twisted and bloody.

'All fucking gone,' Matt cursed. 'Murdering bastards.' He looked around him. 'It's not safe here, we'd better get out.'

207

'I'm not leaving them,' said Johnny, looking at the corpses of men he laughed with, marched with, shared memories of home with, the situation throwing them together so that they became as close as brothers. 'There's bound to be spades, something in the village. We have to bury them.'

'Ozzie's not going to make it far right now, anyway,' said Matt. He was busy applying a tourniquet to the other man's leg. 'Go see what you can find. The bastards will have moved on.'

Darkness had fallen by the time the gruesome task of burying their comrades was completed. 'I can't walk,' said Ozzie. 'You have to go, somehow get back to a unit. Give me some water and a gun and leave me.'

'We'll have a rest, then we'll go and you'll come with us.' Johnny knew he had no more strength left in him and there was little chance that the Germans would return. They would think they'd killed the whole group. He would not leave Ozzie.

After another feed of raw vegetables, they slept for a couple of hours, then dragged their aching bodies upright. There was no more marching, only staying under cover of the trees supporting Ozzie between them and moving ever forward. With the help of a pocket compass, they headed north.

Every night, as he fell asleep in a ditch, or under a hedge, or in an old abandoned barn, Johnny thought of Mary. The last letter he'd from her was all about how she was going to join the WAAF. There had been no mail for months and he wondered what she was doing at this minute.

Chapter Thirty-Four

Mary

'We're having a concert at the weekend,' said Gloria bursting into the barracks. 'They're looking for acts. Can any of you come up with anything?'

'I can sing,' said Mary. 'My mam and I often sang at local concerts back home.' Next to dancing, Mary loved to sing.

'Yes, you can. I've heard you in the shower,' said Trish. 'Very good you are too.'

A concert, it was something to look forward to. Mary had seen Greg on the airfield, so she knew he was safe. He had waved to her and walked towards her. 'Mary,' he said, a wide grin on his face. 'I've been hoping to run into you.'

'Well, you have now.' She spoke sharply.

'How've you been?'

'Fine. Excuse me, but I've got a message to deliver.' She spun on her heel and marched away. She was glad to see he hadn't been hurt, but since he seemed to be spoken for, it was better to stay out of his way. Her heart still leapt when she saw him and any sort of friendship could be disastrous.

The night of the concert, Trish, Janet and Gloria decided to sing as a trio, dressed as tramps. On one of their trips into town, they bought some second-hand clothes and made their own costumes.

Mary thought that since the others were acting the fool, she would sing something serious and chose the Burns song, *Aye Fond Kiss*.

The concert was held in the NAAFI, and an airman who looked too young to be out on his own never mind flying a plane, accompanied the acts on a piano.

Dermot came on with his face blackened and did an Al Jolson number, but he changed the words. The crowd erupted with laughter when he got down on one knee in front of Mary and instead of singing, *I'd walk a million miles for one of your smiles*, he sang, *I'd walk a million miles for a kick at your piles*. There were hoots, cheers and applause; everyone, it seemed, forgot the horrors of war for a few hours.

Trish, Janet and Gloria tumbled onto the stage and marched around singing, *my old man said follow the van...* and were met by a standing ovation. Then it was Mary's turn. She waited until the hoots and whistles died down. She nodded at the young airman at the piano and clasped her hands as he played a few bars. Her eyes swept the hall and stopped for a fleeting second when she saw Greg Cunningham, then flew away when he smiled slowly and gave her a brief nod.

After taking a deep breath, she began, her sweet voice rising, filling the hall. As she sang, her eyes avoided Greg's. When she finished, there was silence for a beat. Then the audience began to clap and clap, some rising to their feet. Mary tightened her lips as tears of emotion stung her eyes. The shouts of 'encore' filled the hall. Mary looked over at the piano player, who raised his eyes as if in question. One of these questions that need no words. *What else have you got?* he was asking.

She knelt beside him. 'Do you know *Green grow the Laurels*?'

'I think so. If you start, I'll follow you.'

She walked back to centre stage. The crowd hushed and silence fell as she clasped her hands together and took a breath.

Before she could sing a note the harsh screams of the siren split the peace. Ever ready, the pilots dashed to the door, struggling into their jackets as they went. Within minutes the evening song was that of planes roaring along the runways.

There was a mad scramble as the girls and NAAFI staff grabbed their tin hats and headed for the trenches meant to protect them. Explosions filled the night. Searchlights lit up the sky. A fierce dogfight took place above them. Then the bombers came closer to the airfield than ever before, the sound of engines filling their ears. For the first time since the girls arrived, several bombs fell directly onto the airbase. Flames of many fires lit up the surrounding countryside and the purring sound of the spitfires faded as the fighting moved further away.

'That was close,' whispered Mary, realising that she and Gloria were clinging onto each other. The girls parted just as the guttural sound of another bomber filled the night along with the terrifying squeal of a falling bomb. The earth erupted in a huge moving wall around them and the dugout where they sheltered rose and collapsed, all but burying them alive. As the girls struggled to get their heads and arms out from under the mud and dust, the terrible noise faded. They were coughing, gasping for fresh air that wasn't there. After what seemed like an eternity but what could be no more than ten minutes, the all-clear sounded and a member of the ground crew ran towards them and helped them out of the trench. 'Anyone hurt?' he asked.

'No we're fine.' Mary felt anything but fine, her body was shaking, her heart thundering, her stomach threatening to rid itself of her last meal and she was sore all over. But since she was still in one piece, she guessed she had no reason to complain.

'Then come on, help us with the injured.'

All round her people were either trapped, wounded or dead.

Mary took a deep breath and knelt beside the nearest man, recognising him as the cook from the NAAFI. One leg was

211

twisted at an odd angle, the bone sticking out of his thigh. Blood was leaking from his mouth. She never felt so helpless, nor so angry. 'Over here,' she shouted to the medics who were already loading bodies onto stretchers. With the medics unable to come at once, all she could do was fashion a tourniquet from her belt and try to stop the blood pouring from the cook's leg. He clutched her hand as he screamed and gasped and prayed in turn. 'Try to relax. I'll get you a cup of tea,' she said, at the same time realising how inadequate she sounded.

'No, don't … leave… me.' He grasped her hand so tightly she thought he might break the bones. She waved to the catering staff who were pushing trolleys among the injured, supplying their own brand of comfort. By the time they came towards her, the hand holding hers had fallen limp, the young man was quiet and still, his staring eyes telling her that he was no longer in pain.

When the planes returned the girls were too busy to count them down. It was only later that they found out that less than half had returned.

It was almost morning before the girls were able to snatch a few hours' sleep.

By the following evening, Mary was so tired she could hardly walk. She dropped onto her bed and lay on her back, staring at the ceiling, trying not to think.

'Don't get comfy,' shouted Gloria. 'I couldn't half do with a drink after last night.'

'And I could do with a sleep,' said Mary, sure the utter weariness that claimed her also rendered her unable to move.

Gloria dropped down on her own bed. 'I couldn't sleep. Come on, have a shower, it'll wake you up. I'll lend you some of my make-up.'

'You go,' Mary muttered, and closed her eyes. But after a few minutes when visions of recent events filled her mind, she realised that Gloria was right. Their sleep would not be easy tonight. She knew most of the dead and injured, if not

212

personally, then by sight. And so many planes had been lost. Young men with their lives ahead of them, wiped out in a split second. Among them Dermot. His loss affected her deeply. She could still see him acting the fool, making everyone laugh. She had not yet developed the knack of controlling her emotions completely, of rising above the pain and devastation going on around her. Wearily, she dragged herself to her feet, collected her towel and soap and made her way to the ablution block.

By the time everyone exited the bus in town, spirits had lifted, as if it were just another day. 'Come on, Mary,' said Gloria. 'I've been longing for this drink for ages.' Then she added quietly, 'it'll wash the dust out of my throat.'

Mary followed the others into the public house where the noise levels blasted her ears and the smoky air stung her eyes. She wanted to relax and join the fun, to force the last twenty-four hours behind her, but she was still too distraught.

'We can't get too emotionally involved,' said Gloria, pressing a gin and tonic into Mary's hand. Her eyes slid over her friend's shoulder and her face lit. 'I know what will cheer you up.'

'What?' Mary gratefully accepted the drink and tossed it back, waiting for it to flow through her and take the edge off the pain.

'Greg Cunningham just walked in.'

Mary looked around. Through the crowd she could see him, half a head taller than anyone else in the room. 'And why should that interest me?' she asked. 'Seems like he has someone else.'

'Come on,' said her friend. 'Nothing's going to last in this war. If you like the man, go for it. He might not be here tomorrow, none of us might.'

Perhaps Gloria was right. In these unsure times, every second had to be treasured, for there might be no future. And who knew? The thing with the pretty blonde might already be history.

'If I do speak to him,' she said, the gin giving her courage, 'It will be to ask him about the lassie he was in town with last week.'

'Go for it.' Gloria lifted her drink in a salute. 'Thata girl.'

Mary moved sideways through the crowd towards Greg. When she was near enough, she grabbed his sleeve. 'I thought it was you,' she said. When he turned and looked down at her, recognition filled his eyes.

'Mary. Lovely to see you again. May I buy you a drink?'

'Thank you. Gin and tonic, please.' She held up her empty glass then followed him through the throngs to the bar.

'Will we find a seat?' He held the drinks above shoulder height as others fought their way past them.

She nodded. They found a couple of seats beside some sailors and their partners, local girls who giggled nonstop.

'How have you been?' Greg asked, raising his voice to be heard over the melee.

Mary shrugged. 'I can't complain.'

'I know what you mean.' He lifted his glass in a salute. 'Drink and be merry for tomorrow we die.'

Mary tried to laugh, but she knew it would never reach her eyes, just as Greg's eyes held the unmistakable pain of having seen too much.

The sailors started singing rude songs and others joined in. It was difficult to talk above the noise.

When they'd finished the drink, Greg leaned close to her and shouted in her ear, 'This is no use. Will we go somewhere we can actually hear each other?'

Feeling reckless, Mary nodded.

The weather had become warmer in the last week as spring made her presence felt. The street was alive with servicemen from every force, laughing and singing as they made their way from pub to pub, girls on their arms, cigarettes dangling from their lips. She felt proud to be in uniform, proud to be part of it. Greg grabbed her hand and tucked it through his arm. He guided her along the road and into a park.

He chatted to her easily, but she only gave him short answers, the sight of him with another woman still uppermost in her mind.

Then he said the one thing guaranteed to get her attention. 'Didn't I promise to take you up in a plane one day?'

'You did and all.'

'Tomorrow?'

'Really?' She forgot to be angry. She had begged rides in any plane for so long.

'Really. Provided there's no more raids of course.'

There wouldn't be, not during the day, she thought. But first she needed to have her say.

'I saw you in town,' she said. 'I'm right glad you and your lady friend made it to safety before that bomb fell.'

He looked surprised. 'Ah yes, that was a bad business as well. I didn't see you.'

'She's very pretty, your friend.'

He gave a laugh and scratched his ear. 'I'll tell her. She'll be pleased. That was my sister by the way. She came up to see me.'

His sister! Relief flooded through Mary making her face light up.

'Surely you didn't think…' He laughed and put an arm around her squeezing her tight. 'Was that why you've been off with me?'

She tossed her head. 'Not at all. It's no business of mine what you do.'

'I'm flattered that you were jealous.'

'Who said I was jealous?'

He lowered his head until it was level with hers, their mouths less than an inch apart so that their breath mingled.

'I am not…,' she started. He cut off her words with his lips and in spite of her resolve, she gave herself up wholeheartedly to that kiss.

He pulled her tightly against him, gently at first, then crushing her. The butterflies in her stomach tumbled and danced as his lips met hers again and he kissed her like she'd never been kissed before. When he pulled away and gazed into her eyes, Mary Rosie was lost.

'Come on,' he said, grabbing her hand, his voice slightly hoarse. She willingly followed him to a clearing by a stretch of water where there was a path and some wooden benches. He sat on one and pulled her down beside him.

'Tell me all about yourself, Mary Rosie,' he said, one finger playing with a strand of hair about her ear.

'There's nothing much to tell. I was born on Raumsey Island, but my dad was badly burnt in the last war and his lungs were bad with the smoke. He needed to go to hospital sometimes so we moved to the mainland. He died when I was eight.' She lifted her eyes to his. 'What about you?'

A shadow passed over his face. 'I was born in Devon. I still live there you know, with my mother. That sounds lame, doesn't it? A man my age still living with his mother. Truth is, since I'm only home on leave, it's not worth owning a place of my own. After the war, things'll be different.'

She looked across the still waters of the river. Two swans sailed gracefully past. 'It's so peaceful here,' she said. 'You'd hardly believe there was a war on.'

He lifted her hand and caressed her fingers. 'If you could be anywhere in the world, where would you be?'

Right now she was exactly where she wanted to be, but she wouldn't say that. 'On a beach.' She thought about pictures she'd seen in magazines. 'And there'd be palm trees and blue skies and deck chairs to sit on and the war would be far, far away.'

'Would I be there, beside you?' he asked with a glint in his eye.

I wouldn't want anyone else, she said inside her head, but the words she uttered aloud were different. 'In your dreams maybe, but not in mine. I'd have Cary Grant.'

He laughed. 'Then I'm a poor substitute. Come on, we'd best get back. I should be at the base.' He rose to his feet and helped her up.

She hadn't wanted the kissing to get out of hand, would have stopped it anyway, so why then did she feel disappointed that he hadn't wanted more?

He looked down at her. 'I only came on the off chance that you would be here,' he said.

Her mood instantly lifted.

They walked back to the pub hand in hand, enjoying a comfortable silence. Outside he glanced at his watch and kissed her chastely. 'I'll see you again, little one,' he said.

You can bet on it, she thought, but said, 'Maybe.' She floated rather than walked inside to join her friends.

The next day, he met her after breakfast as she left the mess hall. 'About that flight,' he said, drawing her to one side.

'Oh, but I can't just go,' she said.

'Don't worry. I've cleared it with your sergeant.' He glanced at his watch. 'I have to have you back by ten though.'

'Come on then.' Full of excitement, she grabbed his arm.

'A Wimpy,' she said, slightly disappointed. She'd imagined a Spitfire.

'What's wrong with a Wimpy?' he asked.

'It's the one plane that makes me nervous. The wings never look safe. They flap up and down.'

He threw his head back and laughed. 'It's all I could organise at short notice. We can do it tomorrow if you'd rather.'

'No, no. I don't care. Let's go up in it.' She'd waited too long to back out now.

'Come on then. Let's get kitted up.'

Once they were in the air, Mary was no longer nervous. She watched the airfield shrink below them and the houses and fields and the town with vehicles like toys moving below. It was the most magical thing she'd ever experienced. Then they were heading back to the airfield again and the ground was rushing up at them. The wheels hit the runway and seemed to bounce and she held her breath as it coasted to a stop. The whole thing was over all too soon.

'Did you enjoy that?' Greg asked after they'd fully stopped.

'It was the most amazing thing,' she said. 'I know now why you love flying so much. Can we do it again sometime?'

He laughed. 'Even if the wings do go up and down?'

'I know that was a silly thing to say, but they do give that impression, like they're a bit loose or something, but I don't mind, really.' With you by my side, I don't care about anything else, she thought, gazing at him.

'I'll see what I can do,' he said.

From then on they were together every spare moment. Like all the others, Greg thought he would be killed, expected it and Mary clung to the desperate hope that he never would. Life was a strain for everyone, always on the edge, waiting for the next raid. In some ways it was a dreadful time, in others fraught with excitement. Everyone on the base lived for the moment and they loved and laughed knowing that by the next night any one of them might be gone.

Chapter Thirty-Five

Johnny

Meanwhile, in France, Johnny and his colleagues were drawing near another village, the outline of the buildings visible in the moonlight. There were a few lights and there seemed to be a fire glowing with figures moving around it.

'Please God,' whispered Johnny, 'Let it be allies.' Crawling on their stomachs, Johnny and Matt sneaked up to the perimeter, where the smell of cooked meat reached them making their already empty stomachs cramp with hunger. The faint hope of a welcome and something to eat was soon dashed; it was Germans and they were everywhere.

'Fuck them,' muttered Johnny, his fingers tightening on his gun. 'They can light fires when we're not even allowed to strike a match.'

His stomach growled, thirst and hunger becoming more unbearable by the minute. He wanted to charge in there, his gun blazing. He had long since stopped caring whether he lived or died and was desperate for revenge. It was only the thought of Mary's photo in his pocket and the hope that by some chance he would find her waiting for him when he returned that made common sense prevail.

They turned away from the smells and crept through the undergrowth. It had begun to rain in the last hour and they were soaked already.

Matt grabbed his arm. 'Over there,' he whispered. Johnny's eyes followed the line of his pointing finger to the dark shape of a building with a chimney, probably a farm house, part of which had been destroyed. There was no light, no smoke, no movement in the grounds, nothing to indicate the presence of either animal or human.

'Careful.' Ozzie lifted his head slowly. 'The Jerries might be in there.'

'Doesn't look like it.' The pull of a night away from the rain and perhaps something to eat was strong. They inched closer, guns clutched so tight their fingers were numb.

'You stay here, keep me covered. I'm going in.' Johnny could hardly feel his feet or fingers and couldn't stand the thought of another night in the open. Crouching, he ran up to the house wall. Nothing. He crept around to a window and followed the muzzle of his gun. Silence.

He turned and beckoned to his companions. The house was abandoned. The beds were still intact but without blankets.

In a cupboard they found some soft biscuits and a tin of bully beef, which provided some sustenance. Outside there was a well with fresh water. Afraid to light a fire in case the Germans saw the smoke, they spent another cold, uncomfortable night in their wet clothes, but at least they were under cover.

By morning Ozzie's temperature had risen. Johnny undid the bandage. The wound was swollen and red and oozing pus. 'His leg's infected,' he said to Matt. Without the means to boil water, they washed it as best they could in cold.

'Leave me,' Ozzie whispered.

'No,' said Johnny, but he knew in his heart that Ozzie needed medical help and quickly.

Matt caught Johnny's eye. 'Maybe we should go. We know where he is. When we find a unit we'll come back for him and at least he's got shelter here.'

'Just give me a gun and water,' pleaded Ozzie.

'There's one chance,' said Johnny. 'You have to give yourself up to the Germans. In a camp you'll get medical attention.' After what he witnessed in the forest, he wasn't so sure, but it was Ozzie's only chance at survival.

'I'd rather kill as many as I can before they get me.'

'Think of yer wife and bairns, man. These men might be different. This lot might even obey the rules of the Geneva Convention.'

Ozzie started to cry. 'I can't stand this anymore.'

'He'll be delirious before long. We can't take him with us,' said Matt.

'Then I'll stay with him. You go, get help. Come back for us.'

'Fuck sake, man.' Matt hit his forehead with the heel of his hand. 'This is our chance to get out.' He looked at Ozzie, groaning and twisting on the ground.

'Hush, listen.' Johnny went to the window. From the distance came the sound of guns and exploding shells.

'Fighting. There must be a unit near here. I'll stay, you try to get through and bring help.'

Matt hesitated.

'It's his only chance, man. He won't last on his own.'

'Right.' Matt grabbed his rifle and a bottle of water.

Still in his wet uniform, Matt crept once more into the forest.

He walked for three days, often through pouring rain and he lost track of time. The sound of gunfire never seemed to get any nearer. His only means of navigation was by the stars at night and only then when the sky was clear. He grew ever weaker; there was no food to be found anywhere.

Eventually he came to a clearing on the edge of a sheer drop.

Peering through the leaves, down into the valley, he saw a wide river with a bridge running through a town. Germans seemed to be all over the place, on the bridge and on the roads.

From here the shelling sounded louder. From across river and over the ridge, plumes of smoke rose into the air. He hoped it was the British, but even if it wasn't, it had to be allies. Knowing he was so near a friendly unit gave him a new boost of energy. He had to get across that river.

At the far end of the field he found a gap in the hedge and rolled down the hill. The weather had taken a turn for the better and he lay where he landed allowing the sun to warm his face. He slept for a time, woke with a start and struggled to his feet. He had to keep going.

Crawling on his hands and knees, he crept upriver to where he was out of sight of the bridge. At the water's edge, he stopped in desperation, berating himself because he'd never learnt to swim. There seemed to be no way across. He continued upriver looking for anything he could find that he could use as a raft. Finally he came across some barges moored at small wooden pier. Again he moved on his belly. They seemed to be uninhabited. After waiting for what seemed hours he crept on board the nearest, all the time his ears straining for any sound. Thankfully the barge had been abandoned, but, as with the houses, everything had been removed. In a corner, he found a stale crust of bread that looked well nibbled by mice. After cleaning the dust from it he ate every last crumb and drank some water left in an old iron kettle.

The desire to lie on one of the bunk beds and sleep for a few hours was almost unbearable, but Ozzie and Johnny needed help as soon as possible. There was no more time to rest. Tied to the far side was a small flat bottomed skiff without paddles. He untied the knots, lay flat and paddled across with his hands.

It took another hour of hiking through blasted trees before he reached another ridge, where the air was arid, but there were no more sounds of fighting. Looking from the ridge, he almost fainted with relief. Down below, the roads were thick with British lorries and troops. 'Thank God,' shouted Matt as he collapsed onto his knees, unchecked tears running down his face.

He slipped down the hill to the road, relief fuelling his adrenaline. British infantry were shuffling past bearing the dazed look of men who had recently seen action.

'What's going on?' he asked one.

'You don't know? We're heading for Dunkirk. They're going to try to evacuate us. France has surrendered.'

'What? We've been defeated?' What had it all been for? 'I've left a couple of men behind. We've got to get them. One's badly wounded.'

'Are you mad, man? We're getting out. No one's going back in. Look around you. The war in France is over. The country's under German occupation.'

'I promised,' Matt said, hoping Johnny and Ozzie were still alive, hoping they would somehow know he had tried his best. All he could do now was follow the crowds.

They came towards another town, the sign read, Poperinge. Here, they walked into a new nightmare. Lorries were burning by the roadside, a long line of horse-drawn wagons moved slowly, dead men lay on the verges and injured horses struggled to stand. Drivers, some in tears, were going around shooting the wounded animals. Smoke hung over everything. As they approached Dunkirk, more and more damaged equipment lay beside the road, eventually forcing them to walk in single file. All the seafront buildings had been bombed and lay in ruins. Finally they came to the dunes where numbers of troops were huddled together, some stumbling onto the beach, others resting.

Matt dropped beside them. It seemed that now all they could do was wait to be rescued. 'Is there any food?' he asked.

One solder gave a wry smile as if Matt's stupidity amused him. Apart from that, he was met by blank stares.

Before them, white sand stretched for miles in both directions and perfect blue water lapped at the edges. Sun shone from a clear sky. A soft breeze dissipated the smoke and caressed his skin. Above him, seagulls rode the thermals. He closed his eyes and his mind conjured up memories of days at the beach as a boy. Perhaps if he slept now, he would wake up and he would be back there, Dad buying ice-cream, Mum rubbing cream on her skin, and he would look at them and say, 'I just had a terrible nightmare.'

He lay as if in a dream before pure exhaustion sent him back into a sleep from which he did not wake up until morning. When he awoke, the sky was heavy and dark and his clothes still wet and stinking. The inclement weather was on their side, however, as the low cloud prevented a German air raid. There were several ships in the bay and smaller boats ferrying the soldiers to their salvation. Too weak to move, he drifted once more into an uneasy slumber.

He didn't know how long he slept before the sounds of gunfire woke him. He eased himself up on one elbow and looked down towards the beach. The sand was littered with abandoned vehicles and bodies, some twisting and lifting even though they were dead as the bullets tore into them.

He lost all track of time and did not know until later that it was Wednesday 29th May, and the raid began at three thirty in the afternoon, when queues of servicemen still snaked across the beach.

'Where the hell is our RAF?' he shouted as the German Messerschmitts swooped from the sky and the queues broke up, scattering as fighters strafed the beaches, slaughtering all in their path.

Although fifteen British ships and four French ships were sunk that day, there was no pause in the evacuation.

Chapter Thirty-Six

Johnny

Back in the abandoned farmhouse, Johnny no longer knew how many days had passed. He accepted now that Matt was not coming back. Ozzie's delirium had ceased and he had slipped into unconsciousness, but even if he wanted to, Johnny doubted if he had the strength to make a run for it. As the cold rendered his fingers and feet into a numb nothingness and his stomach ached with hunger, he imagined his mother's mutton pie with new potatoes and fresh green cabbage, a crackling fire and the banter around the table. He wondered what they were all doing now. He needed nourishment soon or he would die. He might have sneaked into the village. It was possible that the Germans had gone and left behind a morsel of food, but there was no more strength left in him. All he wanted to do was sleep, although it seemed he'd done nothing else for days. As he stared into the darkness listening to his friend's laboured breathing, his mind carried him back to Caithness, the land of his ancestors, and he was running over the heather with Mary, jumping and giggling. The wind lifted her hair which was threaded with daisies and she turned and laughed at him, her lips and tongue stained purple from eating blaeberries.

Holding onto the warm image of the only girl he'd ever loved, Johnny drifted away into the arms of Morpheus once more. He awoke to something hard pressed against his temple. Opening his eyes, he twisted his head to find himself looking along the muzzle of a rifle. The muzzle was drawn back enough to allow him to see his assailant. An old man, unshaven, his clothes dirty and creased, stood over him. Within minutes more people crowded into the room. Two women, one old, one young, and three children of various ages, all thin, dirty and ragged.

Johnny put his hands above his head and rolled onto his back.

'*Anglaise*?' asked the old man.

Johnny nodded.

The man turned to his followers and issued orders in French. The young woman kneeled beside Johnny. 'We must burn your uniforms. It will be dangerous for this family if you are found here. We will give you clothes.'

Johnny looked up into the palest blue eyes he had ever seen and recognised the girl he had met on the road from Paris.

'Suzanne?' He gasped, before he slipped once more into unconsciousness.

When he next opened his eyes, there was a fire burning in the grate and the room was warm. He had been washed and dressed in clothes that were far from clean, but at least they were dry. A girl of about ten or eleven sat by his bedside. When she saw he was awake she rose and ran out of the door. '*Suzanne, il est réveillé.*'

Suzanne came into the room and took a seat beside him. 'How do you feel?'

'I'll live. How's Ozzie?'

'Your friend is still alive. We have no medicine but we've poulticed his wound and offered him some soup made from nettles and the birds we've been able to trap, but he was unable to eat. He's very ill. I've sent Yvette to get some food for you.'

Yvette brought in the soup. It was thin and bitter, but Johnny was ravenous and lifting the bowl to his lips drank it down in several gulps.

'Who are you?' he asked Suzanne.

'My father is English. These,' she indicated the others huddled round the fire, 'are what is left of my mother's family, my grandparents, my aunt, my nieces. I was with them when Hitler invaded. We were hoping to leave, but when we heard that France surrendered, we returned to our farm. Being under occupation might be better than taking our chances on the ocean or in another country. Perhaps I can still go back to England, but I can't turn my back on them. We can only hope the Germans will treat us fairly.'

Johnny thought about the surrendering soldiers shot with their hands in the air and wasn't too sure about that. 'How will you survive? North of Paris is like a desert.'

'I know. I've heard that whole towns are mostly destroyed, though the Germans haven't damaged the churches and cathedrals.' She gave a short laugh. 'They think that God will forgive them more easily for the atrocities. The villages are deserted, the farmsteads empty, but now the people will return. There's nowhere else to go.'

She took a breath and looked around her. 'I'm young and fit. I can hunt. I can't let my family starve. Any farm animals or crops that have survived will go to the German army, then to those who'll work for them. For people like us…' She spread her hands and shrugged. 'We'll hunt when the animals return, grow more vegetables, but in the meantime, maybe I'll be forced to work for the enemy to keep us alive.'

'I have to get home.' Johnny struggled to keep his eyes open.

'We've heard a whisper about somewhere safe. Do not go north. You must go to Marseille, the seamen's mission and ask for Donald Caskie. He'll help you. If you're found here we'll all be shot.' She lowered her voice and bent close to him. 'The less my family know about this, the safer it will be for them, but

227

there are those who will not surrender, who will form a resistance. They will help you, but for now, you are a French peasant, my cousin, and you are a deaf mute. If the Germans come, how well can you act the idiot?'

In spite of the situation, he gave wry smile. 'I won't need to do much acting. Can I see Ozzie?'

Yvette came up and whispered something to Suzanne.

'I'm sorry,' she said, 'your friend has died.'

Chapter Thirty-Seven

Mary

Mary rubbed her aching forehead. A wind had sprung up outside, a high angry wind that brought thick dark clouds, threatening to weep their misery onto the scene below. It was the kind of night that should have brought reassurance, as weather such as this discouraged bombers, but Mary barely noticed.

'Well, what do you think?' Anna's voice grew louder.

'Sorry, what?' Mary's head snapped up.

'You've not been listening to a word I've said. What's the matter? Bad news?'

Mary's fingers smoothed the page of the letter she'd been reading. 'A boy from back home. Missing presumed dead.'

'I'm sorry. We're you very close?'

'We were once going to get married.'

'Oh, that's sad,' Anna lowered herself beside her friend. 'But there's always hope. Missing's not the same as dead.'

Mary thought of the other young men she'd grown up with. 'Aye, but what's the chances? At least my brother's still safe, or he was the last time my mother heard from him, touch wood.' She looked around desperately, then took the pencil from her bedside cabinet and held it in her hand for a moment before replacing it. 'Touch wood,' she repeated.

But Johnny. Johnny couldn't be dead. She remembered him as she'd last seen him, so smart in his uniform, so full of bravado, yet she'd seen the fear in his eyes. She *had* loved him and if she was honest, she still loved him in a way, but it was the slow, comfortable love of friendship, nothing like the wild passion she felt for Greg.

'Don't get too down about it. He could be in a prison camp somewhere. War's like that.'

The hut seemed to tremble with the force of the wind. Mary stood up and took her greatcoat from her locker. 'I have to go out.' She left before Anna could question her further.

Outside, the rain lashed against her face, the wind tried its best to force her back inside and she remembered just such a night, when she and Johnny dodged into a barn, water streaming down her face. She could see him now, forcing the unwilling door shut, while the straw lifted about his feet and the chickens roosting in the rafters above clucked their disapproval. They laughed and fumbled to find each other in the dark and he kissed her. That first inexperienced kiss when their noses got in the way made them laugh again, this time with both embarrassment and wonder.

She wanted to see Greg, felt she needed his comfort, his arms.

She was still thinking about Johnny's gentle lips, when Greg opened the door to her knock. 'Mary. What a pleasant surprise. I was just going to meet a few chaps in the NAAFI. But do come in.' He took her arm and led her to the bed. He removed his jacket, hung it carefully up and smoothed his hand over the material, then he came over and sat beside her. Studying her face, he said, 'Bad news?'

Bad news was the usual reason for tears. He picked up her hand. 'You're frozen.'

She nodded. She didn't want to explain about Johnny. Turning, she looked at him in the glow from the weak lamp. His handsome face was full of shadows and for a second the distortion made him appear slightly menacing. She shuddered. 'Just hold me,' she whispered. She wondered what it was that made Greg so appealing. Perhaps it was something deep behind his eyes, a secret place that he never allowed her to enter. Although they'd been seeing each other for weeks, she knew little more about him than the first day they met.

He removed her greatcoat and threw it on the end of the bed, then he held her while her body trembled and she buried her face in the stiff material of his shirt. He ran his hand down the curve of her spine and pulled her against him with a force that left her breathless. 'Oh, Mary,' he moaned. 'What have you done to me? I want you so much.'

It was about now that, although desperate for his love, she would reluctantly fight him off. No matter how strongly she felt, she would not risk having a bairn. Tonight, however, her body reacted to his touch and she experienced a stronger need. The need to grasp at life, the desperation to connect with someone else, someone warm and breathing, someone who could chase the shadows away, take her to another place for a few blissful hours.

He lowered her onto her back and put his hand first on her knee, then slowly moved upwards. When his fingers reached the top of her stockings, she jumped. He hesitated and when she did nothing to stop him, he slipped his hand up further and inside her blackouts. Wishing fleetingly that she had worn her silk camis, she raised her hips to facilitate his hands and clung to him, encouraging him as he fumbled with his fly. She sighed and relaxed, her lips slightly parted and she waited, her body on fire, for what would come next.

Suddenly the shriek of the siren filled the night.

'Shit,' Greg gasped, sucking air. He took a deep shuddering breath, before leaping to his feet leaving her feeling empty and frustrated.

Mary had little time to reflect on what had nearly happened. No one expected an attack on a night like this. It was not until later, however, that she was grateful for the intervention. Although they'd made love before, they had never fully gone all the way. Tonight, she would have been unable and unwilling to stop.

'You'll come back again tomorrow?' Greg's voice was unsteady. 'I'll be better prepared.'

She nodded, knowing he meant to get a sheath.

'Don't let anyone see you leave.' He grabbed his flying jacket, then, as if it was an afterthought, he lifted a letter from the table. 'Post this for me – in case I don't return.' He thrust the letter at her and they hurried out under a sky that was already strobed by searchlights. Greg ran towards the airfield and Mary ran to the bunker.

Huddled in the trench with the other girls, she listened to the roar as the fighters took off. Her lips still tingled with the taste of Greg's kiss, her body still shivered at the memory of his hands on her. Still high on sexual tension, she couldn't wait until the next time they were together. What would she do if he did not come back? No, she couldn't think like that, she wouldn't.

Four hours later, only half of the squadron had returned. Another hour and a few stragglers limped home. Greg was not among them.

It had happened. The thing she most feared. 'He can't be dead,' she said to Gloria. 'If he was I'd feel it in here.' She set her hand on her chest.

'I'm sorry, love, but we keep going, don't we? It's what we do.'

Although she was bone weary, Mary rose and began polishing her shoes. Her mother's words came to her, 'Hard work is the best salve for a broken heart.'

Night after night, when sleep evaded her, vivid memories of the way he looked at her, the way his eyes lit up at the sound of her voice, the way they deepened in desire, the feel of his hands on her body tortured her. On a still night, when nothing much

232

was going on, they would be together, and it was these nights that were hardest of all to take. Why had she not allowed him to love her properly before now? They could have taken precautions, but even if she'd had a bairn, at least she would have some part of him to keep with her for always.

'It's not knowing,' she confided to Anna. 'For all we know, he might still be alive, be somewhere safe.'

'Maybe,' said Anna, but her look of sympathy told another story. Her friends thought him dead, like so many before him. No figure of authority would tell her anything. She was not his next of kin. She was nothing. But until she heard word that his body had been recovered, she could not believe that he was really gone.

It was two weeks later before there was any news. Anna came bursting into the mess hall and took a seat beside Mary. 'Word has just come in. Greg's alive,' she whispered.

Mary felt her insides turn to liquid. 'Thank God,' she breathed. 'Is he hurt? Where is he?'

'His plane was shot down, but he managed to parachute out. He's badly injured, but he's alive. He's been taken to a hospital in Exeter that's all they know.'

'Then I'll have to find out.' Mary stood up, her appetite deserting her.

'There's no point,' said Anna. 'They won't tell you anything. I was lucky to get that little bit of news. Do you know anything about his family? Maybe if you wrote them a letter…'

'He never really spoke about his family, only that he was brought up and lived in Devon. He even described the house.'

For the next few weeks, Mary was beside herself. Greg spoke of his mother once and he mentioned having a sister. *They* would know. 'I'll just have to go to Devon and find out myself,' she told her friends.

'Do you know how many Cunningham's there must be in Devon?' asked Gloria who clearly thought her mad.

'It was by the sea.'

233

Gloria let out a hoot. 'Devon has two coast lines.'

'They must have his home address on record. If only I could get access.'

'What are you thinking? Sneaking into the office and going through files?'

'How else am I to find out how bad he is?'

'Do you want to be court-martialled?'

'I have to know. This is driving me crazy.' Only then did she remember the letter. 'Wait a minute, he gave me a letter to post.' She ran to her greatcoat and fumbled in the pockets. 'With the raid and everything, I clean forgot.' She studied the envelope. 'It's addressed to Mrs. Sylvia Cunningham. Must be his mother. I can't believe I forgot all about it.' She took a note of the address. 'I'd better post it now.' Then she stopped and pushed the letter back into her pocket. 'Better still, I'll deliver it by hand, now I have his address.'

'Why not just write to her?' asked Anna.

Mary shook her head. 'A letter could take ages and what if she doesn't write back? I couldn't stand it. I've got leave next week. I've got to go.'

However, that plan was interrupted by the news that her Aunt Agatha was seriously ill and not expected to last much longer and asking for her.

Chapter Thirty-Eight

Mary

Katrine met her at the door. 'Mary, I'm so glad to see you, dear.'

'I'm sorry I couldn't get here before. Compassionate leave doesn't extend to Great Aunts.'

'You're here now, dear, and that's the important thing.' Katrine ushered Mary into the front room which was dark and sombre, the curtains drawn.

'Aunt Agatha?' Her heart leapt to her mouth. Curtains were normally drawn after a death.

'She's still alive, dear. She's waiting for you. The doctor's with her now. We'll wait here till he goes, dear.'

'Thank God.' Mary would not have been able to forgive herself had she been too late.

The doctor, a much younger man than Mary expected, came downstairs. 'She hasn't got long. You can go in now.'

Mary followed Katrine into the sick room which was overwarm and heavy with the scent of death. She took a seat by her aunt's side and lifted the pale, wrinkled hand in hers. 'Auntie,' she whispered, 'I'm here.'

Agatha opened her eyes. 'Mary,' the word sat on her breath. 'You came.' She inhaled slowly before she spoke again. 'Have you had any word from Lisbeth?'

Mary shook her head.

'I hope she's well.'

Silence fell again except for Agatha's rattling breathing.

'I'll try to find her,' Mary said.

'We did try, you know. We found the rabbi who'd put her up. He explained what happened. I wish she'd felt she could tell me the truth, I would have understood.' She stopped as if exhausted and closed her eyes before speaking again. 'I said some terrible things about Jews. I didn't know then…what they suffered…It's all come out now… I want to make my peace…'

'Hush. Don't upset yourself. I'm sure she realised.'

'I'm leaving my London house to Katrine. She'll sell it, of course and go back to Edinburgh. Please don't be offended.'

'I'm not, not at all.'

That was to be expected. Katrine had been with her all these years and the look that often passed between them was so kind, so affectionate, that Mary would not have been surprised had Agatha made Katrine her sole heir.

'And you too, of course. I know you'll never leave Scotland, so you and each of my other relatives will inherit a sizable sum.'

Mary wondered what *sizable* was. She assumed it would not be much. Her mother had been one of seven siblings and the aunt herself one of eight. The nieces and nephews must amount to a fair number. On the other hand, perhaps the Aunt was a lot richer than she made known. 'That's not important now, Auntie. What did you find out about Lisbeth?'

'It was too late.' Agatha shook her head and seemed to sink even further into her pillows, her eyes closing.

Katrine took over. 'The baby, that lovely little baby.' There was a break in her voice.

'What about the baby?'

'Killed…an air raid, dear.'

236

'Oh no.' Mary's stomach contracted. 'Little Gussy. I wanted to take them both back home with me to Mam. And Lisbeth? What about her? Did she survive?'

'Yes, she did. The rabbi said she'd gone to be a translator for the government. That's good isn't it, dear? She's a good girl.'

'Yes, she's a good girl.' Mary felt numb. Poor Lisbeth. To go through all that and then lose little Gus. She felt guilty now about having spoken so sharply to her at their last meeting. 'I hope she finds happiness,' she said, meaning every word.

'I always believed she'd come back some day,' Agatha whispered. 'I've worried so much...' Her voice trailed off with a long sigh. 'Don't cry for me. The earth is hungry for my bones and I deserve my rest.' She did not speak again, but sometimes her eyes would flicker open and Mary watched the bright intelligence slowly cloud over.

Aunt Agatha lay in a semi-coma for over a week before she slipped away. Mary accompanied Katrine and the gardener when they brought her body up to London to lie in the same grave as her husband. Mary hoped Lisbeth would see the death notice and turn up for the funeral and, although she had not really expected it, was disappointed when that didn't happen.

Chapter Thirty-Nine

Johnny

Travelling by night and resting by day, Johnny slept in barns and abandoned buildings, ate what crops were left in the fields and drank from ditches. Sometimes he slept in forests which were already healing. Trees closed in over his head, a struggling green canopy, daylight twinkling through the foliage, dancing like sunshine on the sea back home. He imagined the steady breathing of the waves against the shore and he would snatch a few hours' sleep clutching Mary's photograph to his heart. Those were the times that calmed him and gave him the strength to go on.

Eventually, he neared Cambio Les Bains and Marseilles was within his sights. Unable to go on, he lay behind a wall and closed his eyes. He normally chose a more discreet place, but his legs would not take him further. When he next opened his eyes, two young men were gazing down at him, their faces covered in stubble and their eyes battle-weary, beneath the raw lids.

'*Qui êtes vous?*' one said.

Johnny remembered what Suzanne told him. He was dumb. He pointed to his mouth and shook his head.

The peasants looked at each other and laughed.

'Anglais?' said one.

'Yes,' said Johnny, knowing he would never get away with this and he tried to convey that he was utterly exhausted. The men indicated that he should stay low and they moved to the side of the road. They allowed several cars to pass, then one of them stepped forward and waved his hands. A truck slowed down and stopped. They both turned and beckoned to Johnny.

Knowing that if he didn't eat soon he would die, he staggered towards the car, no longer caring whether or not this was a trap.

'Climb up,' said a soft-spoken, well-dressed gentleman. Johnny was so weak he had to be helped onto the truck. The driver exchanged some words with the peasants and drove off. Without having any idea what was going on, he dozed, his head rattling against the side window.

When he next opened his eyes, they were still speeding along the road.

'Ah, you're awake. I'm Mr Abrams,' said the man in perfect English. 'I, too, need to get out of France.'

Johnny looked at him, waiting for more.

'My family and I, we are Jewish, a race condemned by the Nazis. I only stay to do important work. You are a serviceman, yes?'

'I'm a soldier,' said Johnny. 'You have a way to get out?'

Mr Abrams nodded. 'Tonight you must stay with me and my family.'

Too weak to do much talking, Johnny almost cried with relief. He lay back, intermittently dozing and watching the countryside passing. They soon left the fields and woods behind and drove into Marseilles.

The car coasted down a lane and drew up beside a tall, narrow house in a street of other tall, narrow houses. Mr Abrams helped Johnny down from the truck and, still supporting him, he pushed open a door and called out, 'Ruth, we have another mouth to feed.'

A bird-like woman with kind eyes and short, grey, crinkled hair came to greet them. 'Anglais?' She lifted her eyebrows.

'Welcome. We have helped many of your countrymen.' She spoke in heavy French-accented English.

'Scottish,' said Johnny.

'Oui, oui,' she said with a laugh. 'Écossais. Come with me.'

She led the way to the kitchen where she served him with a bowl of strong coffee, thick bread and cheese, followed by boiled fish. The serving was small, but Johnny forgot any semblance of manners as he gulped the food, sucked the bones, then mopped the plate with bread to pick up every last bit of flavour. 'Thank you so much,' he whispered.

'You will see many people coming and going,' said Mr Abrams. 'This household is full of refugees. I'm afraid the conditions are rather primitive.'

Once he was fed, Johnny felt strong enough to wash himself, and fell, uncomplainingly, into a bed which he shared with four other men, none of whom spoke English. He only briefly wondered about their stories and why they were here, but he was too exhausted to dwell on the whys and wherefores and too grateful for the relative comfort. Despite the cramped conditions, he slept soundly for the first time in months. Mr Abrams shook him awake when it was still dark. Groggy and sore, he felt as though he'd had no sleep at all.

'You must go to the harbour, *Le Vieux Port,*' Mr Abrams told him over a breakfast of one bread roll and weak coffee. 'If you're lucky you might get a boat out of here. I'm sorry that we can't give you more help, but many more are arriving daily.'

Johnny shook Abrams's hand. 'I'm very grateful for what you've done already,' he said.

Still dressed in his ragged, dirty clothes, he walked for what seemed to be miles and lost himself in the narrow labyrinth of winding cobbled streets. In the light of the approaching morning, wiry, sun-tanned boys and girls dressed in rags stared at him from doorways or ran into the narrow lanes as he passed by. Gaunt and sick with exposure, Johnny was not out of place in this boiling pot of human misery.

At last he felt the welcome sea breeze and tasted salt in the air. He had found the harbour, which was sadly empty of boats save for a few fishing skiffs. An old man with sunken cheeks and hollow eyes who was seated by the harbour wall looked at him. He waved a hand in the air. 'Last boat gone,' he said, as if guessing his purpose and language.

Johnny swallowed his disappointment. He had arrived too late. 'The mission?' he asked.

The old man nodded and pointed with his stick and repeated an address, as if he'd said it many times before. Johnny moved in the direction indicated until he came across a wooden hut at the end of the road. On the door was pinned a notice.

"SEAMEN'S MISSION. OPEN TO BRITISH CIVILIANS ONLY."

Heartsick and almost expecting to be turned away, he fell against the door and stumbled inside as soon as it was open. The mission was crowded. Without him asking, a pale young man with a prominent Adam's apple helped him into a kitchen and brought him a bowl of tasteless soup and some bread, which he devoured within seconds.

'I was told to ask for Donald Caskie,' said Johnny.

'He's not here. My name's Stuart. Follow me.' He took Johnny to an office where three men in civilian clothes gave him a rigorous interrogation. His name, his next of kin, his regiment, his address in his homeland – an hour of exhausting questioning about his movements since he came to France.

Eventually, Stuart stood up. 'Sorry about that, but we can't be too careful. If we're proved to have been helping British servicemen not only will we be closed down, but we'll be shot.' He gave a shudder. 'Now, downstairs,' he ordered. 'If the Germans come you must hide. German troops raid us regularly and don't be surprised if you are asked to lie under the floorboards for a time. We don't want them to see too many different faces showing up. Do you have papers?'

Johnny shook his head.

'We'll get you some. Rest now and I'll wake you if I need to. Later, when it's dark, we'll go to the Arab quarter and get you a change of clothes. I have to go now. There'll be many more servicemen coming soon.'

Johnny almost fell over a coal heap, behind which he found a relatively clean space with a thin, horse-hair mattress and, after covering himself with a dusty blanket, he was asleep within seconds.

It was black as pitch in the cellar when the weak beam from a torch woke him. 'Come now,' whispered an urgent voice. He staggered to his feet and shook the sleep from his eyes.

A sorry bunch of soldiers, still in uniform, waited at the top of the stairs.

'Where are we going?' one of them asked.

'To the Arab quarter. They sell us clothes and other things we may need. You must disguise yourselves as civilians,' said Stuart. 'I'll go out first, make sure the coast is clear. Don't speak.' He opened the door and, after looking both ways, beckoned to the men to follow him.

In the Arab quarter Stuart purchased them different items of clothing, whatever he could get. Some he dressed in suits of businessmen, others in the rags of a peasants. 'We need to use what we have,' he whispered. 'Now, take your uniforms. The Arabs don't want to keep them here. We'll dump them in the harbour, behind the wall.' He turned to Johnny. 'Keep your clothes. We'll get them washed and use them again.'

Once more they dodged up alleys and hid behind doors all readily open to them and, eventually, they reached the harbour, weighted their burdens with large stones and dumped them into the ocean.

'Tomorrow we'll undoubtedly have more people trying to flee France. The ships that took away the refugees have left the harbour and won't come back. The last one was torpedoed and there were few survivors.'

Johnny shuddered. He'd just missed the last one.

Stuart continued, 'We'll send you over the Pyrenees and into Spain, from where you'll be able to make your own way home.

'The route we often use is becoming ever more dangerous. You will stay here one more night, in the house of a French family. Many French risk their own lives to help us.' He stopped and cleared his throat. 'We cannot trust anyone. We've already been betrayed on more than one occasion, leading two of our escaping parties to their death or imprisonment.'

Johnny was taken to a small house where a man, his wife and niece lived.

'They will look after you today. The niece has been a great help to us. We have to trust her to lead you to the pass. I hope you're ready; we have to leave tonight.'

'I'm more than ready,' said Johnny.'

'May I introduce Marie Maurierre,' Stuart said, when a young woman met them at the door.

Marie was small-boned and fair. She looked very young, too young to be leading grown men through a pass.

'Her looks are deceptive,' said Stuart, as if reading his mind. He turned to go. 'Be at the mission by midnight and stay indoors until then.'

Marie led him into a small room with a stove, a table and chairs and a single bed in the corner. An elderly woman who spoke only French and who Johnny took to be the aunt, served him with bitter coffee and bread that reminded him of his mother's bannocks, made mostly of flour and water.

'You must sleep now,' said Marie. 'We will talk later. In here.' She opened a door he had not noticed in the wall. Inside was a narrow bed and no room for anything else. 'And please be quiet,' Marie cautioned as she shut the door, leaving him once more in the dark. But he could not sleep. He wondered what news of him filtered back home and guessed he would be reported missing. They would think him dead. He imagined his homecoming, his family's tears, and Mary. Please God he would find her unhurt and unattached.

Chapter Forty

Johnny

When the clock struck midnight they entered the mission where the six weary soldiers, now dressed in the new clothes, stood waiting for instructions. Stuart opened the door. 'Good, there's no moon. Collect your gear now.'

He led the men inside where each was issued with a stout pair of boots, a padded jacket and a backpack. 'These are all donated by helpful French,' explained Stuart, to Johnny's unasked question. 'You will be climbing in the mountains. Be assured, this is no easy walk.'

Once kitted out, the party filed through the door. 'Keep close to the wall until you get into the country, then stay among the trees as far as you can. Make as little noise as possible until then and stay in single file. You have the map?'

Marie, dressed like a boy, nodded an affirmative. No one spoke until the streets gave way to scattered farm houses. When there was no sign of pursuit, they relaxed and began to chat quietly.

'Have you always lived here?' Johnny said to Marie as she fell in step beside him.

She didn't reply immediately.

'I think I know your accent,' she said at last. 'You are from Scotland, yes?'

'How do you know that?' Most foreigners could not tell the difference between the dialects.

'Many of your countrymen pass through here.'

'Really? Maybe I know them if they speak like me.'

'I never ask their names.'

The night was still, with only the whisper of the men's feet and their low voices.

They walked for a while in silence. 'Where are you from?' asked Johnny at last.

'I will only tell you that I work for the German army, but that is a cover. Leading stranded servicemen to safety, this I chose to do myself. We had to find a way to get your servicemen out of France. Also there are many British living here. They are in grave danger of being incarcerated.' She fell into silence.

'Are you English?' he asked, amazed by her command of the language.

She shook her head. 'No, but I've already said too much.'

When a grey dawn broke the horizon, Marie held up her hand. We will rest during the daytime,' she said, 'and travel by night. Ahead is Perpignan and an innkeeper there will provide us with refreshments, then we'll grab some sleep in his basement.'

The mountains were tall and rugged, sharp peaks reaching into the sky. They looked almost impossible to navigate on foot, but he had to trust Marie to know what she was doing.

Johnny hoped to get her by herself, to get more information from her, but it was as if from then on, she purposely avoided him.

The innkeeper gave them soup, bitter chicory coffee and bread, and he provided them with blankets. In the morning, after a breakfast of broth and coffee, Marie, looking perturbed, held up her hand. 'I have news that our route has been blocked. We will have to take the alternative.'

Once more, Johnny fell into step beside her. 'You don't look too happy,' he said.

'I don't have an easy feeling. This is most unusual, but it is possible the pass has been blocked by an avalanche. And the message seems genuine enough.'

He tried to engage her in further conversation, but she held her fingers to her lips. 'It is better we remain silent,' she whispered.

As they ascended, the temperature dropped and the men changed into their boots and heavy jackets. Before long, it began to snow. They had all fallen silent, no sound but the crunch of boots on snow and the high wind through thin pines. In places the ascent was steep and they slipped and struggled to keep a footing. Tired, cold, hungry and footsore they continued to drag themselves uphill. Johnny tried to remember how much he'd loved the snow as a child. It meant many hours of fun: sledging, snowball fights, snowmen, snow houses, running indoors to warm frozen fingers and toes, just to rush out again as soon as possible. He imagined a blazing range, leaping flames, hot soup. Ahead of them, Marie stopped and held up a hand. She tilted her head as though sniffing the air.

'Get down,' she shouted, too late.

German soldiers suddenly appeared from behind high rocks and out of gullies, firing indiscriminately. The men dropped like skittles. Johnny grabbed Marie's arm and together they rolled into a ditch, miraculously dodging the flying bullets. Hardly daring to breathe, they lay still until they could not feel their hands and feet.

Even after the gunfire had ceased, they did not move. Unsure if she was still alive, Johnny reached out to touch Marie, relieved when he heard her intake of breath. He indicated that she should remain as she was, and he inched his way to the top of the chasm where he raised his head enough to see what was happening. A few other men hid nearby. He heard the Germans crashing through the undergrowth, shouting at the men they uncovered to get on their feet, then marching them away at gunpoint, hands on heads.

Johnny slipped back down, put his hand on Marie's head and held her face against the freezing ground. He dare not even whisper, only hoped she understood the need to lie still, half buried in snow. Surely, after all he had endured, it could not end now, here like this, when he was so near freedom he could almost taste it. All he could do was press his own forehead against the snowy earth, now warmed by his tears.

If he had been asked afterwards how long they lay there he would not have been able to tell. Time seemed to disappear while he waited once more for death, terrified that his own steamy breath would give away their position. He was not aware of when the Germans left and silence fell on the mountain. At some stage he had rolled over onto his back and drifted away.

When he woke, it was to sunshine on his face. He blinked, eased his aching body upright and looked around. Marie came from the direction of the trees, unhooked her backpack and squatted beside him.

'Have they gone?' he asked.

'Yes. We are all that is left.'

'I'm sorry I fell asleep.' He cursed his own weakness.

'You were already exhausted before we began.' She took a deep breath and her voice became hard. 'Someone has betrayed us.' She took a bar of chocolate from her pack and broke it. 'Breakfast.' She handed half to him.

He ate it slowly, savouring the smooth flavour on his tongue. 'Since there's only us I should tell you my name…'

'Stop. No names, remember?'

'Then what'll you call me?'

She smiled almost shyly, 'Hey, you. It's what the British say, *n'est-ce pas*?'

'It'll have to do,' he answered with a grin. 'What do we do now?'

'Continue towards the border. We should be in Spain before nightfall.'

Spain, safety. He put his head in his hands and would have wept, but tears refused to form.

They did not reach Spain by that evening. When darkness fell, they were still walking. 'You're sure we're not lost?' asked Johnny. By now they were going downhill and the muscles in his legs groaned making the descent harder than the climb. At least the temperature was rising.

Marie checked her compass. 'It's a different route than the one I'm used to, but we're going in the right direction.'

As they walked they talked, but Marie still gave away very little about herself. The desire to lie down and sleep was strong and only Marie's constant questions forced Johnny to remain focussed.

'Where in Scotland do you come from?' she asked.

'A place called John O'Groats.'

'Tell me about it.'

Johnny was happy to describe the firth and all its moods, the grand hotel that once was the home of the Dutchman Jan de Groot who gave the area its name, the flat landscape and the islands to the north.

'And did you leave a sweetheart behind?' Marie asked.

Johnny thought of Mary, of their last conversation. How she promised to write and how he treasured every letter. She, too, would think him dead. Returning home to find her wed to another was unthinkable. Yet she had promised him nothing.

'Yes...Mary,' he said.

'What is she like?'

As the miles passed he spoke of Mary, of Chrissie, of home and his family, and as he spoke he could see himself there, hear the banter of his own folk, warm himself at a blazing stove, satisfy his hunger on home-baked bannocks dipped in thick scotch broth.

'It sounds amazing,' she said. 'You must have been very happy there.' There was a wistfulness in her voice, or did he imagine it?

'I was. And what about you? Do you have a sweetheart?'

She was silent for a long time. Just as Johnny thought she wasn't going to answer, she said, 'I was once in love, but this war, it does no good to linger on affairs of the heart. Now tell me more about the people you left behind. What news do you get from them?'

Johnny surmised that she was attempting to divert the conversation away from herself and he was having none of it. 'Was your sweetheart killed?' he asked.

Once again Marie fell silent and the only sound was the crunch of their feet on the snow and their laboured breathing.

'I'm sorry, I don't mean to pry,' said Johnny, wishing he had not been so direct.

'It's fine. Yes, he is dead.' Her voice was sharp and she speeded up so that she walked in front of him, effectively ending the conversation.

In the early morning they came to a clearing. Two men in dark clothes with red berets were sitting on a rock eating from tin containers. As if hearing the rustle of footsteps behind them, they grabbed rifles from their sides and sprung to their feet, spinning round as they did so.

Instinctively, Johnny reached for his gun, numb fingers closing round the shaft.

Marie put her hand on his arm. She said something to the men in a language Johnny didn't understand. They lowered their guns and approached the couple with wide smiles on their swarthy, lean features. '*Ongi, ongi,*' they said, holding out their hands.

Marie turned to Johnny. 'We are in Basque country. You will be safe now. We must rest and eat.'

They were taken to a low, stone-built house where they were met by a leathery-skinned woman with a scarf around her head and a long sackcloth skirt. Without speaking she ushered them in and gave them water, bread and boiled chicken. Once they were fed, she led Johnny to a small room with a single bed in one corner and a picture of Christ on the cross hanging on the wall. A small table covered with a lace cloth held a candle. Johnny immediately fell on the bed and sank into a deep sleep.

When he rose again it was to darkness. He could hear voices in the next room. Still drunk from fatigue, he made his way towards the sound, where Marie, dressed in her jacket, was easing her rucksack onto her back.

'Are we leaving?' he asked.

'I'm going back. From here on you are safe.'

'No, you can't go back. They'll kill you.'

'They don't know me. I must discover who the informer is.'

'Marie…'

'Do not worry about me. I still have work to do.'

'Will I ever see you again?'

'That is up to God. And…' She reached the open door and hesitated. 'When you get back to Caithness, give this to Chrissie.'

She handed him a small envelope. Through the paper he could feel the outline of a plain ring.

'What? How…Marie come back here…'

The two Basque men grabbed an arm each and prevented him from following as the darkness swallowed the girl.

Chapter Forty-One

Chrissie

Chrissie marched up to the cottage door and gave it a few sharp bangs with her fist. A dog barked inside. Shuffling feet approached in the hallway, a bent shape loomed behind the multi-coloured glass panes in the top half of the door before it opened.

'We're no looking for trouble,' said the beefy woman taking a backward step when she saw Chrissie.

'I've no come for trouble, Johan. I just want to see Jess,' said Chrissie.

Johan's eyes narrowed to slits. 'I've done my best. It's no my fault she's the way she is.' She held onto the edge of the door, barring the entrance.

'What way?' said Chrissie. 'What's no yer fault?'

'She's a good girl, our Jess, always has been. Don't know how this happened.'

'Tell me what ye're on about,' said Chrissie. If the gossip was anything to go by, she already knew.

Johan moved away making room for Chrissie to enter. 'Jess's in the ben room. No been very well. I just want ye to know, I'm the one that's suffering with her dad away and her bringing shame on my head. No had a wink of sleep for months. I suppose it's wagging tongues that's brought you here.'

'I just want to see her,' said Chrissie.

Johan gave a martyred sigh. 'Ye'd better go through then. I suppose your Peter'll not want her now.' She pointed the way. 'It'll be left on my shoulders the way everything else is.'

Chrissie opened the ben door.

Jess gasped and lowered her eyes, her face red. She quickly crossed her arms over her swollen stomach.

'So it's true,' said Chrissie in horror.

Jess didn't answer, but lowered her head even further, so that her hair covered her face.

'Ye could at least have come and seen me, let me hear it from yer own lips,' said Chrissie. She was shocked by the girl's appearance. She'd put on far too much weight and not only her eyes, but her whole face was puffy.

Jess raised her eyes but she didn't look at Chrissie. 'I was ashamed.'

'Have ye told Peter?'

She shook her head.

'And the father? Will he stand by ye?'

Jess shook her head again. 'He doesn't know. I don't want him to. It's Peter I love. I could never love anyone else.'

'A fine way ye have of showing it too,' said Chrissie.

'I was just... so lonely.' Tears shimmered in her eyes.

'How long did you think it would take before I heard?'

'I know I'll lose Peter and that kills me, it just kills me. Mam wanted me to get the bairn adopted and never let on. I can't do that, but she's threatening to throw me out if I don't.'

'So, another child grows up not knowing who his father is.' As soon as the words left her mouth a voice inside her head said, *you're a fine one to talk, Chrissie Rosie.* But her situation had been different she reasoned. She may have been married to Jack Reid, but she *had* been in love with Charlie Rosie when she took him to her bed.

'I've ruined my life and his. I'll write to Peter, but I don't know when he'll get the letter,' said Jess.

A brief vision of Peter in a muddy trench, tired and dispirited, flashed through Chrissie's mind. She remembered too well how Charlie told her that only her love kept him alive during the bitter days after he was wounded. Time enough for Peter to know when the danger was past. 'No, don't tell him. He'll have enough to contend with fighting a war and, God forbid, if the worst happens, let him go to his grave believing you waited for him.'

Jess shrunk even more into herself. 'I'll do what ye think best. I'd do anything to turn the clock back. Anything to make Peter the dad.' The words were wrung from her, full of pain and hurt.

Had this happened to anyone other than her daughter-in-law, Chrissie would have been sympathetic. The girl before her was little more than a child herself, a child who'd made a dreadful mistake.

'Is it someone local?'

Jess shook her head.

'A serviceman then?'

'It was one night. I went to the dance. I sometimes did that, just to forget the war for a time. I had a drink and then another.' She held up her hand when Chrissie opened her mouth to tell her that was no excuse.

'I know what ye're thinking. I shouldn't have. But he was kind and he had suffered in the war too. His family were wiped out in the blitz. Imagine that, to lose everyone. He understood how scared I was that I would lose Peter. I think I cried. We both did, but it's all a bit hazy. I didn't go out after that and I never saw him again.' She burst into tears. 'I tried to get rid of it. I drank gin and took hot baths for a week. Now I'm so scared I've damaged the bairn.'

Chrissie had known women to do this before. It seldom worked and the bairn was usually born healthy enough, but she wasn't about to give Jess any comfort.

'What will ye do if yer mother won't let ye keep it?'

Jess shook her head miserably. 'There's nothing else I can do. I can't work and support a bairn with no help.'

'I'm sorry for ye, lass, but I'm sure you'll do the right thing.' Chrissie left the room, her thoughts in turmoil. It was clear that the girl's health was not what it should be.

'When was her last check-up?' she asked Johan.

'She's not been for any check-ups.'

'She doesn't look well,' said Chrissie. 'It's important you have a doctor look at her as soon as possible. Will ye make sure of that?'

Johan bobbed her head.

'Make sure you do.' Chrissie took her leave, her work here was finished.

Chapter Forty-Two

Mary

The RAF station was buzzing with the news. Hitler had committed suicide on the 30th of April, it was official. The war was almost won. In the camp, morale reached an all-time high and a local band was hired for the dance that night. But Mary couldn't enjoy it; her head was spinning with memories of Greg. Her next leave started in two weeks and she knew exactly how she was going to spend it, if she could get no news of him from any other source, she would go to his mother's. Once Mary explained how close they had been, his mother would weep and invite her inside. It was more than possible that Greg had already told his family about her and she imagined a warm welcome.

She saw herself sipping tea in a large cosy living room. Greg spoke quite posh; his family must be well-off and since he'd never mentioned his father, she assumed he was long dead. Greg might even be there, convalescing but, then, if he was fit, why hadn't he written to her? There could only be one reason, he was too badly hurt and once again her stomach knotted. He should be here and she should be in his arms waltzing round the floor. She missed him so much.

'Come on, love,' said Hilda, a strapping girl from Stepney, 'it ain't no use getting yer knickers in a twist. At least you know he ain't a goner.'

'But it's driving me mad, this knowing nothing. No matter how bad it is, I *need* to know.'

But it was no use. No word about Greg Cunningham ever filtered back to the base.

On Tuesday, 8th of May, Mary sat on the bus that headed out of town, staring absently through the window. Her hair was freshly washed and curled and she'd begged some makeup from other girls. She wanted to look her best when she saw Greg again.

Suddenly the doors of the houses they drove past burst open and people ran into the street, shouting to each other and cheering. A man jumped in front of the bus waving his arms causing the driver to step on his brakes which threw the passengers forward. It had been lucky that the bus was travelling slowly. The driver opened his window. 'What the hell do you think you're doing?' he yelled.

'The war's over. The war's over,' shouted the man. 'Six years of misery, it's over.' Then he started to cry, great gulping sobs. Some of his friends came and hugged him before leading him away.

A loud cheer filled the bus and Mary laughed and clapped as loud as any.

'I'm glad it's over,' said the smiling conductress. 'It was an awful time.'

'It definitely was,' said the driver gruffly. 'Best get going, though. This bus'll not drive itself.'

Mary settled down to enjoy the rest of her journey although the news of peace was marred with the worry of what she would find out about Greg. But no matter how bad his injuries, she thought, she would stay with him and nurse him for the rest of his life.

Celebrations were already underway in every village they passed through. Shops displayed rosettes and tri-coloured button-holes in the windows and men were putting up bunting and flags. A complete stranger to the situation could have sensed the tenseness and mood of expectation.

At last they reached her destination. She asked directions from the conductress who was happy to help. With a fluttering heart, her bag clutched against her side, she stepped from the bus.

Number four Chichester Street. She stood outside the house and it was just as he described it. A two-story, semi-detached villa with a well-kept garden in front, not too posh, but not too shabby either. She cleared her throat and patted her hair, walked up the paved path and rang the doorbell. It seemed like an age before it was answered by a tall, blonde woman, a child in her arms, her face drawn, as if she'd had too many sleepless nights. She looked vaguely familiar.

'Sorry for taking so long to answer. Churchill was just on the wireless. It's really over.' She raised her eyebrows at Mary. 'What can I do for you?'

'I…I was looking for Mrs Cunningham,' said Mary, only then recognising the woman who smiled up at Greg while walking on his arm the day she'd seen him from the café window. Of course, this must be his sister.

Her next words stunned Mary and made her stomach clench.

'I'm Mrs Cunningham.'

Mary's mind raced. His sister-in-law then? But he never mentioned having a brother. For a long moment the words stuck in her throat, her mouth opened and shut and she caught herself.

'I…I'm from RAF base Marham. A few of us, we were wondering how Greg was. They tell us nothing.' Her voice ran away with confusion. Her mind raced for an explanation. Maybe his sister wasn't married, but had a child and called

258

herself Mrs, that would make sense. Yes, that would be it. She tried to look normal and waited.

The woman eyed her suspiciously. 'It's nice of you to come all this way. Miss…?'

'Rosie, Mary Rosie.'

The woman nodded and her next words destroyed any lingering hope that Mary harboured.

'Well, Miss Rosie, he will live, but without the use of a leg. He's still very weak.' She stopped and swallowed. 'I was so afraid my children would have to grow up fatherless.' She paused for a second, cold eyes scrutinising Mary. 'Perhaps you would like to see him?'

Mary refused to hear. The words came out of the woman's mouth, but if it were possible to close her ears against them, she would have gladly done so.

'You…you're his wife?'

The woman frowned. 'Yes. I am, and who exactly are you, Miss Rosie?'

Mary's heart staggered then plummeted to her boots. She had a sense of falling, of grasping at air. Everything seemed to go black for an instant and her stomach somersaulted. Later, she would never know how she managed to keep her face neutral and her voice even, or whether or not she'd fooled his wife.

For a second there was silence, a silence that stretched and grew as loud as thunder, before Mary found the ability to speak.

'No one. Just a spokesperson. His friends were worried and I had some leave due, so I volunteered to come and make enquiries as I was in the area. I hardly know him personally.' She tried to smile, to make her voice light, while she longed to scream, to shatter his world the way he had shattered hers, but the war had enough casualties without adding this woman and her children.

Mrs Cunningham released a breath. 'I'll tell him you called.'

Mary knew by her icy tone that she had not been believed.

'Thanks. I've to be somewhere else now.' She turned away before her distress became even more obvious, before her tears began to course down her burning face, before she threw herself on the ground screaming in grief, embarrassment and frustration. She held her head erect and marched down the path towards the bus stop, not really seeing where she was going, her humiliation complete. The door slammed behind her.

On every street corner celebratory bonfires were being lit. People were already dancing and cheering, hugging each other and crying, but Mary saw nothing. Her eyes were too blurry, her throat too thick. Then she became angry. *Fool, fool, what a fool I've been,* she ranted in her head. She should have known when she saw them together, not been so quick to believe his unlikely explanation. *Fool, fool, fool.*

Chapter Forty-Three

Chrissie

Chrissie had just pulled the curtains against a lowering sky, when she heard a motor car outside, then the sound of footsteps followed by several thumps on the door.

'All right, don't break the wood,' she shouted as she pulled the door open. Dougal Duncan, Jess's uncle, stood before her, his face expressionless. 'Ye've to come,' he said, in his slow manner.

'Come where?'

'Jess. She's having the bairn. Johan says.'

'What's that got to do with me? Get the nurse or take her to the hospital.'

'It's Johan. She says tell nobody. She says ye'll have to bring it into the world and then we'll get rid of it.' He stared at her, his eyes expressionless.

'I do not have to do any such thing,' Chrissie said.

'She's bad. Johan says she'd rather they both die than have a scandal. And she means it. Ye have to come.'

After having met Jess's mother, Chrissie could well believe it. 'Did she take her to a doctor?' asked Chrissie.

He shook his large head. 'Nooo….she'll no have it. Come on.' He grabbed her arm and tried to pull her out.

'God preserve us,' muttered Chrissie and shook him off. 'Wait a minute. I'll get my bag.'

Jess was sobbing and bent over the end of her bed. Sweat beaded her face and her eyes were so puffed up they were almost closed. A strong smell of vomit filled the room. 'Help me, for God's sake help me,' she cried, when she saw Chrissie, and she heaved again. 'It's no just my stomach and back, it's my head too, my head.' Her wails turned into howls.

The next thing Chrissie noticed were the hands that clutched the bed end. The fingers and wrists were badly swollen. She quickly checked Jess's feet and her ankles bulged and hung over her slippers.

'She needs to go to hospital,' Chrissie shouted from the bedroom door. 'Get to a phone and send for the doctor now!'

Johan Duncan stood solidly in the passage. 'There'll be no doctor,' she said. 'It'll be a blessing if the bairn dies.'

'It's no just the bairn. If she doesn't get to a hospital, we'll lose them both.'

Johan didn't flinch. 'You're a howdie. Can't you do anything? If it survives, me and Dougal are taking it to Inverness tomorrow and getting it adopted. It's best for your family as well as ours that no one else knows. Better still if it doesn't survive.'

'Are ye no listening, woman? She's seriously ill. The hospital has drugs I've no access to. Do you want to be responsible for your daughter's death as well as your grandchild?'

Johan's face grew pale, but she still looked undecided. Chrissie turned to Dougal who stood staring at his sister-in-law as if waiting for instructions. A sudden long drawn out scream from the other room sent Chrissie running back. As she reached the door she glanced over her shoulder. 'Get an ambulance, Dougal,' she commanded. 'Now, I don't care what yer sister says.'

Neither the woman nor man moved.

'I said, now, or so help me I'll see ye charged with murder,' Chrissie shrieked before running to Jess's side.

'Come on, lassie, lie down. I have to examine you.' She took Jess's arm and tried to get her onto the bed. 'We'll get you to hospital and help this bairn into the world.'

'I heard what ye said, what she said. I'm scared. If I die,' Jess said through desperate sobs. 'Save the baby. Please do what ye can, just save the bairn. Look out for him.'

'No one's going to die,' said Chrissie. 'Come on now, take deep breaths and try to relax.'

Berating herself for having shouted at Johan when Jess was within earshot, she was grateful to hear someone leaving and the roar of the truck outside.

Jess's fingers tightened around Chrissie's wrist. 'Promise me,' she gasped. 'Save my bairn. Look after him.'

'Ye'll be fine. Ye'll look after him or her yerself.' But Chrissie felt less than confident as she tried to reassure the girl.

'Promise me,' shouted Jess as her back arched and her eyes closed tight. The lips drew back like a rictus grin.

'I promise,' said Chrissie. 'Now save yer strength for the next push.'

When the pain passed, Jess flopped back against the pillow, her face dripping with sweat. 'Thank you,' she breathed, before the next pain built up.

'Your bairn's almost here,' said Chrissie. 'I can see the head.' There was no time now for a hospital birth.

A few minutes later a big, limp baby boy slid into Chrissie's hands. Jess's lips were blue, her eyes had closed and the colour was leaching from her skin. Her breathing was shallow and laboured but Chrissie had no time to attend to her if she were to save the bairn. For less than a second, indecision swayed her. She would do everything in her power to save them both, but it already seemed that it was in God's hands. Where the hell was that ambulance?

'Johan,' she yelled, but there was no answer.

She cleaned out the child's mouth and rubbed his chest. When he didn't respond she lifted him up by the feet and slapped his back. Not something that was recommended by then, but Chrissie was desperate and it had worked for her granny when she was the howdie.

'Jess, Jess wake up,' she shouted as she laboured on the child. She blew into the mouth and rubbed his chest again. She felt the faint flutter of a heartbeat under her hands. She laid her cheek against the blue lips and sensed the faint warmth of a breath. He gasped and stirred and gave a feeble cry. Outside she heard the ambulance finally arrive.

After wrapping the bairn in a towel, she turned her attention to Jess. Her breathing was quick and laboured and her pulse was weak, but she was still alive. Once the medics arrived and began working on her, Chrissie stormed into the kitchen. She wanted to grab Johan and bang her stupid head against the wall.

'How's Jess,' Johan asked, wringing her hands.

'It'll be a miracle if she survives, you...you cruel bitch!' Chrissie spun on her heel and followed the stretcher to the ambulance. She could not trust herself to stay in the same room as that woman a minute longer.

Chrissie sat in the hospital all night, praying that both Jess and her baby would survive. She could not understand Johan's belief that the child would be better dead. To Chrissie who once feared she would never be a mother, every child was a gift from God.

She fell asleep in the chair and woke with a hand on her shoulder. Sinclair was standing over her. She struggled to her feet and threw herself into his arms. Only then did the tears come. 'Have they said anything? How is she?'

'Not to me,' said Sinclair.

The doctor came down the corridor. 'You're Jess Rosie's mother-in-law I believe?'

264

'Yes, I am.'

'All I can tell you is that her blood pressure has come down some. We hope for the best.'

'The baby?'

'We've given him a feed. He's doing well.'

'Can I see him?'

'Of course. You undoubtedly saved his life. We did have a few worrying moments when he first came in, but he's fine now.'

He led her to the nursery where a nurse held the baby up for her inspection. 'Say hello to Granny, wee mannie,' said the nurse.

Two blue eyes stared unblinkingly into hers and at that moment, Chrissie's heart melted anew and she knew she could not hold the mother's sins against an innocent child. Her arms ached to hold the precious babe.

There was still no sign of Johan Duncan.

'Honestly,' she said to Sinclair as he led her to his truck, 'I've never been so angry in all my life. That stupid, stupid woman!'

'What's going to happen to Jess?' asked Sinclair, as they pulled up in front of Chrissie's cottage. She had told him everything on the way home.

'Even if she makes it, she'll be weak for a long time and I don't see her getting much support from her mother.'

'So you've forgiven her?'

'My heart's sore for our Peter, but she was just a weak, lonely girl, who needed to forget the worry and heartbreak of the war for a short time. If she's stuck, I'll take her in myself.' She would, but in truth, she didn't know if she could ever fully excuse her actions.

Sinclair stopped the truck and turned to look into Chrissie's face. 'You're a remarkable woman, Chrissie Rosie,' he said.

The next day, Chrissie took the bus into town. She couldn't wait to see the baby again and find out if they were both doing well.

'Her blood pressure is still up and down,' said the midwife. 'She's not out of the woods, but you can see her.'

Jess lay still and white on the bed in a darkened room. She opened her eyes when Chrissie took a seat beside her. 'Have ye seen him?' she whispered in a weak voice.

'He's a grand laddie,' said Chrissie. 'Ye're just to relax now and not worry about a thing.'

'How can I not worry?' Tears formed in her eyes.

'Has your mother been in?' asked Chrissie.

Jess nodded. 'She's letting me come home, but I'll never hear the end of it. I'll just have to thole it. It's my punishment for what I did.'

'She'll fall in love with the baby, wait and see.' Chrissie was relieved. Although she would have taken the girl in had there been no other support, she didn't want to be put in that position.

'Mam won't even look at me.'

Chrissie squeezed Jess's hand. 'She will in time. What did you call the wee fellow?'

'Donald, for my dad, and Peter. Even if he wants no more of me, I hope he won't mind.'

'Donald Peter.' Chrissie rolled the name around on her tongue. 'A good strong name. I can't speak for Peter,' she said. 'But I do have sympathy for ye and this poor bairn.'

'Please don't hate me,' said Jess.

Chrissie took a deep sigh. 'I don't hate ye, lassie. But what ye've done will devastate my boy and I find that hard.'

'I'm so sorry. But thanks for yer kindness.' Jess turned her head away and sniffed. 'Will ye come back and see me?'

'Of course I will, in a day or two.' Chrissie rose. 'I'll have another look at Donald Peter before I go.'

Chapter Forty-Four

Mary

Mary stepped from the bus. She had told no one that she was arriving today. She wanted no big welcome when so many would never return.

Taking a moment, she set her case on the ground and watched the bus pull away, leaving her alone on the empty road. Her mother's cottage stood at the end of the track, near the shore. Cloud-cover was high and broken allowing sunlight to flit across a panorama of fields in muted shades of brown, sturdy little cottages and arrays of outbuildings with wide, stone walls that defied the worst tempest. Beyond that the stacks of Duncansby poked their heads above the cliffs to become visible for miles around, the Pentland Firth in choppy blue, the horizon broken by the islands of the north. The air had a stinging freshness that she'd almost forgotten.

Is it because I grew up surrounded by this landscape, she wondered, *that made me immune to its beauty?* Once she thought the panorama before her bleak, but now it contained all the life and colour of her childhood. It was a pleasure to stand here with no planes droning overhead, no air raid sirens shrieking or exploding bombs, with no stench of burning, and without the overpowering fear. But behind the relief was a sense of flatness, an anti-climax. Wondering if she would ever be able to settle back to a crofting life, she set off down the narrow road. Outside the cottage the old dog didn't bark. Instead he ran up to her wagging his tail. 'Bob,' she whispered, 'you're still here and you haven't forgotten me.' Bob had been ten years old when she left and she hadn't expected him to still be around. She knelt beside him and ruffled his ears, his tongue giving her an enthusiastic welcome.

She found her mother bending over a pan on the stove. Chrissie stood up, turned around and gasped. 'Mary!' She flew across the room almost knocking her daughter over in her enthusiasm. 'Why didn't you let us know ye were coming?' Her eyes were moist and her lip trembled. 'I would have met ye.'

Mary disentangled herself and lowered her bag to the floor. 'I didn't want a fuss, getting met at the station and all that.' It seemed out of place, the welcome, the celebration of being alive.

'But I've only got saps for tea.' Chrissie wiped her eyes with the bottom of her wrap-around apron. 'Ye'll be hungry. Everything's still rationed. It's even harder to get stuff now, but if I'd only known, I'd have killed a hen.'

'After the muck we've been eating, believe me, saps is something I've dreamed about,' answered Mary.

'Sit, sit down.' Chrissie pulled out a chair then removed a soup plate from the rack above the stove. Into it she ladled the saps made with milk, brown bread and raisins, glistening with melted butter.

'How are ye? Ye look pale,' said Chrissie. Her cheeks were flushed, her eyes moist. She looked older than Mary remembered and she'd lost weight.

'I'm tired, Mam.' Yes, she was, in spirit as well as body. 'Any word of Peter?'

'His last letter said he was on his way home. He's spent the war fighting the Axis forces in North Africa and it's a miracle he's no been hurt, he says. Almost five hundred lads from Scotland have been killed. I've heard nothing since.' She put her hands up to her face. 'I've prayed for this day. The war over and both my bairns safe.'

'Peter's lot, they'll maybe be at sea.' Mary finished her plate of saps and she couldn't remember when she'd eaten anything more delicious.

'Aye, that'll be it.'

'And Jess, do ye still see her?'

'Och, Jess.' Chrissie sniffed. 'She's had a bairn, to one of the airmen.'

'She's … she's left our Peter?' Mary was horrified. They'd seemed so in love and Jess didn't seem the type to play around.

'No. He doesn't know.' Chrissie took a chair and gave a deep sigh. 'I don't know if it's my place to tell him. Do ye think we should warn him or leave it for her once he's safely home?'

'I don't know either.' Mary thought of Greg and all the pilots who'd had affairs and never let on they had a wife at home. Who was to say that Peter was any different? She thought of all the women who hung around the base, even more so once the Americans came, women whose men were fighting elsewhere. The one thing Mary learned was not to judge and, instead of anger, she felt sadness. 'Stuff happens in war,' she said. 'We were living on the edge, never knowing if we'd still be alive tomorrow. It makes you see things differently.'

'He's no the only one to come home and find a wee stranger by the fireside,' said Chrissie. 'Aye, there'll be a lot of explaining to do, I'll be bound. But I liked Jess, and poor Peter, how's he going to cope?'

'He might surprise you. I think we should leave it to them, not interfere,' said Mary and fell silent for a beat. 'And the others? You told me about Rita. Is she still with her mam and dad? I can't wait to see her again.' Rita came home two years ago and gave birth to a baby boy not long after.

'Aye, but they're no happy with the disgrace she's brought on them. The poor lassie has a life of hell, so I hear.' Chrissie shook her head. 'She'll no be the last to come back with a bairn either.'

Mary thought of Greg again and of how easily she could have been one of those women. 'And what of Ellie and Sally?'

'Ellie married an airman. She's settled in in Southampton.' Chrissie took a deep breath, 'I didn't tell ye before. Sally wasn't able to cope with the forces and came back home. She got a job as an auxiliary nurse at the Town and County hospital.'

'And is she still there? I can't wait to see her as well. I've so much to tell her…' She stopped when a dark cloud crossed her mother's face. 'What's wrong?'

'A bomber crashed into the nurses' home. All the crew were killed as well as a lot of the nurses.'

'And Sally?'

'I'm sorry, lass.'

Sally, bright, bubbly Sally, always out for a laugh. 'And I thought I was the one in danger,' Mary said, her heart newly heavy. 'Johnny? Did they ever find out what happened to him?'

Chrissie's face brightened. 'Oh, there's good news about him. He's alive. But he's in hospital in Southend.'

'Badly hurt?' Mary asked.

'I don't think so. His dad told me he's suffering from exposure and malnutrition. He should be home soon.' Chrissie turned and took an envelope from the mantle. 'Some more good news. I got a letter from Aunt Agatha's solicitor. She's left us money. Two thousand pounds. I can't believe it. It's for ye and Peter though. I've no need o' it.'

Two thousand pounds, Mary could hardly take it in. It was a fortune! 'Oh, Mam, it's for you too. You deserve something. Maybe a toilet that flushes and a proper bath. You've no idea how great that is.'

Chrissie coloured slightly. She lowered her eyes and looked almost coquettish. 'There is something I need to tell you, but I'll wait till Peter comes home.'

'Mam, come on, what have you been up to?' asked Mary with a sly laugh. There was no way she was going to wait another minute.

'Nothing, it's... I'll tell ye later.'

'You've got together with Sinclair, haven't you?'

When Chrissie nodded, Mary shrieked. 'Are you moving in with him?'

'Maybe someday, but I want to be home for a while with ye and Peter. But then the house'll be yours as long as ye both want it.'

Mary knew she wanted to add, '*We don't know what state Peter will be in,*' and the unspoken words lay between them, returning the mood to its more sombre state.

'I'm sure he'll be happy for you, too,' said Mary, with confidence although it was something she and her brother never discussed.

While Chrissie busied herself making tea, Mary looked around, drinking in the familiarity of her surroundings, shabbier now that six years had passed. The leather strap where her father sharpened his razor still hung by the fireplace, two cats lay curled on the chair by the fire, a deep contented rumble in their throats, the clock on the mantle still counted the seconds with its steady monotonous tick. All these things jogged her memory sending her back to a place that belonged to a long time ago.

'Do ye mind if I go for a walk by the shore, Mam?'

Chrissie opened her mouth as if to say something, hesitated, then said, 'No, lass. I don't mind at all.'

Mary walked outside and down to the shore. Everything looked the same, yet she knew nothing would be the same again. She fought to banish Greg from her mind. What he did to her would eat into her trust forever and try as she might to erase him, he clung to her memory like sticky cobwebs. He could have been here with her now, holding her hand. It's how she had pictured them.

She watched a small boat bob across the firth towards the mainland, a liner materialise from the horizon, a steam drifter sail towards Orkney, a flock of seabirds in its wake, and she marvelled at the normality of it all.

The sun sank and the sky and the sea and the windows of houses along the beach front turned to fire. Suddenly realising how cold it had become, she shivered and tightened her cardigan around her shoulders. She stood up and started. The shape of a man stood as still as a painting at the top of the rise. The sunset behind him turned him into a mass of shadows and angles. She walked towards the shape until she knew who it was.

Johnny stood before her. Johnny, still whole, still bonny, but with the innocence of youth gone from his eyes and replaced by hard evidence of the things he had seen.

'I thought I'd find you here,' he said.

'Johnny. When ...?'

'Yesterday. I didn't want to see anyone. Then Da told me he'd seen you get off the bus.' He held out his hand. She grasped it and he helped her up the rise.

She studied the gaunt, tired face. He appeared much older than the image she carried in her mind. 'What happened to you in France? We thought you'd been killed.'

He instantly retreated behind his eyes. 'Aye, but I'd rather not talk about it yet.'

She understood. 'We've a lot to tell each other. You'll come home with me...see my ma?'

'Of course I will. I've something to give her. Nothing's the same anymore is it?'

Mary shook her head and together they walked up the rise.

Epilogue

It was a fine spring day when the Church bells rang for Mary and Johnny. Little Donald toddled up and presented her with a horseshoe.

Chrissie was glad to see her so happy. She was also heartened to see Peter and Jess together. She had worried about the girl and her baby left alone with a cold, uncaring mother, and she felt sure there would be no more mistakes on her part.

'It was war,' Peter had explained to his mother. 'I can understand Jess's reasons but whether I can ever forgive is a different matter entirely.'

'Were ye an angel all the years ye were away?' asked Chrissie.

Peter had looked at her, his face drawn as it usually was since his return. 'I never betrayed her like that. All I know is that I need her with me now. I'm no easy to live with since I came home and there's no many would put up with the way I am now. We're no the same people we were, never can be, but we both want to try and that's the main thing, isn't it?'

'I'm proud of ye, son.' Chrissie squeezed his arm.

'And ye, go and be happy, Mam,' he said. 'I see the way ye and Sinclair look at each other.'

'And ye don't mind?'

He gave a strangled laugh. 'Why should I mind? Jess's happy to move into the cottage and we've even planned an extension. We need to be near ye, so you can do a bit of babysitting. Is that not so, love?' He pulled Jess to him and kissed her forehead.

She nodded and gave a thin smile.

With one arm round his wife and the other round his mother, Peter followed the wedding party to the hotel at John O'Groats for a meal and dancing. Thanks to Aunt Agatha's money, Mary had been able to have the kind of wedding she once could only dream about. Afterwards, she and Johnny were to travel down to Inverness for a week in a hotel.

Little Donald didn't seem able to stand at peace and, as Jess left to pull him down from a wall he was now trying to climb, Peter took a deep sigh.

'He's a lovely laddie,' said Chrissie. 'I'm sure ye'll be a good dad to him.'

'I will. In a way, I'm glad he's not my blood,' said Peter.

'Why? asked Chrissie, surprised.

Peter ran his fingers through his hair. 'My real....Jack. He was mad, wasn't he? I'm fine, but I worry about what I'll pass to my children through my bloodline.'

Chrissie understood that he couldn't bring himself to call Jack his father. She looked up at his handsome face and gasped. The young Charlie was clearly superimposed there. He slowly smiled at her as if sending her a message. Words froze in her throat and just as suddenly, he was Peter again.

'Are ye alright, Mam? For a moment there you looked as if ye'd seen a ghost.'

'I'm... fine.' Until this moment she had always thought Peter was like *her* father, like *herself*, bearing no resemblance to either man who might have fathered him.

'I don't think ye need worry about passing on bad blood,' she stated, her mouth dry. 'There's something I've got to tell ye, but we'll leave it till another day.'

'What...?' But before he could question her further, Donald ran at him wrapping his arms around his legs and screaming, 'Daddy.'

'You speak to him. He'll no listen to me,' said Jess, coming up behind him.

274

Peter lifted the child and blew a raspberry on his neck and Chrissie knew she need have no worries about the love between them. Her heart grew large with pride.

'We'll speak later, Mam,' Peter said, as they followed the others into the hotel.

After the madness of war, Mary looked forward to peace and the challenges of her new life as Johnny's wife and mother of their potential children. She loved Johnny and was sure their future would be happy and fulfilled. Before she climbed into the taxi that waited to take them to the railway station, she closed her eyes and threw her bouquet into the waiting guests behind her. It rose in the wind and Chrissie stepped away, but it spiralled towards her, leaving her no option but to catch it.

Peter clapped her shoulder.

Mary giggled, delighted.

'Come away, love,' said Johnny taking Mary's arm.

A seagull sailed on the slight breeze and from somewhere came the distant drone of an aircraft. 'Give me a minute,' she said, and she gazed up at the perfect blue of the sky.

'The beginning of a lovely life,' said Johnny, as he stood back and waited.

Mary watched as the small plane neared, swooped above their heads and shot away into the distance.

'The taxi's waiting,' shouted Johnny.

She took another minute. 'I'm coming,' she said with a poignant smile, reached for Johnny's hand and allowed him to help her into the waiting vehicle.

About the author

Born and brought up until the age of nine on the Island of Stroma, she heard many stories from her grandparents about the island life of a different generation. Her family moved to the mainland at a time when the island was being depopulated, although it took another ten years before the last family left

An interest in geology, history and her strong ties to island life has influenced her choice of genre for her novels.

Since first attending the AGM of the Scottish Association of Writers in 1999, Catherine has won several prizes, commendations and has been short-listed both for short stories and chapters of her novels.

In 2009, she won second prize in the general novel category for '*Follow the Dove*'

In 2016 *The Road to Nowhere* won second prize in the Barbara Hammond competition for Best Self Published novel.

The follow up, *Isa's Daughter* won 1st prize in the same competition the following year, 2017.

Catherine Byrne lives in Wick, Caithness.

www. catherinebyrne-author.com